Books of Merit

THE HUNDRED HEARTS

ALSO BY WILLIAM KOWALSKI

Eddie's Bastard

Somewhere South of Here

The Adventures of Flash Jackson

The Good Neighbor

THE HUNDRED HEARTS

WILLIAM KOWALSKI

THOMAS ALLEN PUBLISHERS
TORONTO

Library and Archives Canada Cataloguing in Publication

Kowalski, William, 1970–
    The hundred hearts / William Kowalski.

Issued also in electronic formats.
ISBN 978-1-77102-300-9

I. Title.

PS8571.O985H86   2013   C813'.54   C2012-908447-6

Editor: Janice Zawerbny
Cover design: Michel Vrana
Cover image of painted wood: iko/shutterstock.com

Published by Thomas Allen Publishers,
a division of Thomas Allen & Son Limited,
390 Steelcase Road East,
Markham, Ontario L3R 1G2 Canada

www.thomasallen.ca

ONTARIO ARTS COUNCIL
CONSEIL DES ARTS DE L'ONTARIO

Canada Council   Conseil des Arts
for the Arts   du Canada

The publisher gratefully acknowledges the support of The Ontario Arts Council for its publishing program.

We acknowledge the support of the Canada Council for the Arts, which last year invested $20.1 million in writing and publishing throughout Canada.

We acknowledge the Government of Ontario through the Ontario Media Development Corporation's Ontario Book Initiative.

We acknowledge the financial support of the Government of Canada through the Canada Book Fund for our publishing activities.

13 14 15 16 17 5 4 3 2 1

Text printed on 100% PCW recycled stock

Printed and bound in Canada

For Alexandra,
whose heart is endlessly big

As for your own end, Menelaus, you shall not die
in Argos, but the Immortals will take you to the
Elysian plain, which is at the ends of the world.
There fair-haired Rhadamanthus reigns, and men
lead an easier life than anywhere else in the world,
for in Elysium there falls not rain, nor hail, nor snow,
but Oceanus breathes ever with a West wind that sings
softly from the sea, and gives fresh life to all men.

— HOMER, *The Odyssey*

They call it the American Dream because you have to be
asleep to believe it.

— GEORGE CARLIN

PROLOGUE:
THE PSYCHOPOMP

HELEN MERKIN passed away on August 3, 2011, at the age
of sixty-six, having been ill just three times in her life—
never seriously. The women in her family didn't get sick.
They lived, in fact, to enviable ages. Her mother had carried
on to ninety-four, her life beginning at the tail end of the age
of horse and carriage, progressing thence through the ages of
automobiles, flight, a World War, radio, another World War,
the atomic bomb, the moon landing, and the computer epoch,
to name just a few. Her grandmother, who was born in the back
of a prairie schooner during the Garfield presidency, and who
as a child had survived two attacks by Kickapoo warriors, made
it to ninety-eight. These were the genes that made up Helen,
strong genes, genes like cinder blocks but made of something
even more obdurate—like quartz, or obsidian, or elements she'd
never even heard of that had cooked for eons in the heart of a
star a million light-years away and then flown across the universe to accrete briefly in her being, as they do in all of us.

Yet in the end, her body, made of eternal star parts though it
was, failed her like a cheap Battery Park watch. The cause was
chronic severe sleep apnea, which had plagued her for most of
her life—especially in recent years, when she'd begun to plump
up due to her love of her own baked goods. Normally, when

Helen's snoring choked off her breath, she woke in a flailing panic. But this time she simply stopped breathing. Helen's last thought was therefore not a thought at all. It was a dream.

It's a dream about something that really happened. She's nine years old again, breastless and wiry, back on the farm in the emerald-toothed Tehachapi Range where she'd grown up. Her parents are sheep farmers, as they were in real life. Her father has just given her a motherless lamb to care for, a sweet female that creeps up to her deferentially on spider legs and sucks her little finger. Helen is delighted. There are no other children living nearby, and her brothers are vastly older; her playmates are either animal or imaginary, and none of them need her the way this lamb does. It will die without her. No one has ever before depended upon her to survive. She feels her heart expanding to include it, feels a new sense of importance. Her uterus ticks into life; she feels tiny twin flushes in the places where someday her breasts will grow. Within a year, in a gush sparked by this moment, she'll begin to menstruate.

She names the lamb Agnes. Agnes, Agnus, Agnus Dei, Lamb of God. It makes her religious mother happy. This is the reason for many of the things Helen does.

Things are not exactly right. Somehow, in this dream, Agnes has learned to walk and talk like a person, albeit with sheep-like tendencies. She looks, in fact, like a little girl with a sheep's head. This doesn't exactly disturb Helen, but her dream is calling attention to itself, and to this she is not accustomed. Rarely does she remember her dreams at all, but this one is as vivid as the OMNIMAX movie she went to see with Al in 1990 in Los Angeles—the one about the whales.

Agnes greets Helen with affection. When she hugs her, Helen can feel her woolly face against her cheeks. After a moment of hesitation, she hugs her back.

"Let's go for a walk," says Agnes, because in this dream she can talk. Her breath is grassy, her muzzle articulate and pink, its fine white hairs glinting in the sunshine. "I've got something to show you."

"Where are we going?"

"The river," says Agnes.

"What river? There's no river here."

"There is now," says Agnes.

They walk toward the far end of her father's fields until they come to a spot that looks familiar, though Helen can't remember when she was here before. The path indeed ends at a river, a wide, eddying spill of slow silver, where there grows an ancient cottonwood with arms broad enough to shelter a whole village. On the far bank is a green hillside ramping up to the sky. Helen thinks it's very pretty, and says so. Then she ventures the suggestion that they'd better be getting back.

"Getting back where? We've arrived," Agnes says. "This is the place we go."

Only then does it dawn on Helen that she's not dreaming, and that Agnes has led her here on purpose. She feels tricked. And she doesn't like what Agnes has said: This is the place we go. As if this had been the destination all along.

"I want to go home," she says.

"There is no home."

"What do you mean?"

"Hold on," says Agnes. "Someone is coming."

"Who is it?"

"Someone important to you. You'll see soon enough," Agnes says.

It seems to Helen that she's both nine and sixty-six; she has the body of a child again, but she remembers her entire life, growing up and getting married and becoming first a mother and then a grandmother. How can this be? She doesn't care for this dream, and also she has the dawning sense that it's not really a dream at all. A snake of dread climbs up her ankles and settles around her middle. She feels tricked, disoriented. She's certain she knows every inch of this farm, and there's no river on it. Someone is playing a joke on her. Not Agnes. Someone even more mysterious.

"Why am I a little girl again?" she asks, looking down at her slim tummy, her sticklike legs. "I used to be a grown woman. I know I was. I remember."

"We're all the age we want to be," says Agnes.

"I don't like it here. I want to go home," Helen says again, and she begins to cry.

"You ca-a-an't just go home," Agnes says. In her impatience her voice reverts to lambiness. "Don't you understand? We're going across. You don't have any choice."

Helen sits on the ground and crosses her arms over her chest. "You go across. I'm not going. I want to see my family."

"You will see them."

"When?"

"Right now. But they won't see you."

"Why not?"

"Because," Agnes explains, as if to someone very slow, "you don't have a body anymore."

This news comes as less of a shock than it should. Indeed, Helen feels some sense of relief. Ever since the day she noticed the first speck of blood on her panties, followed by the painful swelling behind her nipples that made them puffy and unsightly, her body has felt like an ever-growing burden, an extra layer she must haul around with her everywhere that obscures the real her. She'd gotten plumper with every passing year, her breasts sagging and her behind expanding, until she was embarrassed to look at herself in the mirror. She would be glad to leave all that.

"How can I see them?" she asks.

"Look," Agnes says, pointing to the water. "You can see everything in the river."

So Helen looks.

In the water she sees Al Merkin, her husband, as he finds her gray and lifeless, a statue of herself. It's Al's habit to come into her room first thing in the morning and wake her to place his breakfast order. First he freezes in shock; then he recoils at the touch of a dead body, the first he's seen in many years. Finally, he holds her and weeps. He berates himself aloud for not knowing she was dying. Had she called out for him? Had she reached for his hand, even though they hadn't slept in the same bed for years? Would she be alive if he hadn't insisted on his own bedroom? He will never know. It bothers him tremendously that he'd been lying in the next room during her last moments, probably fantasizing about Theresa Talley-Graber, who had let him molest her once during a dance in high school and who, though he hasn't seen her in well over half a century, has crept back into his thoughts in recent days.

Helen, watching him in the river, approves of the emotion he shows; it's only the second time she's seen her husband cry. She can see all of his thoughts, so she knows full well that he's been thinking about Theresa Talley-Graber, but she forgives him. Sex had begun to seem stupid to her long ago, and now it's almost comical, the squishy, squirting japery of mortals who are really no better than dogs and cats when it comes to mastering their baser instincts.

"Look at him," she says to Agnes. "He's acting like a little boy."

"We're all children," says Agnes. "Just old children, that's all."

"Is that why I'm a child again?"

"No. You chose this form, whether you remember it or not. This was how you thought of yourself. You always felt like a little girl, even when you were grown up. Didn't you?"

"Yes. Now that you mention it, I did. But how did you know that?"

"Everything is known here," Agnes says. "Every single thing that ever was or will be."

Now they're lying on their stomachs in the grass, Helen's chin on her hands, Agnes's on her hooves, looking into the water. Then Helen hears the plash of water on oars. She looks up to see a man rowing a boat at a gentle pace. He's still some way downriver, but he's coming closer. His broad back is to them, so she can't see his face. He wears an olive-drab T-shirt and sports a military haircut. It sounds as if he's whistling. The tune is familiar. In the stern of the boat, a dog stands, its tongue a damp flag flopping in the wind, tail waving upright. The dog looks familiar too.

"Hey, there's Proton!" says Helen, standing. "Jeremy looked everywhere for him! Here, Proton! Come on, boy!"

"He'll be here soon," says Agnes. "Just be patient."

So Helen sits and waits for the ferryman to arrive.

1

THE TOWN of Elysium, California, lies halfway between Barstow and Bakersfield on Highway 58, near the western edge of the Mojave Desert. The desolation of the Mojave takes many forms, including blinding-white salt flats, incisor-like ridges, and hellish valleys. Here, it's a vast plain of rusty dirt, home to foul-smelling creosote bushes and Joshua trees upthrust like gladiators' fists, and populated by serious, sunburned people who are accustomed to feeling as insignificant as insects in the howling wasteland. It's so hot that one's bones go rubbery and tend to bend in the wrong places. To compensate, people develop a stiffness to them, an unwillingness to yield. Jesus is King. The government is out to get you. The right to bear arms is sacred. These are the beliefs that have sustained them for generations. With every passing year, they become more firmly entrenched.

Jeremy Merkin thinks of Elysium as a dried-up zit on a whore's ass. It's a rather indecorous thought, but he learned to think this way while in the army, and though he's been a civilian for almost five years, he finds it a hard habit to break.

The developer who dreamed up the town, a Greek immigrant named Ouranakis, had been a great lover of ancient mythology. This was before he himself passed into a mythology of his own creation, which is still occasionally repeated around dinner tables in the homes of older Elysians, of whom Jeremy's grandfather is one. The original Elysium was the eternal paradise to which the Greeks believed their souls went after they died. This was portrayed on a billboard by the artificial lake in the center of town, on which a man in a toga stands before endless green fields, hoisting a goblet of never-ending wine, his chipper Hellenic features badly weathered by the California sun. On the billboard, some wit has spray-painted a speech balloon coming from the Greek's mouth, with the words WELCOME TO HELL.

Thanks to Ouranakis's showmanship and talent for self-promotion, a real estate boom had been expected here once. People talked about it as if it were a physical thing, like a train, that might be showing up at any moment. Ouranakis built several neighborhoods and promised a hundred more. He was even gracious enough to accept down payments from hopeful homeowners, to the tune of nearly a million dollars. An extensive network of streets had been bulldozed into the desert and paved with asphalt, and many miles of sidewalks and driveways had been laid.

The boom never arrived. Decades later, streets still end abruptly without leading anywhere. Sidewalks run through neighborhoods that have no houses in them, only empty concrete pads. It's as if a giant vacuum has come along and sucked up everything that wasn't attached to the earth, including children and dogs. And maybe Ouranakis himself. He disappeared one day as if he'd been Hoovered into the clouds, and he wasn't rediscovered until 1973, when he died on the Greek island where he'd been living like a prince.

This is where Jeremy grew up, in a town that looks as if it was laid out for a community of ghosts, partly real but mostly imaginary. American flags snap in the mad rush of the Santa Ana winds, reminiscent of the whips of teamsters who once drove the borax mule trains down from the hills. Two or three times a day, the ground is slapped by sonic booms from nearby Edwards Air Force Base. Occasionally a dark shape sneaks beneath the sun, casting a deltoid shadow. It's the stealth bomber, emitting a quiet roar, conducting practice sorties, its crew pretending to drop bombs on their unsuspecting countrymen. The strangeness of things reaches an extreme here, and so does the temperature, and the hugeness, and the isolation.

America has always been a big, weird place. And nowhere is it bigger or weirder than the Mojave Desert.

A month after they've consigned the remains of his grandmother, Helen, to the flames of the crematorium, Jeremy sits in his car in the parking lot of Sam "The Patriot" Singh's Fortress of America Motel, a crumpled note in his hand. The note had arrived today in his faculty mailbox. It's written in pencil on a piece of ragged-edged notebook paper. The handwriting is decidedly feminine. He knows whose it is. In just a few weeks, he's learned to discern the penmanship of most of his nearly forty students. He'd wrestled with himself over whether he should open it, sensing that whatever it said, it would get him into trouble. But in the battle between curiosity and discretion that took place in his mind, curiosity had discretion on the ropes.

Room 358. I need you, Jeremy.
You're the only one who can help.

Help with what, he doesn't know. Merely being in possession of this note makes Jeremy nervous. He's already received a lecture from Peter Porteus, principal of Elysium High School, on the importance of propriety: don't let yourself be caught alone with a female student, for God's sake, and if you do, keep doors open, keep hands to self, et cetera. It is preferable to wrap yourself hermetically in plastic and stay on the other side of the room.

"You're a man, so you're a potential criminal," Porteus told him. "That's the way it is these days. We're all rapists. Even if you've never raped anybody. So just don't do anything that might be misconstrued. Keep your johnson in your pants, don't get into any situations, and everything will be fine."

Jeremy didn't think he would have a problem with that. The only time he'd ever removed his johnson from his pants in a work-related setting was seven years earlier, during his tenure as cone dipper at the Freezie Squeeze, when he and Samantha Bayle, his assistant manager, had gone to town on her desk—a mildly acrobatic feat of which, thanks to his war injuries, he's no longer capable. And technically speaking, it had been she who removed his johnson from his pants, not he.

That had been in a different era, prewar, pre-IED, and it's a performance he has no intention of repeating. He's done his best to assure Porteus of this in so many words, and he's also promised not to get into any "situations." Porteus hasn't said anything about going to motel rooms with students, but that's probably because it's so blindingly obvious.

This, Jeremy thinks, definitely qualifies as a situation.

The car rocks from side to side as it's buffeted by the Santa Anas. Jeremy rocks with it, allowing his head to sway loosely on his neck as he continues to regard the motel room door. He cannot make up his mind. Go in or go home? He has the distinct sense that his life branches at this point, and it's precisely at such moments that indecision completes the paralysis that's been stalking him ever since April 7, 2007, the day the bomb went off. He really ought to just leave. But he finds that his hand is not obeying his brain's order to turn the key in the ignition. So he sits, waiting for a sign.

When you're in sign-seeking mode, you see them everywhere: in the patterns of clouds, the tracks of insects, the ticking of a cooling car engine. Or in the numbers on motel room doors.

358. There's something familiar about those numbers. After a moment he realizes what it is: 358 was also the number on Proton's license. He'd been the three-hundred-fifty-eighth dog registered in 1999, when Jeremy had rescued him from a Lancaster puppy mill. He'd gotten him cheap, after a coyote had broken into the breeding pen and impregnated one of the bitches. Nobody wanted a dog that might rip your head off while you were sleeping. Proton turned out to have not an ounce of aggression in him. As a watchdog, he was useless; he would play ball with anybody.

Proton had disappeared five weeks ago, just before his grandmother died. Jeremy had walked everywhere looking for that stupid dog, or at least as much as his reassembled spine would allow. But he was gone. Al, his grandfather, said Proton had probably been bitten by a scorpion or a rattlesnake and crawled off into the desert to die. That was typical of Al; mostly he seemed glad Proton had saved the sixty bucks it would eventually have cost to put him to sleep. So Jeremy chose not to tell Al that he'd arisen before the sun every morning for seven days in a row and called Proton from the end of every dune-drifted street, wandering among the waist-high scrub brush until his spine threatened to buckle. Proton had been his dog. He'd bought him with money he'd earned at the Freezie Squeeze. Everything and everyone else had changed while he was in Afghanistan, the people getting older and fatter, and the town somehow greasier and sadder, but when he'd walked in the door as a civilian again, Proton had bounded up to him and deposited a tennis ball at his feet as if the whole war had merely been a lengthy interruption of their endless game. For that, he felt gratitude. On the seventh day of his search, he surprised himself by weeping, unable even to choke the dog's name out. That morning he returned home to find his grandmother had died in her sleep and the house in chaos. After that he didn't look for Proton anymore.

There's something else about the numbers 3, 5, and 8 that he recalls. Taken as individual digits, they are Fibonacci numbers. One day, out of nowhere, Smarty, his best friend in the army, had turned to him and said, "If there is a God, and I think there is, then the Fibonacci sequence is proof of His existence."

This was the sort of statement of which only Smarty was capable. His real name was Ari P. Garfunkel, but nobody ever called anybody by their real name in the army. To most of the guys in the squad, Smarty was a mystery, an academically oriented anachronism. He kept up a running commentary that sounded, to the uninitiated, like a string of non sequiturs. Jeremy was the only one to understand that these were merely the termini of whatever streams of thought had been coursing through Smarty's formidable brain most recently.

Jeremy had never heard of the Fibonacci sequence, but then he'd never heard of half the things Smarty talked about. While the rest of the squad listened in eye-rolling bemusement and did other squadly things, farting MRE-induced gas and cracking jokes and endlessly adjusting their balls, Smarty had explained, in his calm voice that was the only sane thing in that insane country, that the Fibonacci sequence was a series of numbers. It was repeated everywhere in nature, from the proportions of trees and mountains to the placement of seeds on the head of a sunflower. It was a cosmic code, a rare revelation of the matrix glimpsed through the skin of the physical world. Zero, one, one, two, three, five, eight, thirteen, twenty-one . . . You constructed it by adding the last number to the one before. That was all there was to finding out the secrets of the universe.

"How do you know these things?" Jeremy had demanded.

"I read," was Smarty's reply. That was how he got his name: he read all the time. There was more knowledge contained in his gluteus maximus than in the rest of the platoon put together. Jeremy did not just admire Smarty; he envied him. For this, he realized, was the secret knowledge that lent Smarty his equanimity in the face of all things crazy-making: the dust, the heat of day, the cold of night, the lunatic Captain Woot, the pinging bullets, the whumping mortars, and the fact that the rest of the army seemed to have forgotten all about them, leaving them stranded in their forward operating base with dwindling food and ammo supplies. The only thing they had plenty of was body bags. On cold nights, they slept in them.

And now here these numbers are again.

"Goddamn it," Jeremy says to himself. He considers beating his head against the steering wheel, but decides this will hurt too much.

Finally he gets out of the car. The Santa Anas are a blow-dryer in his face, scouring the sweat from his skin before it has a chance to settle. He's been sitting too long; his legs have gone numb. He limps to the door, tries the knob, and finds it's unlocked.

In the moments before his eyes adjust to the dimness, he smells a dozen smells, all of them familiarly unpleasant. Hair spray. Cigarette smoke. Cheap perfume. Shampoo. Wet towels. Mildew from the swamp cooler. That indefinable motel room smell overlaying it all—the smell of fugitive despair and ruined family vacations, perhaps. These odors do not enter his nostrils so much as they ram their way down his throat. He's always hated motel rooms, though he's forgotten that until just this moment. Reluctantly, he closes the door.

He'd been right about the handwriting. He'd pegged it as Jennifer Moon's, and here she is, sitting on the edge of one of the two double beds, hands in her lap. She's seventeen, small for her age, with a face that is both round and elfin, framed by stringy hair dyed black. One ear is pierced all the way up to the top in a jeweled crescent, and another stone glitters in her nostril. In her tongue, he knows, resides a miniature silver barbell that she absentmindedly clacks against her upper teeth. She's also in the habit of wearing long-sleeved shirts, which in this climate is unusual; normally the people of the Mojave try to wear as little as possible.

Jennifer is one of his quietest students—polite, certainly, but not terribly engaged. In fact, she has yet to turn in any homework. Not that many of the three dozen teenagers he deals with every day seem to have much interest in the laws of physics. Why should they? These laws govern them whether they pay attention or not, and they're of no help in the endless quest for beer, popularity, and sex. No zit-pocked teenager ever got laid because he could draw a wicked vector diagram. Jennifer spends most of her class time staring out the window or doodling, and often looks intently into her lap, as do most of the others, staring at their crotches as if they are the most fascinating things in the world. This generation has become adept at secret texting. Jeremy gave up telling them to put their cell phones away on day three of the school year. He is now on day twenty-one. The rest of his career is looking incredibly long and depressing from here.

"Jeremy," the girl says. "You came. You're so awesome." She stands up, and he has the sinking feeling she's about to hug him.

"Hi, Jennifer," says Jeremy. He peeks out through the drawn curtains, deflecting her attack. The intelligent thing would have been to check to see if anyone was watching before he got out of his car. To the list of careers at which he would be terrible, he adds *spy*. "I got your note," he adds, unnecessarily. "What's going on? Everything okay?"

"Not totally," she says. "Call me Jenn, okay? That's what my friends call me."

"What are you doing here, anyway?"

"I . . . well, I ran away," Jenn says.

Her dramatic pause is a clue that she expects this to have some impact on him, but a lot of people have said a lot of crazy shit to Jeremy, and on the grand scale of things, this ranks rather low. So he stands, waiting.

"Okay," he says. "You ran away."

"Yeah. I took your advice."

"My advice?" Jeremy gapes, uncomprehending. "I don't remember saying—"

"You inspired me, that's what I mean. You gave me the courage to do it. That great talk you gave us about sticking up for yourself because no one else will. And you said the struggle for survival was something you didn't have to ask anyone's permission for. You just had to do it. It was like you could read my mind. I could have sworn you were talking to me. You were, weren't you?"

Jeremy closes his eyes as he tries to remember what the hell she's talking about. Vaguely, he recalls an off-the-cuff speech he gave to a roomful of bored adolescents a few days ago, on one of the increasingly frequent occasions when the lesson plan he'd labored over for hours had turned out to occupy approximately fifteen minutes, leaving him with a yawning chasm of half an hour to fill. Something strange happened to time when he stood at the head of the class; it dilated, so that seconds stretched into minutes. Nothing in the online classes he'd taken had prepared him for this—but then they hadn't prepared him for much of anything. And he hadn't planned on becoming a teacher anyway. He'd only applied for the job because he'd heard the principal of Elysium High would hire anyone, even someone with no training. It was impossible to attract qualified people to this corner of the world. What had he planned on doing, once he graduated and received his virtual diploma? He doesn't even remember.

"Okay, look," he says. "That was just a bunch of stuff I got from some movie somewhere. I didn't mean you should run away. I mean . . . why did you? What's going on?"

"Things are bad. Really bad. I had no choice. My, uh . . . my stepbrother . . ."

Mentally, Jeremy sorts through the complicated web of familial entanglements that bind this town together. "You mean Lincoln?" he says after a moment.

"Yeah. Him."

"What about him?"

"I just really need to talk to someone," Jenn says.

"What is it? What's going on?"

But now she won't look at him. She huddles on the bed, knees drawn up to her chest, an armadillo of emotion.

"Jenn, look," Jeremy says. "If you want me to help you, you have to talk to me. I really shouldn't even be here. If someone saw us, they'd think . . . some not very good thoughts. You understand?"

She looks at him, her eyes dark with makeup. Her fingers move unconsciously to the inside of her wrist, lifting her sleeve. Jeremy already knows why she wears long-sleeved shirts in the hundred-degree weather of late summer. He's seen the fine map of scars on her wrists; in class, she has the habit of tracing them with her finger, unaware she's betraying her own secret. He's been told to report things like that, so he'd mentioned it to the secretary, Mrs. Bekins, who also functioned as an unofficial school nurse, at least to the extent that she distributed tampons to the needy from a box she kept in her desk. She's a cutter, Mrs. Bekins explained to him. Mother ran off a few years ago. Father was in Gulf One, came home crazy. Bad home life. Jeremy had nodded sagely and then gone on the Internet to look up what a cutter was. A cutter was someone who cut herself repeatedly and on purpose, often with a razor blade. They were almost always girls.

"Oh, yeah," Jenn says. "I understand."

"Maybe you need a professional," Jeremy says. "You know, a doctor or somebody. Somebody you can talk to."

Jenn seems to find this amusing. Her upper lip lifts a fraction, and she exhales in derision. "I am talking to someone. I'm talking to you."

"But . . . you don't really know me."

"I can tell you're not like the other teachers. You let us call you by your first name. You talk to us like we're people. None of them care about anything. It's like they're zombies or something. You're different, though. You're not brain-dead yet. You still have a soul."

"I'm glad you trust me, Jenn. I really am. I want to help you. But you have to understand that I'm just a . . ."

Various possible descriptions of himself appear in his mind: A twenty-five-year-old who lives in his grandfather's basement. A cripple with a marijuana problem and a raging case of PTSD. A veteran whose disability, percentage-wise, was just a little too low to stay home and watch television for the rest of his life. A loser who hasn't had a girlfriend in years.

". . . a guy," he says finally. "I'm just me. I don't have any power."

"But you're a teacher," Jenn says. "You're an authority figure. You can do something."

"Do something about what? Something about Lincoln?"

She doesn't answer this. She just keeps tracing her wrist.

"Is it something you should maybe go to the cops about?"

"He is a cop," Jenn says.

"Lincoln is a cop? Since when?" He remembers Lincoln from school, though he's a couple of years younger. He'd been an angelic-looking little boy who grew into a cool, assured teenager with overlarge brown eyes and long eyelashes and a tall, rangy body. Jeremy hasn't seen him since he came back, or maybe he wouldn't have recognized him if he had. So many of his classmates had already transformed into unrecognizable older versions of how they were stuck in the flypaper of his memory. Boys had become fathers with bald spots and paunchy guts; girls had become mothers with depleted breasts and varicose veins. Everyone looked forty, fifty, one hundred. It was as if Afghanistan were a black hole that halted time for him, but back home, far from the war, it had speeded up.

"He became a sheriff's deputy last year. So he's one of their own. And they always protect their own. That's what he told me himself. I said, 'What about me? We practically grew up together. Doesn't that make me one of your own too?' And he just laughed. You know what he said? The cops are his family now, he said. His real family. That's what he told me."

She begins to cry, her thin shoulders quivering. Jeremy must fight the urge to put his hands on them. Don't touch her, he tells himself. You want to keep this job, stay out of jail? Wrap yourself in plastic and stay on the other side of the room.

"I've been saving up money," she goes on in a tremolo. "I have four hundred bucks. I spent some on this room, but still, I have enough to go somewhere. Look." She reaches into her purse and pulls out a wad of cash. She begins to count it. The desperation in her voice makes Jeremy want to tear out his own pancreas. "One hundred, two hundred, three hundred, three-twenty, three-fifty—"

"Wait, don't tell me," Jeremy says. "You have three hundred fifty-eight dollars."

Jenn looks at him, her eyes wide. She holds up a five and three singles. "How did you know?"

Jeremy rubs his face. Spirit of Smarty, he thinks, activate your magic powers. Turn me into a whirlwind or a superhero or some fucking thing.

"I counted from here," he says.

"So how much would it cost?"

"How much would what cost?"

"To have you kill him," Jenn says.

Jeremy reels backwards, a bull's-eyed carnival duck, an inflatable clown with a weighted bottom. This conversation started out weird and has progressed to insane in a matter of minutes.

"Jenn!" he says, shocked. "What the fuck do you think I am, a hit man? I'm your physics teacher!"

"Yeah, but you were in the war, right? You've killed people before. I hear it's a lot easier after the first time. Everybody says you're like some big war hero or something. It would be easy for you."

"You have to be kidding me."

"Please, Jeremy," she begs him, her makeup running down her face. "I wouldn't be asking you if I thought there was any other way. There just isn't."

Suddenly he feels weak, and his head begins to swim. He recognizes these sensations. No, no, not now, he thinks. Usually they're set off by loud noises, or by images on the television, or articles on the Internet that he shouldn't have read. But he hasn't had one of these episodes in months. Lola Linker, his counselor, had hinted that he might be cured. But he doesn't feel cured. They still haven't solved the mystery of the day that's missing from his memory, the day the bomb went off, the day Smarty and two others got smithereened. And he's been getting headaches lately, too. Bad ones. They emerge from somewhere inside his skull like a knife blade appearing point first. Each time, the blade is a little wider, a little sharper; and each time, it opens the gap between the hemispheres of his brain a little more.

"What's happening? Are you all right?" says Jenn.

"I . . . don't know."

"What is it?"

I feel heavy, he wants to say. I feel like I'm on Jupiter. But he can't find the words. There's something squeezing his chest from the inside, trying to pop his heart. He sits on the bed opposite her, puts his head down, and tries to breathe.

"Are you okay?" she asks. She sounds scared. "Jeremy? Is this like a heart attack or something?"

"It's okay," he says, wheezing. "Not a heart attack. It'll be gone in a minute." But it could be much longer than that, he knows. Sometimes they last for hours. He rests his head on his knees and breathes deeply. Irrational thoughts fly through his head, a murder of crows screeching the news of his imminent destruction. Once, during one of these attacks, he'd become convinced there was a gang of Pashtun tribesmen waiting for him in the shower, intent on slitting his throat while he sat on the toilet. This had lasted for two days, during which he had to shit into a plastic bag because he was too afraid to go into the bathroom. He'd hid it in the same can where he put Proton's dog crap. He hasn't even told Lola Linker about that one. Some stuff is too crazy to tell your shrink.

"Do you want me to get you anything? You want a glass of water?"

"Okay," he says, because why not?

She goes into the bathroom. He hears water running through pipes that creak and gush under the floor, and in a moment she comes back with a glass containing a swirling mass of tepid, brownish liquid. Desert water, pumped up from subterranean depths through rusted pipes and treated unmercifully to make it potable. His grandfather's entire career at the pumping plant had been about bringing this water over the mountains. It was supposed to end up in Mexico, Al had told Jeremy once. But America got it first, as was America's right. Tribes of Indians south of the border had had to pick up and move because their rivers had dried up, finishing as swimming pools in LA instead of making the ancient journey to their ancestral home. Well, fuck 'em. If they had the chance, Al has explained, they'd take our water, too.

Jeremy takes the glass of stolen Indian water and sets it on the nightstand. "I'm sorry. These happen to me some—"

Suddenly he knows that despite any intentions his legs might have to the contrary, he must run for the bathroom. He barely manages to close the door before his lunch comes up in a hot rush.

A memory comes to him then. He realizes with surprise that it's one of the missing ones, rescued from the chaos of his unconscious, a single straw extracted from a jumbled pile. He remembers a stereo blasting rap music—must have been Jefferson's. He never turned that thing off. And he remembers a man with a hose down his throat, arms and legs zip-tied, surrounded by soldiers, one of whom was Jeremy himself, as Cap'n Woot poured water into the hose through a funnel. The man's abdomen swelled visibly. Then Woot had stomped on his stomach in time to the music. Water erupted from his body the same way Jeremy is puking now. Fuck waterboarding, Woot had said. This is why they call me the Water Method Man, boys! This is how we do things in the Spitting Cobras!

Who was the man? He can't remember.

Why were they doing that to him? He can't remember that either.

He spends several more minutes hovering, waiting for more to come, but nothing does. The music still pounds in his head. I's a mothahfuckin' killah, yeah, a loony with a gun. I chase them raghead niggahs and I smoke they ass fo' fun. I'm a homicidal maniac, a baby-shootin' brainiac, a totally insaniac . . .

Finally he rinses his mouth out as best he can. With no toothbrush, no mouthwash, nothing, he must abide the tang of his own stomach acid until he gets home. He looks at the window, and a wild idea comes to him: he'll crawl out of it, walk around to his car, go home, and pretend none of this ever happened. But he can't do that. He can't abandon her the way he's been abandoned, the way he's abandoned too many other people.

I's a mothahfuckin' killah . . .

He steps out into the room again. Jenn is huddled on the near bed, staring over her kneecaps at nothing. She rouses herself when he opens the door.

"You okay?" she asks.

. . . a loony with a gun.

"Yeah, I'm good." He needs his medication, at least three or four grams of Humboldt County hybrid. If he had a joint on him, he'd spark it up now, even in front of her. He needs to get to his stash.

"My dad throws up a lot too," she says. "He says he's been throwing up for twenty years. Spent plutonium, he says. Fucking government, huh?"

"Listen," says Jeremy. He sits down across from her. "We gotta talk. Because, uh . . . I think you have the wrong idea about me."

"I do?"

"Yeah. You know, what you asked me to do. I don't, uh . . . I mean, I'm not like that." Anymore, he adds mentally, and he can almost hear the laughter of the squad in his head, which is the only place most of them exist anymore. "I don't, uh . . . I don't believe in violence." Anymore. "I think it's wrong." Now. "And it wouldn't solve your problems." Except one.

"So you never killed anyone?" Jenn asks.

Suddenly he wants to smack the wide-eyed expression from her face. Instead, he gets up and paces. I'm the niggah on the triggah and I see you in my sights. Gonna waste your mom and daddy, gonna fuck yo ass all night. Jesus Christ. He needs this music out of his head.

"I'm sorry," says Jenn. "Maybe that's none of my business."

"Yeah, maybe it isn't," says Jeremy. "Maybe you should never ask anyone that fucking question again."

"I'm sorry," Jenn says again. "I didn't mean anything."

"You're sorry? You don't even know what sorry means. You wanna see sorry, I'll show you sorry. And maybe you should fucking think before you start shit up like this. 'Cause you don't know what you're waking up." Then he stops, clamps a hand over his mouth before he goes to town on her. It's always this way after an attack. He wants to rage the walls down.

Who was the guy, anyway? Why can't he remember his face?

He's scared her now. He breathes deep. The knife blade is edging forward again, slicing its way through whatever softness is left inside him. Not much at this point.

"I think I better go home," says Jeremy.

"Okay," she says. She looks relieved. Because he's leaving. Shit. He's out of control. Still.

"Jenn, I'm sorry. I didn't mean to, uh . . . I didn't mean to yell. I'm sorry. Really."

"It's okay, Mr. Merkin," Jenn says. Her attitude has changed. She's demure, sitting upright, looking down at her hands. Trying not to set him off. "You're right. I wasn't thinking."

"So. What are you gonna do?" he asks her. He tries his best to sound normal. Too little too late, but he doesn't want to be one more name on the list of devils in her life. Goddamn it. Why did he come here? He should have thrown that note away. Because he could kill this Lincoln asshole, no problem. He could sneak up behind him, run a knife across his throat, and then kidney-fuck him with it. Just like riding a bike. How had she known? Could she tell just from looking? Could she see the mark of Cain on his forehead?

"Stay here, I guess," Jenn says. "For tonight. I'm safe here, at least."

"Maybe you should tell your dad."

"Yeah, right. Great idea."

"He won't help you?"

"My dad's not exactly stable," she says.

"Listen, Jenn. If you don't tell someone, I have to tell Porteus. It's the law. I'm your teacher, and you're a minor. Once I hear something like this, I can't unhear it."

"What?" she shrieks. "Not Porteus! Fuck, Jeremy, it'll be all over the whole school in an hour!"

"No it won't," Jeremy says, knowing she's right, but knowing also that he has no choice. "Besides, it won't stop until you tell someone. He's not just going to stop on his own."

"Please, Jeremy, please please please. I'll blow you. How's that?"

"Oh, fuck, Jenn, no, don't go there. Now I'm really leaving. Watch me. Here I go." He gets up again, but he tries to move too fast and a hot rapier of pain nearly brings him to his knees.

"I'm great at it!" Jenn screams. "I get lots of practice!"

She stands up on the bed, her face purple, the cords in her neck standing out like she's being strangled by her own rage. She hasn't even noticed he's almost collapsed. She looks as if she's going off the rails. He's seen people lose it before, most recently the guy in the mirror, and the expression on his face had been very much like hers. He has no idea what to say, so he says nothing. Now he's the calm one. Pain has that effect on him. It flattens him, puts everything into perspective. This is why he's sometimes grateful for it. He just waits.

"Okay," she says finally, her chest heaving. "Okay. I never came right out and said it, anyway. Did I? So you can't report something I didn't say."

"I guess not," Jeremy says.

"I only hinted. I could be totally full of shit. You don't know for sure."

"Yeah."

"I could be making up the whole thing. You don't know. Right? Right?"

"Okay," says Jeremy. "Okay, I won't tell."

"Thank you," Jenn says, utterly calm now, and she gets off the bed and sits again, hands folded in her lap as before. She looks exhausted. "Jeremy."

"Yeah."

"I'm . . . sorry about what I just said. About the BJs. I was just carried away. I know you're not that kind of guy."

For a moment Jeremy thinks she means he's not the kind of guy who enjoys BJs, and he's actually about to argue this point, but then he understands what she really means: that he's not made out of the same stuff as her stepbrother, Lincoln Moon, who does deserve something particularly nasty to happen to him—if not death, which was after all too easy, then at least something extremely painful and of long duration. Too bad Woot isn't here, Jeremy thinks. He'd torture him all day long. But Jeremy himself no longer has the stomach for it. That part of his life is over.

"Give me your phone," he says.

She hands it over. He keys in his number and hands it back. "I shouldn't be doing this, but if you get in any trouble, text me. Let me know what happens anyway, one way or the other. Okay? So I know you're okay?"

"Okay. Thanks. And I'm sorry if what I said got you upset."

"It's all right," Jeremy says. "Forget about it. I . . . have a few issues I need to work on."

"Jeremy."

"What?"

"You really scared the shit out of me for a second."

"Sorry," he says, thinking, What, are we just going to keep apologizing to each other?

"Don't be," she says. "It was very manly."

She gets up and comes toward him, grabs his face, brings it into hers. But he pushes her away, not bothering to be gentle anymore, because who is this stupid little bitch anyway, to stir things up in his head like this? Five years of therapy out the window. He doesn't even wait to see if she falls on her ass. He just walks out the door.

He makes it half a mile down the road before he has to pull over. He lies across the front seats so no one will see him. Now the knife is working madly side to side, like someone stirring a pot.

He digs his fingers into his head as if he could pull out his whole brain, just toss it there by the side of the road and drive on. If someone knocks on his window, he's afraid of what he will do. At least there's no one around to hear the noises he's making. There's only the wind, which doesn't give a shit.

2

AL MERKIN sits in his living room, waiting for someone to come home and make dinner. On the other side of the room, Henry lolls splendidly in his recliner like a clam on his shell, blinders firmly on as he listens to the television, hands resting on his prodigious belly. Smitty, his teddy bear, is on his lap.

It's 4:35. Dinner is to be ready at 5:30, but unless Henry undergoes a psychological metamorphosis and becomes capable of actually doing something, that's not going to happen. Al's already decided that he's going to explode in moral outrage at the first person who walks through the door, though he plans on making it look spontaneous. It seems that Helen's death has unwound the precise sense of timing he's depended upon to keep his family together. Up until five weeks ago, things had moved along in a predictable, if occasionally jerky, rhythm. They were all planets in Helen's orbit. Now, without her gravity to hold them, everyone's suddenly become unbound—almost gleefully so, it feels to Al, as if they'd just been waiting for an excuse to fling themselves away from the center. He's aware that some people, such as hippies, prefer to live amongst the chaos of achronicity, but to Al this is little better than lying down with pigs. Clocks were invented for a reason. So where the hell is everyone?

He knows he can try calling people on their cell phones, but Al is convinced that everyone finds cell phones as startling as he does. Rita's probably at the restaurant. Imagine: her phone rings as she's shouldering a tray full of dirty dishes—pandemonium ensues, broken dishes everywhere, irate customers with soup of the day in their laps or scalding coffee in their faces. The world is full of accidents waiting to happen, potential energy coiled and ready to spring the moment you let your guard down. Jeremy could be driving, and he might collide with another car. Then there is Jeanie Rae, who is out somewhere, but who knows where, and doing God knows what. She's been a mystery to him ever since that day nineteen years ago when she announced she was pregnant and had no intention of revealing who the father was, so don't ask, ever. His main fear about calling her is that she might answer.

Meanwhile, there's a freezer stuffed with brick-hard chickens, roasts, and chops. He's the one who worked to provide these things. Damned if he's going to be the one to cook them too. This was the arrangement he had made with Helen: he would make the living, and she would make the living worthwhile. He doesn't see why that arrangement should be adjusted now just because she's dead. There's a vacancy in the house, and it yawns at him, an empty tooth socket, a movie flickering in a deserted theater.

"Daboo," says Henry.

"What?" says Al.

"I wanna possicle," Henry says.

"Get up and get it yourself. You're not completely helpless."

"No, *I* wanna possicle," says Henry, as if Al has misheard. "Praise the Lord."

"The Lord has nothing to do with Popsicles," says Al. Or anything else, he adds to himself. Religion had been Helen's foolishness. That and sugar products. Maybe now that Helen isn't here to stuff the boy's face, he'll start to lose some weight.

It's an outright disgrace, he thinks. Porky kids everywhere you look. In the old days, if a kid was fat, you teased him about it until he got thin. Bullying has an evolutionary purpose. Nowadays they send you to prison for it, which is why the human race in general, and the American race in particular, has ceased to progress and is now slowly spinning in a lame circle, mired to the waist in its own lard.

Al sits, determined, feeling his house snug around him like a carapace. He'll never get used to this creeping silence. Helen had abhorred silence. She was always making some kind of noise, humming a tune or talking to herself or chattering to him whether he listened or not. Half the time it drove him crazy. Now, despite the blathering of the television, it's so quiet the walls are echoing his tinnitus.

Al thinks back to when they moved here, twenty-three years ago. They'd bought this place because it had four bedrooms. Rita had moved out by then, and he'd assumed Jeanie would soon be going too. One bedroom was to have been for Al and the other for Helen, since sharing the same bed was a form of marital torture. Al thrashed his way through his nights, fighting off a never-ending stream of imaginary attackers like some kind of somnambulistic kung fu master, while through Helen's nose emerged the noise of a shovel scraping along bare cement. Nobody ever believed him about Helen's snoring, least of all Helen herself, until one night he'd recorded her and played it back in the morning. She'd accused him of doctoring it, so he'd gone to the extraordinary step of purchasing a brand-new Sony video camera and setting it up on a tripod in their bedroom. Then there was no denying it: there she was, flowered nightgown and all, head thrown back and an ungodly noise issuing from her throat. To his amazement, that whole incident was his fault, somehow. She'd walked around with a wounded attitude for days, but right was right and Al had won. He got his own room, and rejoiced.

The third bedroom was to be Al's office, and the fourth was meant to be used for Helen's crafts. She was a heart maker. She took the balsa wood hearts that Al shaped for her on his jigsaw and painted them a deep, arterial red, with cute sayings written on glued-on paper scrolls in the calligraphy she'd learned in Home Ec decades earlier. Some said *Home is where the heart is*, and others *A dream is a wish your heart makes*, and some just said *Heart to heart*. She was always trying to think of something more clever to put on them, but she never succeeded. It didn't matter to her what they said, as long as it had the word *heart* in it. She sold them for three dollars and fifty cents apiece. The hearts also took the form of Christmas tree ornaments, which was achieved by screwing an eye hook in the top and then attaching a loop of colorful ribbon. For this, she charged an extra dollar.

But she was also famous for giving the hearts away at every opportunity. Every one of their acquaintances had a small collection. Some displayed theirs prominently all year round, others only when it was known she would be coming for a visit. If a craft fair or a flea market was held anywhere within a twenty-mile radius, Helen would be at one of the tables, doing a slow but steady business. All in all, when she considered her expenses and her time, she might break even. But then, making hearts was never about the money. It was about the small amount of warmth she felt as she watched each one find a new home. Helen had believed that no one ever used a heart for bad purposes, nor could they see one without remembering that they were loved. The more hearts in the world, the better. When she had once heard herself referred to as the Heart Lady, she told Al, her own had swelled with pride.

Now Al has a closetful of hearts in various stages of completion. They mock him every time he looks for his shoes. They need to be dealt with; he can't bear to look at them. What does one do with such things? Chucking them in the trash is out of the question. No charity would want them. He's not about to set up a table at a craft fair or something like that; the very phrase "craft fair" makes his balls hurt. Maybe a yard sale is the answer. The basement and garage are full of other shit that needs to go too, twenty-three years' worth of stuff that has accumulated like flotsam after a flood.

But the thought of that is exhausting. These days, he can barely summon the energy to get out of his LongLax lounger. He cannot imagine allowing hordes of strangers onto his property to paw through his stuff in search of bargains. The way he feels these days, stupid, old, and thick, he would mistakenly sell his whole house for five bucks to some sharper and be out on the street. And this house is all he has.

Al hasn't told anyone, but his retirement fund was wiped out when Lehman Brothers went down the drain: nearly six hundred thousand dollars. He'd been able to hide it from Helen because money made her nervous, which meant it was his job to read the statements every month and plan their spending accordingly. That was three years ago. After the crash, he'd been left with about a hundred thousand, but all that remains of that, after various expenses, is about thirty. That, he knows, will not be enough. Not even close.

And this is why he's planning to kill himself, as soon as he can work up the nerve.

Helen spared herself a thousand smaller deaths by dying too soon; watching her family descend into penury would have broken her heart. And the whole prospect of his own death seems much more palatable now that she's gone first. He looks forward to it the way he looks forward to sleep. The time is coming. He can feel it. Really, the only thing holding him back is the paperwork. He wants to sign everything over to Rita beforehand, in order to avoid any problems with probates or inheritance taxes or any of that nonsense. Al's hatred of bureaucracy is such that he dreads the paperwork more than suicide itself, even though he has yet to decide how to do it. He does know one thing for sure: no matter what, he's not going to do it in the house.

When they bought this house, they'd been assured that Elysium would soon become the next LA. This was the vision that crooked little Ouranakis had had, an LA for the right kind of people, and even though Ouranakis had been dead for decades, his small but devoted coterie of real estate agents still soldiered on, a second-generation platoon of acquisitive acolytes who specialized in convincing the gullible that Elysium was a fabulous and far-sighted investment. It seemed that it was not enough simply to buy in Elysium; one had to believe in Elysium.

Well, the joke was on them. Al had never actually believed, though he'd pretended to. If he had wanted to live in any kind of LA, he would have simply moved to the real LA. Al bought precisely because he knew Ouranakis's dream would fail, and it was his life's work, water, that allowed him this secret knowledge—because he knew there was no way they would ever manage to get enough water pumped in here to support fifty thousand people, let alone millions. Nobody ever thinks about water, Al often reflects smugly, because everyone is stupid. As a result of Ouranakis's ignorance, which was typical of so many foreigners, the empty town has an air of exclusivity that he enjoys immensely. Driving the streets until they dwindle into the desert, he has the feeling that he's one of the few to have discovered a well-kept secret—perhaps a little too well kept for Ouranakis's taste, but just fine for Al's. There is no traffic, and there never will be. No muggings, no rapes, no car theft, no crime at all but for a little vandalism. He and Helen planned on savoring every thermonuclear Mojave day in peace and quiet.

But none of this ever came to pass, because Rita had moved back in with them, taking up the bedroom that was to have been Helen's craft space. She'd brought Jeremy along, and Henry had appeared shortly after, occupying the bedroom that had been Jeanie's. Then the market crashed, and Al had reason to regret buying a house that was never going to appreciate.

At that moment, a car squeaks to a halt outside. It's Jeremy, driving the Saturn. Al can tell there's more dust in the brake pads now than there was this morning. The car always sounds worse after Jeremy's been driving it.

Al stands as his eldest grandson opens the door. "Where have you been?"

Jeremy shrugs. "Staff meeting."

Al's prepared speech evaporates. He hates to see the boy so gimpy. He himself managed to get through two tours without getting wounded. Not a scratch. It had been a running joke among his buddies: he was probably going to get hit by a bus on his first day back in the world. But his war had not touched him, not the way it had the other guys. If not for his dreams, he would wonder if any of it really happened.

"Oh," says Al.

"Hello Jermy," says Henry solemnly. "Where did you go?"

"I went to my job, Henry," says Jeremy. "Remember? I'm a teacher now."

"Can I come with you tomorrow?"

"No, Henry, you can't. Sorry."

"Why not?"

"Because, buddy. What would you do all day?"

"I would help you send the bad kids to detention."

"*Now* he wants to go to school," Al says.

Jeremy closes the door after him and goes through the living room. "Did Henry take his afternoon pill?"

"I have no idea," Al says.

"Henry, did you take your afternoon pill?"

"I have no idea," Henry says, in a perfect imitation of Al's detached tone.

Jeremy sighs. "Grandpa. We gotta stay on top of this. He's gonna have a seizure if we don't."

"Because I am electric," says Henry.

"Epileptic," says Jeremy. "Where's Mom?"

"At the restaurant," Al says.

"What about Jeanie Rae?"

"Gone," Henry says mournfully.

"I don't know where she is," Al says.

"Has anyone started dinner yet?" Jeremy asks.

"No," says Al.

Jeremy stands, rocking side to side, the way he does when his back is bugging him. "Look, Grandpa, you gotta pick up some of the slack around here. Mom can't do everything. It would be nice if she could come home to find food on the table just once in a goddamn while, wouldn't it? Isn't it enough she has to work her ass off serving people all day?"

"Listen," said Al. He doesn't know how the boy can speak to him so, without a trace of embarrassment. It's appalling. He hadn't always been this way. Just since he came home. Simply refuses to recognize Al's natural superiority as patriarch of the clan. If Al had spoken like this to his own grandfather, the entire family would have applauded as he was hauled outside and given a switching. Nowadays, if a man tries to lift a finger to remind people who's boss, he gets his picture in the paper and has to appear before a judge. They were standing ankle deep in the shards of the convictions that had sustained this country through its first centuries of existence. This was what it felt like when the world had already ended, but people were too stubborn to admit it.

"Yeah, I'm listening," says Jeremy, but this is a patent lie; he's already headed for the basement, where he lives.

"Jermy, I wanna possicle," says Henry.

"You can get your own Popsicle, Henry," says Jeremy. "You know where they are. You know how to open them. You're not a baby anymore."

"Yup. I am a man. I am eighteen years old," Henry announces. He sits in his recliner and looks with supreme smugness at Al, as if a major point has just been conceded. Both of them listen to Jeremy's feet pound on the vibrating stairs.

"I'm so tired," says Al.

"Praise the Lord," says Henry.

"Okay," says Al. "Whatever." He goes into the kitchen, takes a chicken out of the freezer, and addresses himself to the micro-wave.

3

JEREMY has lived in the basement of this house on and off since he was five years old. He dwells in a netherworld into which people from the Upper Sphere venture only to do laundry, or to hunt for elusive hardware-related items: paintbrushes, screwdrivers, oil cans, and the like. There was a time, many years earlier, when it had the feeling of a secret clubhouse, but now he feels entombed in a miasma of radon, and several feet of dead desert dirt. He is kin to the slaves buried alive with their lords in ancient times, that they might serve them into the afterlife. This is how he feels, even though, as an American, he is supposed to be free. Things are not great, he thinks; but imagine how much worse they'd be if he'd been born somewhere else. This is what Al would say.

Jeremy goes to the utility sink, pees in it, then fills his electric kettle from the tap. When the water boils, he pops a fat knuckle of Northern Lights into his teapot and leaves it to steep. Then he lies down on his bed and stares upward. Another happening Friday night in Elysium. Overhead is the tramping of feet, the creaking and bellying of the plywood ceiling. He can tell who is who by how much the wood gives. Al has the lightest feet and is the smallest of them all. He still possesses the same stealth with which he crept through the jungles of Vietnam forty years ago; Jeremy understands now how such habits could become learned in a matter of hours but ingrained for a lifetime. Rita and Helen had been hard to tell apart because they weighed about the same, but Rita was younger and moved faster. Henry is the biggest and slowest of them, even though he's also the youngest, and when he goes from room to room, the house shifts to accommodate him. Someday, Jeremy believes, Henry will come crashing down through the floor. With his luck, he'll land right on Jeremy's face, and if he doesn't crush him to death right away, he'll smother him slowly.

From upstairs, he hears Henry's dim voice: I wanna possicle. Al's blank expostulations, footsteps again, the sound of the freezer door opening and closing.

Henry and his goddamn Popsicles.

Once, an embedded reporter had asked Jeremy what he was fighting for. It was the noobest question someone could ask. It was beyond noob. Of course, they were not fighting for anything. Everyone knew that. They fought because if they didn't fight, they would be killed by the assholes who kept sneaking up on their FOB and trying to cut their heads off. Was there a better reason than that?

Yet it was Henry's rotund face that swam before Jeremy's eyes, and it was only the thought of Henry that allowed Jeremy to keep his cool and inform his questioner that if he ever asked him something so stupid again, he would pound his balls up into his body and rip them out through his asshole. The entire squad had roared its approval at that. They loved it. Go Merkin, go Merkin! They went into their tribal dance then, the way they did when Woot whipped them up into a frenzy, and Jeremy feinted at the reporter as if he was going to grab his nut sack. He'd never seen a man run so fast before. A reprimand came down from the colonel that evening, but Woot covered for him. Woot was good at making up lies to cover bad behavior.

But scaring the reporter didn't make him feel better. For the rest of that day, and for many days after, he continued to see Henry's face everywhere, and he wondered why. Finally, he'd decided to talk to Smarty about it.

And Smarty had explained:

"You're thinking about Henry because he's really what you're fighting for. You keep seeing Henry's face because you protected him all his life. Right?"

"How the fuck did you know that?" Jeremy asked, amazed.

"Because you've told me yourself about fifty times," Smarty said patiently. "So when you think of fighting, you think about Henry. Even though he's not here. It's an association. You dig?"

"Yeah, I dig," Jeremy said. Once again, he was embarrassed at his own stupidity. He always felt that way during a SmartyTalk. The cool thing about Smarty was that he never rubbed it in. That was why everybody loved him. He had a way of explaining things that made everyone feel as if he was some kind of knowledgeable older uncle, although he was no older than the rest of them. Even Cap'n Woot would fall silent, nodding, as Smarty launched into an explanation of this or that, forgetting for the moment that he—Woot—was a bloodthirsty motherfucker. Smarty wasn't afraid of Woot. He wasn't afraid of anything.

Woot. Jeremy thought he'd forgotten about him. But Woot still lurks just underneath the surface, popping out of his memory every time he gets upset about something. He supposes that most veterans throughout history have had nightmares about the enemy. Very few of them, he believes, had nightmares about their own commanding officers. But when Jeremy gives in to his panic attacks and imagines them coming for him, it is not just a bunch of raggedy, dusty men in turbans toting Russian rifles and RPGs that he sees. Sometimes it is Woot, a cigar sticking out of his mouth and a forage cap sideways on his head, a demonic grin on his face; and it is not the things he would do that Jeremy fears, but the things he would order Jeremy to do. And the fact that Jeremy knows he would obey.

His tea has long been ready and is now cold in the pot. Jeremy hoists it up and swigs directly from the spout. Then he lies down again, folds his hands behind his head, and waits for the analgesic effects of the herb to kick in. At that moment, his phone announces the arrival of a new text. It's from Jenn: ˉ

U BASDERT!!!

Jeremy regards this blankly for a moment. Jenn's work is usually sloppy and often wrong, when she bothers to turn it in at all, but bad spelling isn't one of her faults.

He types back: *EXCUSE ME?*

He waits for an answer to ping back. But all he gets is his own message, marked undeliverable.

When he's next aware of anything, it's that he's just had the blank nightmare again: no images, just smoke and burning flesh. This is the only way he is able to remember even a little bit of what happened: shards of recollection gleaned from the aftermath of dreams. Of the explosion itself, he remembers nothing.

The smell lingers after he heaves himself into a sitting position, and so after a moment he realizes he'd fallen asleep, and someone has burned something upstairs in the kitchen. He's not back in Afghanistan.

Automatically, he checks his phone. No new texts, no new emails. Upstairs, he finds Rita picking through a sink full of dishes, an archaeologist combing through the submerged relics of some ancient suburban society. The remains of a pizza sit on the cutting board. The digits on the microwave inform him that it's nearly seven o'clock.

"What the fuck is that smell?" he asks.

Rita sighs. "Would you please stop with the fuck? I'm your mother."

"Sorry."

"Your grandfather decided to nuke a chicken on high for an hour," says Rita. "We ordered out." She nods in the direction of the trash. Jeremy lifts the lid and sees a carcass that looks as if it first exploded then mummified. He ties the plastic loops of the bag together and carries it out into the garage. Flies hum from the bowels of a can that's already overflowing with trash. He missed the last pickup day. The garage reeks. He crams the bag in, balances the lid on top, and opens the automatic door to let the stink out. Then he goes back into the kitchen.

"I didn't want to wake you," Rita says. "You looked like you needed to sleep. I guess you must have been tired, with all the work you did today." She gives him an arch look.

"What do you mean?" Jeremy asks, cautious, sensing he's in trouble.

"I saw you at the motel."

"What?" Jeremy is startled. "How?"

"Because I was there."

"Why were you there?"

"I was with Sam," she says.

"Oh."

"What do you mean, *oh*?"

"Nothing. Can't a guy say *oh* without getting the third degree?"

"You don't like Sam."

"You know what people say about him."

"What?"

"He's a terrorist."

"Oh, for Christ's sake, Jeremy, he's not a terrorist. He's a Sikh."

"I know that," says Jeremy. "But who else around here knows the difference? All they know is he wears a rag on his head."

"It's a turban. It's a symbol of his faith."

"I—know—that—too," Jeremy says, with exaggerated patience. "I'm not talking about me. I'm talking about the people of this town. That's who I'm talking about."

"Since when do you care so much what other people think?"

"I don't. I don't even know why we're having this stupid conversation. I don't want to hear about your love life. It makes me want to puke." He picks up a slice of pizza and begins removing the mushrooms, tossing them one by one into the sink.

"Well, how do you think I feel, seeing you pull up there and going into that girl's room?"

"How did you know whose room it was?"

"I have eyes, Jeremy. I saw her go in."

"Great. Who else saw her?"

"Sam. He only rented her the damn room."

"Oh, boy."

"And then somebody else showed up," she says.

"What? When?"

"About twenty minutes after you left. Some guy in a pickup truck. Had a ponytail. Old enough to be her dad."

"Oh, great," says Jeremy. "What happened then?"

Rita shrugs. "He went in, and I stopped watching. I've got better things to do than sit at the window all day. But you'd better not mess with her, Jeremy. She looks like trouble."

"I'm not messing with her," Jeremy says. "I went there to talk with her."

"Oh, yeah, right. How'd that conversation go?"

"I'm serious. She's got major problems."

"What kind of problems?"

"I can't talk about it. I promised."

"Whatever it is, don't get involved."

"I already am involved. The girl's in trouble, Mom."

"Can't she go to someone else? You don't need this drama, whatever it is."

"She's afraid."

"Can't you go to someone else?"

Jeremy doesn't answer this. He removes the last of the mushrooms and starts eating. Rita grabs a plate from the cupboard and sticks it under his face. Jeremy takes it and goes out to the table. Rita follows him and throws a napkin, which lands on his head.

"Come on, Jeremy, please," she says. "Manners."

He removes the napkin from his head with as much dignity as he can muster. Al has resumed his post in the living room in front of the television. Jeremy looks at the screen, where American tanks are rolling through Paris for the millionth time. Cheering Frenchmen wave. It's weird to look at a crowd of thousands of people and know that all of them must be dead now, even the children. They must have thought their liberation would last forever, but in the end everyone just dies, and they couldn't be liberated from that. This thought underscores the pointlessness of everything, from Hitler's invasion of France to the act of eating this pizza, and yet his jaws go on working and he keeps on swallowing, until the pinprick of this moment dissolves. He must do something to help Jenn. But what?

Henry sits at the other end of the table, wearing an ancient Walkman that once belonged to Rita. Frank Sinatra leaks from the headphones. Henry sings along: New York, New York . . . a hell of a town. Only Henry doesn't say *hell*, he says *aitch ee double hockey sticks*. Helen had taught him about the evils of swearing. He's poring over a black leather-bound book, his lips working as he labors to sound out words and numbers. Jeremy recognizes Rita's address book.

"Whatsa matter with you?" Jeremy asks around a mouthful of pizza.

"My mom is gone," Henry says.

"Mom," says Jeremy through the doorway.

From the kitchen: "Yeah?"

"Isn't Jeanie back yet?"

"No, she is not," says Al.

Rita appears in the kitchen doorway again and gives Jeremy another eyebrow. Jeremy gets up and goes back into the kitchen. She runs water in the sink to cover the sound of her voice.

"Where'd she go?" he asks, sotto voce.

"Her stuff is gone," she tells Jeremy. "She just up and left again."

"Fuck me," says Jeremy. He rubs his face, forgetting for the moment that his hands are covered in pizza grease. "She didn't say anything?"

"Nope." Rita shakes her hands semi-dry and grabs a corner of her apron. Licking it, she goes for Jeremy's face. He ducks out of the way, protecting himself with his arms.

"Quit it," he says.

"I'm your mother."

"That's what I mean." She desists. Jeremy straightens, wary.

"All right. I give up. Wipe your own face."

He does so, gladly.

"It's not like she was going to stay forever anyway," he says. "She was only home for the memorial service."

"That's not the point, Jeremy. She does this every single year. She comes back, she makes promises, she leaves. She doesn't even say goodbye. It's hard on the poor little guy."

"Little? He weighs three hundred pounds," Jeremy says.

"Now he's going to mope for days and days," says Rita, as if she hasn't heard. "I might have to take him back to the doctor if he keeps up like this. This kind of stuff can bring on more seizures."

"Henry doesn't have seizures anymore."

"That's because he takes medication. And he avoids stress."

"I'll say he avoids stress," says Jeremy. "Did you try her cell phone?"

"It goes right to voice mail. She's on a plane, probably."

"Or screening her calls," he says.

"And that pisses me off. Who are we, a credit card company? I'm her sister. I could be calling with more bad news."

"You are. We exist. That's the bad news."

"Yeah, well," says Rita. "I don't know why I thought things would be different now, just because Mom is gone. I guess I thought it would make her grow up. Or maybe make her remember that Henry is hers. But she couldn't get out of here fast enough. And to not even say goodbye? Come on."

Jeremy looks over his shoulder at Henry. His blinders ride high up on his forehead. He stares down at the book. Not even the Lord can save him from these moods.

"I'll talk to him," says Jeremy.

"Please do," says Rita. "You're the only one who can."

At bedtime, Jeremy sits on the edge of Henry's bed. Henry lies with the sheet pulled up under his chin, tucked in as tightly as possible to create a perfect seal against ghosts and monsters. In the years that Jeremy was away, no one tucked him in correctly at all, Henry has informed him repeatedly. Not even Nanny. No one tucked him in like Jeremy did. Smitty lies next to him, gazing up at the ceiling with a calm, one-eyed knowingness.

"Watcha thinking about?" Jeremy says.

"Nothing," says Henry.

"Nothing at all?"

"Hmm."

"Pretty hard not to think about anything at all."

Normally Henry would rise to this bait, in his own fashion. Conversations with Henry are not really conversations, even when he's at his best; they're like lobbing a softball into the air and watching it slump back to earth. But now he just lies there, looking up at the ceiling.

"Don't be sad, champeen. You gotta be tough."

"I miss Nanny."

"I know. I miss Nanny too. We all do."

"She's in heaven."

The only time Jeremy can go along with this lie is when he's talking to Henry.

"Yup. She's in heaven."

Henry nods. "With a lamb."

"There are lambs in heaven?"

Henry nods again. "Proton is there too. Praise the Lord."

"Proton is in heaven too? With Nanny?"

"Oh yeah," Henry says. "For sure." He wrinkles his brow, thinking about something. "How far is New York New York? Is it on the same ground we're on?"

"It's too far, Henry. Crazy far."

"Do you have to take an airplane there?"

"Yes."

"Can you drive there?"

"Yes, but it would take a long time."

"Can we take a bus?"

"You can't go to New York, Henry. It's too far away. And too big. There are lots of people, and they're all in a big hurry. All kinds of loud noises, which you don't like. Your mom knows you wouldn't like it there at all. And if you lived in New York, you would never get to see Daboo or Rita or me or Nan—"

He stops himself, hoping it's not too late. The litany of names is so familiar that he knows it will be years, if ever, before he can remember to abbreviate it. But Henry appears not to have noticed. He has a faraway look.

"Henry?"

"What?"

"What's on your mind?"

"The Green Witch," says Henry.

"What green witch?"

"The Green Witch has my mom."

"There are no witches, dude," says Jeremy. "Witches aren't real." He tries to deduce where Henry might have gotten this from. Running through his mental catalog of witches, one leaps out at him: the Wicked Witch of the West. The Wizard of Oz must have been playing on one of the roughly four thousand television channels that come in through Al's pirated satellite signal.

"You've been watching television," Jeremy says accusingly. "Henry, you can't do that. You have to keep your blinders on." He will have to talk to Al about having the TV on all day, he thinks. But Al will only shrug his shoulders and say he can't keep an eye on the kid every goddamn minute. That had been Helen's job. Maybe installing the parental control password is the way to go, except that will confound Henry and Al.

"Stop worrying about witches," Jeremy tells him. "They're just make-believe. Your mom is fine. Do you trust me?"

Henry looks at him solemnly and nods. "Yes, Jermy. I trust you."

"Your mom is fine. Now go to sleep."

"Okay. Jermy?"

"What?"

"I love you."

"That's nice, you homo."

"Jermy. Say it."

"No. I'm not saying it."

"Say it, Jermy. Say it. Please."

"All right, all right," Jeremy says. He makes a show of looking over both shoulders, to make sure no one else can hear. "Henry is my buddy. Henry is a cool guy. Henry is tops of the world."

"Henry is my bestest friend," Henry suggests.

"Yeah. Henry is my bestest friend. And if he doesn't go to sleep, I'm gonna break his arms and legs with a sledgehammer. Yaaaay, Henry."

"You still didn't say it, Jermy."

Jeremy sighs. "I love you, Henry."

Henry giggles. He rolls over and is asleep by the time Jeremy has gained the door. He can tell by the sound of his breathing.

4

LATE THAT NIGHT, Al sits in his LongLax lounger, feigning sleep. This is the only way he comes to know things. Nobody tells him anything; the best he can hope for is that people will forget he's there and talk around him. He can see Rita through one quarter-open eye, sitting alone at the kitchen table, looking at her address book. He already knows it's open to the page with Jeanie's Greenwich Village address and cell number, which now bears Henry's thumbprint in pizza sauce. She's called her three times already, but Jeanie still isn't answering. Rita hasn't bothered leaving messages. Al knows she will try her again every half hour until she answers.

Then she'll go to Sam's, where they'll get up to God knows what. The disturbing thing about Rita is that she is a woman, and Al knows women must get fucked on a regular basis or they start to go crazy. He doesn't want to admit these things about his own daughters. He feels he cannot both accept this fact and still believe they were ever his girls, for when it comes to women, he feels the natural contempt that the one who fucks feels for the one who gets fucked. He was hoping his girls would turn out to be different, somehow. Above the whole thing. Better than him. He's not sure he can forgive Rita for being human. She certainly hasn't forgiven him for it. Jeanie, he wrote off long ago.

He must know how to take care of her, that Sam. He probably strokes her face, tickles her back, caresses her body. He probably unwinds his turban and show her his most glorious secret: his hair. Everyone thinks Al is an ignorant fool, but he knows that Sikhs have long, flowing locks under those diapers they wear on their heads. Sam keeps his hair hidden during the day, but at night, only for her, Al bets he lets it fall streaming over his shoulders. He bets he sits naked before her, brushing it, while she watches and pretends he's some kind of exotic Indian prince, and she his concubine.

Al imagines Sam's bedroom to be decorated in gold-leafed wallpaper, like an Indian restaurant, with a golden carpet as thick as an Ohio lawn. Pictures of holy sites and ancient temples adorn the walls. Incense smolders in a brass holder on his nightstand. He worships strange gods and eats with his hands. It's not that Al despises these outlandish foreign religions; he despises all religions. They're ridiculous, each and every one of them. The country has long been overrun with right-wing zealots, hypocrisy dripping from their voices like blood from a blade. He cannot defend them any more than he can defend the liberal idiots who think that everything that's wrong with the world is America's fault. This is why he votes Libertarian. Anyone who follows any religion is a complete idiot. There is no God.

He sees, through his heavy-lidded eye, Rita looking at him. He snaps his eye shut and fakes a snore.

So Jeanie is gone again. What else is new? It would have been easier if she'd just never come home. Something broke in her after Henry was born. You could see it in her eyes. Being pregnant had begun to crack her, and giving birth had finished the job. She was never the same after that.

Rita is eight years older than Jeanie, which sometimes seems like a whole generation. Jeanie certainly had a completely different childhood. Al knows that if either of them had a reason to leave, it was Rita, not Jeanie Rae. In the old days, Al often didn't return home from work until ten o'clock, and then it was Rita, not Jeanie—who, after all, was only a baby—who got hauled out of bed to answer for bad report cards, for a mess left in the kitchen, to explain why a boy had called the house and not left his name. He cringes inwardly for the millionth time. He's never let go of any of this. He sees his own finger wagging in her face, the flecks of his spittle landing on her cheeks. Once, she had dared him to just hit her and get it over with. He wondered for years why she'd said that. He thinks he has it now: because at least then she would have been able to name the kind of pain she felt. So she could finally point to a real reason why she hated him. He knew she hoped that one day he simply wouldn't come home from work. She would rage at him for fighting with Helen. She was so tired of his excuses, she said, but they were not excuses, they were real: it was a long commute; he worked hard; if he stopped to pick up a six-pack and drink it in the parking lot of the Legion with his friends, he didn't have to answer to anyone.

In the morning he would see her at the breakfast table, looking as exhausted as he felt, dreading another day of school, her eyes foggy and her face a storm-wracked beach. Her father's daughter. Homework not done again, because the abyss in her stomach made fractions and spelling not only difficult but irrelevant. He could see all of this in her, and more besides. Helen was always being called in to talk with her teachers; he was too busy working or sleeping to bother attending these meetings. He couldn't stomach listening to women talk. They never listened to each other, they just ran their mouths. But he always got the full report later. Rita doesn't listen in class. Rita doesn't get along with other children. Rita is antisocial. Rita is not academic material.

Rita's father is an alcoholic, Al had often wanted to point out. But you do not use that word to describe yourself; you wait for someone else to point it out. And no one had ever had the courage to say this to him. So it was not his fault.

Jeanie managed to avoid his worst years. Except for a couple of spectacular falls off the wagon, Al had quit drinking when she was still a child. She didn't know the Al Rita had known. Was Rita happy or sad about this? Al couldn't tell. What he knew was that Rita was torn between loving her sister and hating her. Jeanie was a princess, and Rita a statue. He had hewn his elder daughter out of stone.

I'm sorry, he wants to say. But he pretends to keep on sleeping.

Theirs was a family of bad sleepers: Helen rasped, Al had his nightmares, Rita didn't fall asleep until one or two in the morning. Jeanie became a sleepwalker. Sometimes, Helen told him, she awoke to find Jeanie standing next to their bed, staring at her creepily. She would lead her back to her bed and tuck her in, unnerved by the way the girl looked, as if she was in one of those movies about demonic possession. At other times, someone might hear her stumbling around the house, and they would find her making bizarre concoctions in the kitchen out of lettuce and eggs, or vacuuming the living room rug with the vacuum not even plugged in. One night, Al heard the front door open and close. He ran outside in his underwear, clutching his .357, to find Jeanie walking down the street, out like a light, on some kind of mission. Everyone was uneasy after that incident.

"You share a room. It's your job to make sure she doesn't do that again," Al said to Rita, because this was in the old house in Lancaster, before they'd moved to Elysium. "If she gets out, it'll be your fault."

Nothing must happen to the princess.

And then there was the time they found her heading for the lake, with the infant Henry in her arms. Better not to think about that, he decides. He fakes another snore.

Rita could not graduate from high school fast enough. Apparently her life needed a fast-forward button. On graduation night, she went out with a gang of friends. Al lay awake in bed, worrying. He knew what was going on, but she was already beyond his control. Beers were being consumed. Vomit was being projectiled. Sex was being had. How was it Jeanie had been the one to get pregnant? He heard her come stumbling in at three a.m. to find ten-year-old Jeanie Rae waiting up for her.

"I'm telling on you," Jeanie had said.

"You're asleep, Jeanie," Rita told her.

"I am?"

"Yes. This is all a dream. Go back to bed."

That kid would believe anything.

The next year, a grown woman of nineteen, Rita fast-forwarded into adulthood. College was out of the question. Al prayed she would meet someone rich. Instead, she went to San Francisco to live with Wilkins, the manic-depressive artist she'd met at a concert in the desert—the kind of concert you did not simply attend so much as become a citizen of, for a brief but life-altering weekend. Jeanie and Helen sobbed as Rita said goodbye. Al leaned against the trunk of his car, arms folded, at a loss to express or explain the hollow feeling in his chest.

"I want to be grown up and beautiful like you," Jeanie said to Rita.

Rita gathered Jeanie into her arms, promised she'd come back for lots of visits as soon as she could get away. She gave the same kind of hug to Helen. She hugged Al too, but fast, arms straight down at her sides, with him patting her shoulder blades, turned awkwardly away so he wouldn't feel his daughter's breasts pressing into his chest. She did not understand this about his hugs; she thought he hated her. He sees that now. He was only trying to be proper. No one ever understood anything he did. You try to do the right thing and everyone assumes you're doing it for the wrong reasons.

Rita didn't come back, as long as things were good with Wilkins, which they were for that first year. The only year, as it turned out.

Jeremy was born fast. Rita brought him home for visits. She didn't bring Wilkins, who couldn't be bothered to make the trek south. Al could tell he despised him and Helen, and the feeling was mutual, as far as Al was concerned. Well, lost that one, he thought. Maybe there's hope for the other one.

But there wasn't. One day he woke up and found that Jeanie was no longer a gawky, stick-thin adolescent but a gorgeous demigoddess, a teenager with the body of a twenty-five-year-old. There was no hint that Jeanie had been cursed with the kind of beauty that caused traffic accidents until it sprang upon her almost overnight. Then her future was foretold; Al could see it in the shape of her face, in the gentle swell of her hips and breasts, like wavelets foretelling a great disturbance out to sea. She'd won some kind of genetic lottery for which Rita held the losing ticket.

Rita was not an unattractive girl, dark complected, a nice face, but he knew she thought her ass was too big, her tits too small, her eyes too far apart, nose too flaring. All this was her own assessment of herself, which as a teenager she used to share with Helen during her frequent lapses into self-pity, and which Helen had relayed to him during his infrequent check-ins on the status of his so-called family.

"She's had her share of boyfriends," Al told Helen. "What's she complaining about?" What he did not say was that Rita was the lucky one, not Jeanie Rae.

"It's just hard for a girl," Helen said.

"What isn't hard for girls? Every goddamn thing is a personal crisis. The drama in this house is unending."

By the time Jeanie Rae was sixteen, her beauty had achieved a level that made people want to whip themselves. She had the kind of looks other women paid thousands for and never quite achieved: thick, nearly blond hair, a generous chest, thin waist, ass and legs as perfect as if she'd selected them from a catalog. Her cheekbones were high and sharp, her jaw well defined, her ski jump of a nose small and perky. Her one flaw was a gap between her two front teeth, but as a child she'd turned this to her advantage by learning to squirt water through it, and after she emerged from her cocoon it had the same effect as a beauty mark, a tiny imperfection that emphasized the rest of her.

Al could barely stand to look at her sometimes. It astonished him that he'd had a hand in the creation of this person. There had once seemed to him to be something untouchable about beautiful women, something divine, mysterious, and unknowable, and it was strange to think not only that was this untrue, but that he was the man behind the curtain all along, that someone like him had sparked her into being. As he approached the end of his life, he could see that everything he'd believed at the beginning of it was completely wrong. This was a great joke, wasn't it? Except no one got it but him.

He couldn't stand to walk in public with his younger daughter, because of the stares of other men. His fists were clenched in anger so often that his knuckles ached. He began to avoid even the most casual family outings, not that he wasn't already practiced in this area from the days when alcohol had come before everything else. Helen bore this kind of sexual scrutiny differently. That was the way nature worked, she explained. Someone had to be the ogler and someone the oglee. Al said on more than one occasion that he understood now why the ragheads kept their women wrapped from head to toe and forbade them to leave the house without male company. He'd always thought that was backwards of them, but when Jeanie blossomed, he began to feel that this woman-wrapping was actually a mighty fine idea.

Rita echoed Al's complaint whenever she gave in to Jeanie's constant requests to take her somewhere interesting, to the movie theater or the mall in Lancaster, or all the way to LA if they were feeling ambitious. She and Jeremy were back in Elysium by then, Rita having had it with Wilkins: the fights over whether to spend money on his drugs or on food and clothing for Jeremy; his crying jags; his general uselessness. She would leave the toddler Jeremy with Helen, and she and Jeanie Rae would go star-spotting on the Strip, or to wander the board-walk in Santa Monica. Jeanie had loved these excursions with her older sister, but she came back from the last one in tears. No matter where they went, she said, the men appeared, swarming around her like insects seeking to lay their eggs. Rita said she had to push them away bodily. She hated the greasy feel of their muscles, she said, and Al imagined them sliding like live things under their sunscreened skin.

Helen pumped Jeanie for information on what had happened. Jeanie finally confessed that they'd gotten back in the car, Rita shaking with anger and fear. She'd thought it was all a game, so Rita had taken it upon herself to explain: They want to fuck you, she'd said. They want to fuck you and tell all their friends about it, and then they want to dump you. Because they're guys, and that's what guys do.

Well, Al thought, after receiving this latest bulletin. Isn't that the way it is? The world is a shitty place. People want to fuck my daughter.

This thought made him crazy enough. What made him cra-zier was the fact that she might like it. He'd never been able to wrap his mind around the fact that women welcomed the desires of men. It seemed like a travesty. He knew the thoughts that men had, because he'd had them. He'd believed for much of his youth that women were clueless about these urges, that they actually fell for the smokescreens men put up around their constant ploys. It had been a stunning and disheartening revela-tion to realize that not only did they know all along, but they wel-comed it. They were whores, all of them. Even his wife. Even his daughters. He wanted to kill himself for having such thoughts. But he could not unthink them, and he did not see where he was wrong.

Rita appeared to have gone a bit too far in her explanation of how things were. Jeanie stopped asking her to take her places after that, and instead she began going to church. This surprised everyone. But it made sense, too. Church was safe; it was a sex-free zone. Rita said she felt guilty. She hoped she hadn't traumatized her sister into becoming a fundamentalist, or maybe even a nun.

Al was delighted. He did not believe Jeanie Rae had it in her to become truly religious, but he rejoiced nonetheless that perhaps she was trying to overcome the natural faithlessness of her gender. And the more time she spent in church, the less she would be exposed to the sordid world of swinging cocks, which was a truly disgusting place. Because that was the other thing Al believed about women but did not say: they were lucky not to be men.

Jeanie's transformation sparked in Helen a renewal of her own faith, which had sustained her throughout her childhood and the early days of her marriage, while Al was away in Vietnam. Maybe now Jeanie would forget this ridiculous dream of becoming a model, which had been planted in her head somehow, and instead bring her feet down to earth.

Helen and Jeanie started going to church together. They visited a squat, flat-topped building that looked more like the offices of a utility company than a stepping-stone to paradise. It was a nonthreatening, non-demanding denomination that dealt in vague exhortations to be nice to each other, with none of the gruesome displays of the more orthodox versions of Christianity—no hanging corpses, no talk of cannibalism or eternal punishment. The pastor, a former double-A quarterback named Reverend Till, received them both gladly. He treated Jeanie as if she were any normal person, which Al believed was because the Reverend was mostly blind, the result of a nasty head injury that had cut short his college career. The Reverend could not be led astray by the sight of Jeanie's body, which had derailed so many other trains of thought.

But Jeanie got knocked up anyway.

It happened at the end of her junior year of high school. After doing the math, Helen told Al it must have had its roots in a weekend church retreat, during which boys and girls had been permitted to sleep in the same general area—apparently without adequate adult supervision.

Maybe her own warnings had been a bit too subtle, Helen said. Maybe she should have simply sat Jeanie down and cautioned her about the dangers of penises. But Rita said that she remembered her own conversations with her mother about this kind of stuff, in which Helen had hedged delicately around the issue of eggs in wombs fertilized by swimming seeds, as if reproduction were a kind of genteel underwater farming.

"I told her myself, Mom," Rita said. "Because your advice was basically useless. So I told her exactly what could happen."

"Useless?" said Helen.

"You rambled about pollen and flowers. What a joke. Cocks and pussies, Mom. That's what it's all about."

"Rita!" said Helen.

"Jesus Christ," said Al. "Who's the father? That's all I wanna know." Because he had plans for the little bastard, whoever he was.

"She won't say," Helen told him. "She's keeping it a secret."

"Oh, bullshit," said Rita. "I'll get it out of her."

"Yes," Al said. "Get it out of her." He wasn't sure whether he meant the truth or the baby. He was surprised at his own resignation to this whole pregnancy thing. But he had prepared himself the way every man with daughters prepares himself: he'd known all along it was just a matter of time.

But Jeanie wouldn't tell Rita either, no matter what threats she levied or promises she made.

So Al paid a visit to Reverend Till, who was abject in his apologies. He interrogated every boy who was at the sleepover, but none of them confessed. Jeanie herself was mum, as if she'd taken some sort of oath. Al was on the verge of forcing every male in the congregation to submit to a paternity test. He would gladly have paid for it himself. It wasn't that he wanted revenge; he wanted accountability. He didn't plan on paying for someone else's goddamn mistake. Babies were expensive.

"What the hell were we thinking?" he said to Helen. "Sending her off to be watched over by a blind man? We might as well have just hung a sign around her neck and put her out by the curb."

"These things do happen," Helen said. "Sometimes you just have to make the best of it."

"Nothing just happens," Al said. He'd never approved of the way Helen saw the world, as if events were utterly beyond anyone's control, and it was simply up to people to react. This, to him, embodied the very worst aspect of femininity: the inability to make things happen. "Someone is always responsible."

"Well, it did happen," said Helen, "and there's no use getting upset about it now. We have to help her. That's all that matters."

"Why won't she say who it was?" Al moaned. "What good is all this secrecy?"

"Maybe she's afraid you're going to kill him," Rita said.

"Rita, hush," said Helen.

"Well, she is," Rita said. "It's not like you haven't done it before."

Al felt the floor falling away from him. He wasn't even mad; he simply thought he was going to faint.

"Rita, that will be enough," said Helen.

"What do you know about it?" Al whispered.

"You were in a war, weren't you?" Rita said.

"Rita," said Helen. "You shut your mouth right now."

"Well, why does it have to be some big secret? That's what wars are."

So Rita didn't know the truth about him. She only assumed. All the same, he had to go into his garage workshop to hide the panic attack that marched up out of nowhere, tapped him on the shoulder, and knocked him cold with an uppercut, like a sucker punch in a bar. All these years he had managed not to think about these things; had thought, even, that he'd succeeded in pushing them so far down they would never see daylight—yet all it took to bring them up again was one offhand comment from his daughter, who didn't even know what she was talking about.

Al and Helen had had to stop sleeping in the same bed because of the nightmares he'd had nearly every night. She used to wake up and show him where she was black and blue on her shins and arms from the pummeling she received from his heels and elbows. One awful night, she claimed, he'd climbed on top of her and grabbed her by the throat, speaking in a language that sounded like rats hissing, and with his eyes open but blank as hubcaps he'd squeezed her windpipe until she was sure she was going to die. Only the fact that he'd woken up on his own had saved her. Then he'd crawled into the bathroom and wept; that was the first time he'd ever cried in front of her. She acted afraid of him for months after that, and that was when she gave him the ultimatum: he had to quit drinking or leave. Finally he'd listened, though why this event had been enough to tip the scales when nothing else had was a mystery. Maybe he was just tired of it all. After a while he began to smooth out around the edges, though his core was still a volcano.

While Al collected himself in the garage, Helen hauled Rita off by the arm to give her a talking-to. But Helen had never seemed to understand that there could be no secrets in this house; the network of swamp cooler vents prevented that.

"Don't you ever say such things to him again," he heard through the vent.

"But what's the big deal?" Rita asked.

"He shouldn't have to think about it, that's all," Helen said. "He's never talked about it. Ever. And you shouldn't bring it up. Especially as if it was a joke."

"I'm not joking. Jeanie really thinks Dad is going to kill him, whoever he is."

"Rita," said Helen, in a tone Al had never heard her use before or since. "Don't."

Everyone thought he was deaf and stupid. He knew Rita was not pleased to be back home. He knew that the mere sound of his voice set her teeth on edge. But she had no choice. And she was still smarting from her failed relationship with Wilkins, which had not been without its violent moments—although Wilkins was apparently more into acid than booze, and he was the victim of her flying fists rather than the other way around.

"It's like he's made of glass or something," Rita said. "Why do we all have to be so careful around him?"

"He wasn't always like that. Before he went away, he was a lot of fun. The Al I married went away to Vietnam and never came back."

"Dad was a lot of fun? I find that hard to believe."

Al turned on his circular saw just to shut them up.

So for his wife, there were two versions of him: the present one, who was an asshole; and a younger, sweeter version, who had never managed to get on the transport plane home but was still stuck in the jungle, lost and wandering in the heat and mist like a wraith.

Sorry, Rita, he thought. Vietnam ruined your father.

And now Afghanistan has ruined her son, he thinks. Jeremy the little boy was friendly, curious, outgoing, sweet, affectionate. Now he seemed to have just two modes: angry or silent. At least Henry is safe from the clutches of the goddamn military. Maybe being born retarded was the best thing that could have happened to him. Maybe, Al thinks, America won't be safe from itself until every single person in it gets a lobotomy.

He hears Rita pour herself a glass of wine. She dials Jeanie's number again, apparently gets voice mail again. She hesitates after the beep, trying to condense her complicated mood into one or two short, pithy sound bites. But the words pile up in her head too fast, so she hangs up again.

Al fakes another snore.

There were two versions of Jeanie too: pre-birth and post-birth. Henry had nearly failed to survive his entry into the world, which was prolonged and difficult. Jeanie hadn't allowed anyone from the family into the delivery room, except Helen. Of course, that was fine with Al. He hadn't seen his daughters naked since they were very young, and in fact had often gone to elaborate lengths to prevent such a thing from happening by mistake. The last thing he wanted was to see his youngest spread-eagled on a delivery table. The cord had been wrapped around Henry's neck three times. Later, Helen would say that her superstitious farm mother, who lived by a complex code of portents and omens, would have found this to be a sure sign of something or other, though Helen couldn't remember what—and he'd failed to breathe after being expelled from Jeanie's teenaged womb. After some frantic work by the nurses, he began to turn pink, though he didn't cry the way a normal baby should, and he failed his reflex tests miserably. The signs were all there. They still didn't know who the father was.

This was in the late summer of 1993. Jeanie lay in bed for months, long after the physical wounds of birthing had healed. She refused to nurse the baby, so Helen took over, feeding him warm formula from a bottle every few hours and readopting the sleeping schedule of a new mother at the age of forty-eight. Rita helped as much as she could, but she had Jeremy to deal with. Helen said Al was no help at all, though he would protest in his own defense that if she didn't think bringing home a paycheck was any help, then she could try living without one for a while and see how she liked that.

Now Helen had a houseful of children; and two of them were grandchildren, which rendered her nearly speechless with joy, even if one of them was simple-minded.

But Jeanie appeared to be stuck in neutral. When her senior year began, she stayed in bed. She showed no indication that she was ever going back to school. This galled both Helen and Al, but since Jeanie Rae had become a mother, Al felt she was beyond his reach; she'd followed Rita into that mysterious female zone where his influence couldn't be felt. There was no way for him to talk to her anymore. She was one of Them now.

Helen asked Rita to talk to her sister, but Jeanie wasn't speaking to Rita, for reasons that Rita was unable to determine. Actually, she wasn't speaking to anyone. When she did deign to rise from her sleeping chamber, it was to gravitate to the new family computer, which was now connected, via means Al didn't quite understand, to the telephone lines. The future seemed to have arrived, although there were still no jet packs, no underwater cities, no meals in pill form. All through the night the family could hear the plasticky clack of the keyboard and Jeanie's stifled giggles. They had no idea whom she was communicating with, or about what, and if they snuck a peek over her shoulder, all they could see was a strange language of symbols and abbreviations. She reserved all her efforts at conversation for her cyberfriends, not for her family. Or, for that matter, her own child.

It was clear to Al that Jeanie wished Henry had never happened. He was the unfortunate result of a stupid mistake: a wrestling match in the church basement, perhaps, that had gotten out of hand; a sneaky sleepover sperm leaping across the room in the night and finding its way into her; a toilet seat upon which some nasty boy had exuded his seed with the diabolical intention of impregnating the next girl who sat there. Jeanie had never actually seemed very interested in boys. However Henry had arrived, he had not been gotten in the normal way.

And then one day Jeanie announced that she was leaving for New York. Nobody believed her, but the next day she was gone, and she'd left Henry behind. It didn't appear that she'd even considered taking him with her. And she didn't say goodbye. Later, Helen admitted to Al that she'd known ahead of time she would leave. When Al asked why she hadn't told him, Helen said:

"There was nothing you could have done. She was going one way or the other."

"You wanna bet?" Al said. "I could have locked her in her room."

"Oh, give it up, Al. She's a grown woman. You can't treat her like a child anymore."

"I can if she acts like one," said Al.

"You're talking like she's still here. She's gone, and we're not going to get her back," Helen told him.

"Well, what are we going to do about Henry?" Rita asked.

"We're going to take care of him, of course," said Helen. "He's ours too."

"If I decide to just drop all my responsibilities and let you raise my kid for me, will you give me a pass too?" Rita sneered.

"You goddamn well better not," Al told her.

Everybody stopped speaking to everybody else for a while after that; but eventually, with two kids who needed looking after, communication resumed, first at a stilted pace, later approaching normal levels. The Merkins, now minus one of their own, felt a hole in their middle where Jeanie had been; but a house with children is busy and loud, and this was what allowed the hole to close gradually, until they simply got used to life without Jeanie Rae.

Rita dials once more. There is still no answer. This time she doesn't even wait for the false-chipper message to finish playing. She clicks off the phone and smacks it down on the table.

"Rita, I'm sorry," Al says. Only he doesn't really say it. The words stick in his throat. He mumbles it incoherently. His eyes aren't even open. He sounds as if he's talking in his sleep.

What she says next shocks him.

"Oh, fuck you, Dad," Rita says.

Then she storms out of the house, fires up her Escort, and pulls away.

5

SATURDAY MORNING. Jeremy gets up and pees in the utility sink. The lip is just an inch too high to be a comfortable reach, but stretching the fire hose is still easier than walking up the stairs with a full bladder. For the thousandth time, he contemplates building himself a short stool to stand on. Then he promptly discards this idea. Building anything in this house means entering the sacred workshop, but before this can happen, Al must conduct a lengthy preliminary interview in order to determine just what one wants to build, why one wants to build it, how one plans to build it, why one intends to build it that way and not some other more practical and time-tested way, and what materials one intends to use, and finally comes an outright denial of workshop usage, meaning that in the end Al says he will build the thing himself, whatever it is, except he never does because he has better things to do and is not a factory or a servant. So Jeremy pees on tiptoe.

Then he goes upstairs, makes himself a bowl of cereal, and is about to head back to the basement with it when Al appears in the kitchen.

"I hope you're not peeing in the sink down there," Al says. "I thought I smelled something funny the other day."

"I'm not," Jeremy says.

"Good. Because that's what toilets are for."

"I know what toilets are for, Al," says Jeremy.

"My friends call me Al. My grandson calls me Grandpa. Or maybe even sir."

"Or Daboo," says Jeremy.

"Are you mentally retarded?"

"Not to my knowledge."

"Then you don't get to call me Daboo."

"I am!" says Henry from the living room. "I am mentally retarded, Daboo!"

"No you're not, Henry," calls Rita from her bedroom down the hall. "You're a special guy, you hear me?"

"And another thing. There's a chore list waiting for you, when it suits your highness," Al says to Jeremy.

"I thought we agreed we weren't going to use that word in this house," Rita says. She's appeared in the doorway now too, in her tank top and sweats, nipples disturbingly prominent, hair wild.

"I'll get to it," says Jeremy through his teeth.

"I sincerely hope so," says Al. "Because otherwise all car-borrowing privileges will have to be revoked."

"Are you two listening to me?" says Rita.

"I do pay rent here, you know," says Jeremy. "I'm not free-loading. Most tenants don't have chore lists."

"Are we having a fight?" Henry says from the living room.

"Most tenants don't get to borrow their landlords' cars, either. That would be a separate fee. In fact, maybe we need to discuss that. The IRS allows me a certain amount for depreciation and mileage every year, and I think maybe you ought to be making an equal contrib—"

"You mind if I eat my breakfast in peace, Al?"

"Fight! Fight! Fight!" Henry chants.

"Jesus Christ, it's like talking to two brick walls," says Rita, and she goes back into her room.

"A grown man sits in bed eating cereal and watching cartoons on his goddamn computer like a five-year-old kid," says Al. "I thought those things were supposed to make the world a more advanced place."

"They do," says Jeremy. "And I don't watch cartoons."

"Oh, no? What would you call them, then?"

"Animated shorts," says Jeremy.

Downstairs, he makes himself comfortable on his mattress and eats his double-frosted sugar bombs while watching the latest Japanimation classic Rico's Dropboxed him. Then he pours himself a cup of tea. Now that he has a job, the guilty edge these mornings used to have has faded. He leans back against his pillow with a sense of pleasantly high contentment. Nowhere to go, nowhere to be, nothing to do. Monday is a light-year away. If he were a truly dedicated teacher, which he isn't, he'd already be thinking about what he was going to teach next week. Tomorrow night he'll hop on Google and see what lesson plans exist out there for him to steal.

The last three weeks have been a panicky time. He hasn't been teaching; he's been doing his best imitation of a teacher. Porteus knew he didn't have any experience when he hired him, but he'd assured him he'd be fine, that he could tell he'd be a natural in the classroom. He can see now this was a blatant lie; Porteus was desperate for a warm body.

In his naiveté, Jeremy had believed he could simply engage his students in Socratic dialogues of the sort he and Smarty used to have, and together they would wing their way through the world of knowledge, delighting in the mysteries of the universe. Maybe he could even teach them about the Fibonacci sequence. He'd somehow forgotten the crushing load of ennui that high school students carried with them everywhere, the blank stares, the hostile resistance to doing absolutely anything. He'd hoped to find out what interested them and build a curriculum of sorts around that, but he'd realized within about two minutes that they weren't interested in anything, at least nothing he was allowed to discuss.

He'd also thought, for some insane reason, that the students would respect him because he was young. Instead, they seemed to think this meant they could get away with anything. On the first day of school they'd aligned themselves into groups, boys on one side, girls on the other, cool kids in the back, dweebs in the front, and had begun to talk amongst themselves as if he wasn't even there. Engage them, Porteus had said; teaching is info-tainment. But Jeremy was not an infotainer. In his vocabulary, to engage meant to lay down heavy fire, to shoot to kill. During his very first class he'd felt a panic attack coming on, and he'd only been able to prevent it by pretending that getting to the end of the period was an objective, and that his job was to attack and hold that objective until reinforcements arrived. He's still not sure how he's made it this far. Sometimes he looks at their glazed-over faces and thinks, If only you could see what I have seen. But he'd been trained to see those things so other people didn't have to see them. That was the role of the army: not to fight for free-dom, whatever that nonsense meant, but to see the unseeable, do the undoable, and later to try to forget the unforgettable. And to somehow try to fit back into a society that had no clue.

His phone buzzes. He checks the screen:
U R SO DED IT IS NOT FUNY!!!!!!!!!!!!

Jeremy thinks, It's a good thing whoever this is used all those exclamation points, or I might not have known he was serious. Because at this point he's fairly sure it's not Jenn.

This silliness has gone on long enough. More importantly, he's almost out of pot. It's time to go see Rico.

Half an hour later, showered but not shaved, he pulls up in front of a neat little bungalow with a front yard of pebbles, a giant yucca growing in the center. A tricked-out lime green Honda

Civic with gaudy rims sits in the driveway. The car is Rico's, but he never drives it, except once a month when he visits his uncle's organic pot farm in Humboldt to pick up another shipment. It's enough for him to stare at it sometimes, and to rub it lovingly with a fake sheepskin.

On the door is a sign that reads, in both English and Spanish:

MEDICAL DISPENSARY, LIFE VISIONING,
LOVE THERAPY
BY APPOINTMENT ONLY

He walks in without knocking, as he has done for the past fourteen years. The living room has been turned into a waiting area, with two pleather couches along the walls and a coffee table piled with magazines in the center. Quietly inspirational synth music issues from unseen speakers, trickling into Jeremy's ears in a soothing stream designed to affect him on a vibrational level. On one wall are various framed posters: a decidedly Mexican-looking Jesus healing the sick; Earth as seen from space, with a caption reading LOVE YOUR MOTHER; a photograph of a massive effigy going up in flames, surrounded by thousands of whooping hippies in various states of intoxication and undress; and the Virgin of Guadalupe appearing in the sky over a flabbergasted farmer. On another wall are perhaps a dozen smaller photographs of people such as Padre Pio, the Dalai Lama, Thich Nhat Hanh, and Mother Teresa. There are also pictures of several other men and women whose callings in life, judging by the candid nature of their portraits, were more pedestrian, but whom Jeremy happens to know are distinguished by the fact that they're dead. Among them is Rico's father, Enrique, who'd met his end twenty years ago when a demonstration for the rights of migrant farmworkers had gotten out of hand. A small television on a corner table plays a muted *telenovela*: a beautiful Latina in hysterics wrangles with a mysterious, brooding man who has a tendency to grab her by the shoulders and shake her to get his point across.

A vibraphone tone has rung out upon his opening the door, and from the rear of the house it summons a plump, short Latina woman about fifty years old, who has shoehorned herself into a pair of tight jeans. A diaphanous blouse of bright red flows to her waist, through which he can see the rolls around her stomach.

"*Buenas días, Yeremy,*" says Rico's mother, Elizabeta. "*Cómo estás?*"

"*Buenas días, señora,*" Jeremy says. "*Rico aquí?*"

"He's in el basement," says Señora Bustamente. "How you doing, honey?"

"Good. Fine. Great."

"Mmm, no," she says matter-of-factly.

"No? I'm not great?"

"You got troubles. Your aura is different."

"It is?"

"You got peoples around you again today," says Elizabeta. "They come in with you. I see four, five peoples. Who are they? You want me to talk to them?"

"Señora, no offense, but it really creeps me out when you say that." For weeks now, Elizabeta has been telling Jeremy this same thing: there are spirits following him like patient dogs.

"Ah, you still don't believe. Science, computers, these things you believe. But these things are not real. In the real world, you don't believe." She smiles. "Maybe is gonna take something bigger to make you see. Is not gonna stop, Yeremy."

"What's not gonna stop?"

"The messages," she says.

"Señora, what messages? You mean . . . the ones on my cell phone?"

"*Ay, Dios mío.* No, not your cell phone. Never mind. Is okay. You hongry?"

"Hongry? No, I . . . well, whattaya got?"

She beckons, and Jeremy follows Elizabeta into her ever-providential kitchen, where a plate of white flour tortillas is eternally warm on the stove and a pot of carne adovada has never, in all the time Jeremy has been friends with Rico, become empty. With the skill of a short-order cook, Elizabeta makes him two small soft tacos and puts the plate in his hands. He picks one up and bites into it. The pork dissolves in his mouth like sunlight, assuaging his munchies.

"You getting fat," she says, poking him in the stomach. "You and Rico, you need to do some exercises."

"Yeah, I know," he says.

"Why you don't go yogging?"

"I can't run anymore."

"Ah," Elizabeta says. "I sorry, Yeremy. Sometime I forget."

"Yeah, well, I've forgotten it too, so no worries on that count."

Elizabeta nods. "You know, you should let me help you. Maybe you need a session."

"A session?"

"A counseling session. I can help you remember."

"How would you do that?"

"Is vibrationing."

"Vibrationing?"

"I close my eyes, I listen. I feel them."

Them, Jeremy knows, refers once again to the spirit world, through which Elizabeta apparently moves like a commuter at rush hour.

"Ha-ha," says Jeremy. "You need your own TV show."

"Mmm, no," Elizabeta says. "I too fat for TV. Who is she?"

"Who is who?"

"The girl you is worry about."

Jeremy's never wanted to venture too far into this part of Rico's life, not since that first conversation in which Rico had explained, without a trace of irony, that his mother was a spiritual medium who sold dope on the side. Jeremy hadn't believed him, but that very day Elizabeta had offered the boys some Kool-Aid, and Jeremy had said yes to be polite, but the fact was he didn't like Kool-Aid because it gave him a headache, and she'd looked at him strangely and said, "Why you say yes if you don't like Kool-Aid?" After that, he was sold on the fact that she was wired in in a way most other people weren't, but because Rico made no big deal about it, neither did he. He preferred to stay off her psychic radar altogether. There were too many things he didn't like to think about. The idea that someone else could know them was unnerving.

"Okay, Señora, we've been over this before," says Jeremy. "Remember? You're not supposed to read my mind without my permission. It's not cool."

"I sorry, Yeremy," she says. "I just see you in so much pain."

"Yeah, well, the stuff your brother grows really helps with that. Much better than any pills I ever took."

"That not the kind of pain I mean, sweetie." She sighs, picks up a rag, wipes some nonexistent dirt from the counter, folds the rag neatly, and hangs it from the oven door. "When you ready, I have some things to tell you. Okay? When you ready."

"What things?" Jeremy says.

"Never mind. You not ready. You go down there and tell that lazy boy I say wake up. Is almost time for lonch and he not even have breakfast yet."

Rico is another basement dweller. At the foot of the stairs, Jeremy passes through a plastic curtain and enters a room with the climate of Central America, controlled by humidifiers and ventilation fans and illuminated gently with a couple of halogen floor lamps. This is for the benefit of the product of Tío Adelmo's Humboldt County farm, of which Rico is the sole Kern

County purveyor. It's all perfectly legal—or else it's completely illegal, depending on which authorities you ask, state or federal. Rico and Elizabeta live with the mild threat of a DEA invasion on a daily basis. It hasn't affected their appetites much.

Water trickles in a corner fountain, cascading off imitation river rocks and splashing gently into a tiny pool, where there gapes a single lonely betta. Rico has named him Columbine. At Jeremy's suggestion, Rico had once bought Columbine a friend, another betta, but he'd eaten him. The lesson in that, Rico told him, was don't fuck with a loner. In the center of the room is a circular conference table, a Vesuvius of dope rising from the center. Rico is asleep on his mountainous mess of a bed, snoring gently, one hand in his boxer shorts.

Jeremy contemplates this appalling sight and wonders how best to mess with him. One would never know, he thinks, watching in revulsion as Rico caresses his morning hard-on, that Rico is modestly famous, on the Internet at least. He runs a blog on which he posts articles that are antiwar, antigovernment, and anticorruption. He is opposed to everything that is opposed to life and freedom. He posts pictures too, and these are what he's most known for: families killed by errant drone missiles, the aftermath of Baghdad car bombs, videos of police brutality. These images are emailed to him by witnesses from all over the world, and he puts them up along with the accounts of those who were there and saw everything. He gets thousands of hits a day, and the revenues from the ads on his site have begun to add up to a nice chunk of change. But Rico is forced to spend most of it on the services of a group of anti-hackers, who have erected a magic wall to protect him from the mysterious forces constantly circling his site like sharks around a mangled surfer, trying to take it down through denial-of-service attacks. Rico is convinced that most of these bad hackers work for one government or another, and he can usually figure out which one is currently after him based on which country his most recent post casts in a bad light. Sometimes it's China, sometimes it's Iran, sometimes it's Mexico. But most of these attacks, Rico is certain, are rooted in the U.S.A.

A picture, Jeremy thinks. That's it. He hunts around until he finds Rico's cell phone. Then he sneaks closer to the bed and pops off a shot. Rico struggles into wakefulness with a snort.

"The fuck?" he demands.

"Nice one," Jeremy says, admiring the image on the screen. "You should post that."

"Fuck off," Rico says, and he struggles upright, his belly poking out from under his shirt. "This is how you wake me?"

"Your mama said get up, dude."

"Dang," says Rico. "What a harsh reality."

"It's like lunchtime."

"Fuck," says Rico. "Who cares? I live by no man's clock."

"Say that to your mama. I dare you."

Rico gets up and slides past him to the bathroom. He closes the door, and soon Jeremy hears the shower running. He contents himself with positioning his nose over Mount Mary Jane and inhaling. He dares not touch the product, lest he render it inorganic. You are only allowed to touch the pot with gloves on. His back protests at his current position, so he lowers himself onto a musty couch that has become glued by condensation to the cinder block wall. The THC in the air is making him giddy.

After a while Rico comes out again, clad in his work uniform: T-shirt, sweatpants, and a bathrobe.

"Wassup," he says.

"Check this out," says Jeremy, holding up his phone. Another text has just come in:

I AM GOING TO ROON UR LIFE!

"The fuck is a roon?" says Rico.

"I think he means *ruin*. I've been getting these since yesterday."

Rico grabs his phone and scrolls through his texts. "Who they from?"

"This girl," Jeremy says. "Except they're not from her."

"Who they from then, her boyfriend?"

"I don't think so. I think they're from her brother."

"What's he got against you?"

"Man, something really fucked up happened yesterday."

"What was it?"

"She told me not to tell anyone."

"I'm Rico, bro. People tell me shit."

So Jeremy tells him.

"Fuck me," says Rico, handing his phone back. "That's sick."

"You're telling me," says Jeremy.

"You know what?"

"What?"

"You're *completamente chingow*."

"Why am I *chingow*?"

"Because, dude. If her brother is a cop, and he's got a hate-on for you, you're in big trouble. You got to get him before he gets you."

"I thought you believed in nonviolence."

Rico looks at him, squinting in disapproval. "I'm not talking about killing him, bro. Jesus, the shit you white people come up with. I mean going public. Telling the higher-ups."

"But I have no proof of anything," says Jeremy.

"These texts are proof of something. Proof he's harassing you. Right? This is not a joke, man. I know how these guys think. He's after you, and he's not gonna stop until he gets you."

That is apparently all the latest panic attack needs to hear to get under way. It always starts as a weird kind of self-consciousness, not so much a feeling as an idea—the strange notion that he's outside his body looking at himself, and not particularly liking what he sees. Then his cheeks get hot. Hyperventilation follows soon after.

He lays on the couch, grabs a pillow, and stuffs it over his face. But the pillow is firmly removed by Rico, who's sat in his office chair and wheeled it close, his expression psychiatric.

"Mira," he says. "Relax. You okay?"

"No," Jeremy gasps. "Not okay."

"Come on, dude. Just breathe. You're gonna be fine. Come on. I'm gonna talk you through this."

Jeremy sits up. He's embarrassed to realize he's crying. He wipes his eyes and snuffles. He takes several deep breaths. Sometimes he can just breathe his way out of these things. Two in two days. Things are definitely getting worse. Rico pats him awkwardly on the kneecap.

"I didn't mean to freak you out, bro," he says. "I shoulda remembered how you get."

"It's not your fault," says Jeremy. He breathes. After a few more lungfuls, his heart rate slows again, and he heaves a deep sigh. He's never cried in front of Rico before. He has a feeling that soon he's going to have cried in front of everyone he knows.

"Feeling better?" Rico asks.

"What am I gonna do? Now I got a cop after me. Fuck."

"Come on, man. The old Jeremy wouldn't get upset about this."

Jeremy wants to laugh at that, because the old Jeremy doesn't exist anymore. Sometimes he's not sure Rico understands this. He himself had fallen into the trap of thinking he was the only one who had changed while everyone else had stayed the same; but while he was gone, something had happened to Rico to make him change too. He'd always had a hardness and an angriness to him, which was partly the bitter core of a bullied fat kid and partly because of what had happened to his father. Enrique Estevez had been found in a San Diego jail cell with his hands cuffed and his head smashed; his death had been ruled a suicide. Rico barely remembered his father, but this was the thing that accounted for his quietness, his serious attitude, and it was also what had eventually launched him on his current trajectory in life, which was dedicated to exposing the underbelly of the establishment whenever the opportunity presented itself.

In recent years, though, he'd developed a new kind of fatalism about things, and now this has come to dominate his personality. Rico is seriously worried about the way the world is going. It comes out most strongly in his blog posts, in which he describes the entire system in the most depressing terms: the poor would always be trodden upon, the government would never give a shit, the only way out was revolution. Talking to Rico lately gives Jeremy the feeling the war has followed him home. It is the same sensation he used to get whenever he saw a dead body, that this is what it all boils down to: in the end we're nothing more than a pile of meat, and the people who cry over us are meat too.

"I have the solution," says Rico. "Let's get high."

"That's your solution to everything."

"That's because it *is* the solution to everything."

Rico, humming, packs an absolutely immense bong, the bowl of which looks like Darth Vader's head. He sparks it up and inhales. He passes it to Jeremy, who considers refusing it and then decides that, under the circumstances, that would be foolish in the extreme. He holds the cool smoke in his chest and breathes out slow. He becomes immediately and undeniably high. Slowly the attack begins to fade.

"There, see?" says Rico. "I got the prescription for your conniption."

"Thanks, dude," says Jeremy.

"Listen, I gotta do a few things on the site. I been getting a lot of pictures from Syria lately. Ugly shit. I gotta get 'em up."

"You want me to leave?"

"Naw, man. You just chill here. But don't look at these pictures. They'll send you right over the edge. When I'm done, we can watch a few flicks." He wheels himself back to his worktable, where his MacBook Air sits waiting, and pops in his earbuds. Soon the histrionic strains of his beloved mariachi music reach Jeremy's ears.

Jeremy lies back on the couch, staring up at the ceiling, where some decidedly nonorganic mold has begun forming a pattern. He ponders the shape of the mold growth, ringed like the inside of a tree trunk, idly measuring it with his eyes. The Fibonacci sequence, he realizes, might apply to this too. The top of the pattern is three times longer than the sides. The central ring is five times larger than the inner ring, and the biggest ring is eight times larger. Maybe his entire existence is ruled by this sequence of numbers. Maybe the dimensions of the universe are constructed according to this blueprint. Maybe everything is proceeding according to some kind of plan. And maybe nothing is.

Or maybe he just falls asleep. Jeremy slowly becomes aware that Rico is saying something.

"What?" he says, rousing himself.

"I said, I just got an email from Mama. She wants you to come upstairs."

"How come?"

"She wants to see you in the consult room."

"Seriously? Why?"

"She says she has something to tell you," says Rico, and as if to emphasize his words, there comes a gentle but insistent thumping on the ceiling. Jeremy recognizes the sound. So does Rico.

"Uh-oh," says Rico. "That's the broom handle."

You did not ignore the broom handle. Jeremy begins to stand, but the rush of blood to his head—or away from it, he can't be certain—forces him to abandon that plan temporarily.

"Jesus," he says. "I am fucking stoned."

"That's Star Wars for you," Rico says, proud. "New strain my uncle Adelmo came up with. I named it myself."

"Smell you later, homes," says Jeremy.

"Not if I smell you first," says Rico.

"Hey, I almost forgot," says Jeremy. "I'm almost out of *herbo bueno*."

Rico reaches into a drawer and pulls out a fat bag. He flips it to Jeremy, who catches it and stuffs it in his pocket.

"That hold you?" Rico says.

"For about a week. What I owe you?"

"Merry Christmas," says Rico.

"And God bless us, every one," says Jeremy.

6

JEREMY hasn't ventured into the consult room since the time he was eleven and mistook it for the bathroom. On that occasion, he'd stumbled across Elizabeta caught up in a deep embrace with someone who at first looked like a ten-year-old child, until Jeremy realized that the person's face, which was blissfully buried in Elizabeta's modest bosom, bore a beard. The man was a dwarf, and he was starved for love, which Elizabeta gladly provided to anyone who needed it.

"Everyone needs a hug," she'd said to Jeremy at the time, and the dwarf, eyes leaking tears of joy, had nodded his agreement. Elizabeta's affection was offered on a purely emotional plane, and it was part of her counseling services, which also included astrology, tarot cards, the I Ching, and communing with dead friends or relatives in order to pass on messages.

Jeremy is relieved to find this time around that Elizabeta is alone, or at least sans dwarf. She's never really alone, she often says; the spirit world follows her everywhere, even to the bathroom. He finds her waiting for him in her wingback chair, upholstered in a soothing yellow cloth embroidered with yin-yang symbols. Another similar chair sits across from her, and between them stands a table with a Tibetan prayer bowl on it. The room is dim and smells of incense.

"Come in, Yeremy," she says. "Sit." She indicates the empty chair.

Jeremy is about to obey, but he halts after a step. "Look, I don't—"

She holds up her hand. "It don't matter if you don't believe. About thirty peoples follow you in here, Yeremy. More coming all the time. Is like a parade. Something big is going on. So, it don't matter if this is your thing or not. This is their thing. Siddown. Come on. I won't bite you."

Jeremy thinks about simply turning and walking out, but the fact is he trusts Elizabeta, who hands out hugs the way other people deal out casual curses. So he will humor her. He sits.

"'Kay," she says. "So you gonna go see your dad."

"My . . . dad? You mean my father?"

She doesn't answer this rather stupid question. Instead, she merely smiles, leaning forward, spine straight, hands folded on her knees.

"How come?" Jeremy says.

"Because he gonna tell you something. There's a thing you gotta learn that you don't know. He knows. He's gonna tell you."

"But I don't talk to my father," says Jeremy plainly. "He's nuts. I mean, I know a lot of people say that about their parents, but he's got the papers to prove it. He destroyed my family."

Elizabeta shakes her head again. Jeremy feels himself growing impatient with her.

"I know he got problems," she says. "That's like so obvious. But he can't help himself. His problems are inside. He didn't choose to be the way he is. At least, not that he remembers," she adds. "We choose our lives when we're still on the other side, before we come in, because we know what we need to learn."

"You mean I chose this life?"

"Uh-huh."

"So what do I have to learn?"

"Jeremy," says Elizabeta, "I trying to tell you right now."

"Oh."

"Anyway, you gotta forget you're mad at him and just go talk to him. Okay? Because he did not destroy your family. You was already going that way when he met your mother. Is not his fault, what happen. You gonna do that as soon as you can."

"And what happens if I don't?" He fights the urge to look over his shoulder, just to see who's standing there. He knows he won't see anything except the door.

Elizabeta gives him a long look. "*Escuchame, hijo*. I know you a long time, right? You was friends with my son when nobody else would talk to him, and I love you for that. I always will. That kind of thing mean more to a mother than I can csplain. I feel about you like you are my own boy. But since you come back from you-know-where, you are not the same person. I can see you got something is bothering you. Something need to change. If you saw a person walking around with an arrow sticking out of his head, wouldn't you tell him about it? Wouldn't you take it out?"

"There's an arrow sticking out of my head?" Jeremy says.

"Is an espression. What I mean is, you gotta let me help you, Yeremy. I can't stay quiet no more. There are lots of other things I see I am not saying right now. You are not ready to hear. You are too closed up. You are like a—" She searches for the right word, then brings her palms together vertically. "What's this little animal with a shell?"

"A clam?" says Jeremy.

"A clan," says Elizabeta, nodding.

"Cla*mmm*," says Jeremy.

"Clammm. But this one thing I can tell you. Go see your father. Please. Do it as soon as you can. Okay?"

"But why?"

She shakes her head. "This not gonna come from me. It's gonna come from him. You got choices, *hijo*. I can't force you to do nothing. All I wanna do is tell you the best choice. You wouldn't know this if I didn't tell you. I'm saving you some time here. Maybe many years."

"Years of what?" Jeremy asks.

"Years of wandering," she says, only maybe it's "years of wondering"; sometimes her accent is hard to punch through. But before he can ask her to clarify, the vibraphone sounds, and she stands up.

"I got someone," she says. "So I gotta go."

Which, Jeremy knows, really means that he's the one who's gotta go. So he stands up, but before he can turn to the door, Elizabeta holds her arms out, and Jeremy falls into them, even though he has to stoop to do it. This position is unacceptable for L1 through L5, but he feels Elizabeta's hand move to the small of his back and begin to rub him there, and as if by magic, the pain disappears under her touch, just for a moment. He hasn't felt this much relief in years.

Her tomato-like form radiates a heat that is utterly different from the kind that awaits him outside as he heads back to the Saturn, already knowing without holding an inner debate that of course he's going to listen to her, because he's never felt so lost and confused, and also because she's Rico's mom, and he loves her like a mom, even though certain thoughts of a sexual nature had flitted through his mind when he felt her boobs poking his stomach—only because it's been so long since boobs have crossed his path—and even though he'd gotten embarrassed by these thoughts, then by the fact that he was thinking about having these thoughts, then by the realization that she probably knew he was thinking about thinking about these thoughts—but finally was soothed by the calm knowledge that she just didn't care.

7

JEREMY goes home and spends the rest of the day in bed, and he thinks: I'm a clam with an arrow through his head. Whatever this means in the language of the spirit world, it doesn't sound good. Luckily, Star Wars tea forces these thoughts out of his head. He should maybe stay away from Rico's for a while, he thinks. Shit there is getting too real.

Dinner is a somber affair. Henry mopes. Al soliloquizes. Rita fumes. Everyone is worked up about something. Jeremy eats as quickly as he can and goes to bed.

In the morning, he wakes up early. He can hear Rita moving around in the kitchen, so he goes upstairs and allows her to make him breakfast. The dreadful suspense of a Sunday hangs over the house.

"How you doing these days, Jer?" Rita asks him.

"Why do you wanna know?"

"Because I'm your mother. Don't get all defensive. You've seem kinda preoccupied or something. Like something is bothering you."

"I'm fine. There's nothing bothering me. Everything is A-OK."

"It's been a while since you've had an attack," she ventures.

He pours himself some coffee and decides to tell her. "I had one the other day. Actually, I've had two."

"What? Why?" Her hand goes automatically to his forehead, as if fevers had anything to do with panic attacks. Jeremy pushes it away.

"The first one happened in that motel room," he says. "The room where nothing happened. When I went to see that girl."

"Why? What set it off?"

"I never know what sets them off. But I think this time it was the smell."

"What smell?"

"The smell of the room. Just . . . it hit me funny. It made me sick to my stomach the minute I walked in."

"Sam keeps those rooms pretty clean," says Rita. "No one else has ever complained about it."

"It wasn't that it smelled bad. It just smelled . . . funny. Familiar. Like it reminded me of something."

"Probably your father," says Rita.

Jeremy looks up from his toast plate. Mention of his father is rare in this house.

"Why do you say that?"

"Because of that time when you were little."

"What happened when I was little?"

"When he took you. Don't you remember?"

"When he . . . took me? What are you talking about?"

Rita sits at the table across from him. She narrows her eyes, as if she suspects him of pulling a fast one. "You really don't remember?"

"Mom, remember what?"

"Maybe you were too little. You were only about five. No, not even. Four and a half. It was right before we moved back home. In fact, that was what started the whole thing. That's when he went completely off the rails."

"I have no idea what you're talking about," says Jeremy. "What happened?"

Rita sighs, leans back, crosses her legs. She's gearing up for a story.

"Your father picked you up from preschool, on a day that you were supposed to take the bus. Even though the goddamn teachers and the goddamn bus aides and even the goddamn principal had all been told that he was not, under any circumstances, allowed to come anywhere near the goddamn school. Those idiots. I had a restraining order and everything." Rita pauses to get control of herself. "And he disappeared with you for almost a month."

"What? Just like that?"

"You disappeared into thin air. I thought I was going to lose my mind. He kidnapped you, Jeremy. Walked into the school like he owned the place and took you like you were his to take. You were on the news. You were on a goddamn milk carton."

"What?"

"You were gone for weeks. And I really went insane. I didn't sleep and I didn't eat. And when you came back to me, you had a T-shirt on that said *#1 Kid*, and you had a big cut on your back that you said you got from when you were trying to fly." Rita's eyes are tearing up. "Don't you remember?"

"No, I don't remember this at all."

"Well, I'll never forget it. Apparently you were living in motels all over southern California. That's there they found you—in a motel room. The cops said the floor was covered in fast-food wrappers, and that son of a bitch was just lying in bed watching TV, completely ignoring you. So I think what happened was that you smelled that motel room and you remembered, even though you think you don't. I'll bet that's what happened. You told me—" She puts her hand to her mouth for a moment to get control of herself. "You told me you used to pray every night I would come and find you and take you home again, because you missed your goldfish."

"Mr. Chips," says Jeremy.

"You remember goddamn Mr. Chips and you don't remember being kidnapped."

"I guess not," says Jeremy. He wonders if maybe he just has a particular talent for blocking things out. It would be nice, he thinks, if just once I could discover something about myself that I could put on a résumé. Instead, it's just one fucking crazy thing after another.

"Well," says Rita, "in some ways that is a blessing."

"What did we do all that time?"

"I never knew." Rita wipes her eyes. "Wilkins never told anyone. And you were too little to explain. But I don't think you did anything at all. He didn't know what he was doing. It's not like he had a plan or anything. He wasn't going to hurt you, at least not on purpose. He was off his medication. He told the cops he wanted to raise you on his own. In a motel room. Because he didn't trust anyone else to do a good job with you. And he said you were being tracked by the CIA because you were the result of some experiment that had gotten out of control. That was when they locked him up again. And he's been there ever since."

"I was kidnapped?" Jeremy says. It's a quality as substantial as a tattoo he hadn't known he possessed, or the fact of actually being Armenian. He tries this new image of himself on for size, that of a kidnap victim. It doesn't fit.

"Yeah," says Rita. "And it seemed like I just blinked my eyes and you were in the army. And the whole time you were over there, I felt just like I did when you were missing. Like you were ripped away from me." She lays a hand on his arm, and for once he doesn't shake it off. "Don't get in trouble over this girl. I couldn't stand it if something happened to you because of her. You've been through enough."

"What makes you think something's going to happen to me?"

"You could get arrested. You could go to jail."

"Jesus, Mother, she's seventeen, not twelve. And I keep telling you, nothing happened. You're overreacting," he says, and he gets up as slowly as an old man and limps toward the bathroom.

"Jeremy," says Rita.

"What?"

"I want you to keep seeing that therapist. That Lola woman. She was good for you. It seemed like she really helped."

"I can't. She's not taking insurance anymore."

"I'll pay," Rita says.

"With what? The bags of money you bring home from the Coffee Mug?"

"I have some money put away," Rita tells him. "I don't mind. What else am I going to spend it on? High fashion? I'm not Jeanie Rae."

Jeremy pauses between kitchen and dining room, leaning against the door frame. He can't bear to look at her just now. His mother loves him so much it makes him uncomfortable.

"No, Mom," he says. "Save it for something important."

"But she said if you could only remember what happened—"

"I don't want to remember. I just want these attacks to go away."

"But if that's the way to make them go away—"

"No," Jeremy says. "I'll remember on my own."

He showers, gets dressed. Under the running water, he thinks about Elizabeta, about Rita, about himself on the back of a milk carton, and a plan occurs to him. He locates Al in the garage.

"I need the car," he says.

"You gonna take out this garbage?" says Al, indicating the overflowing trash can with his chin.

"Pickup is tomorrow. If I put it out tonight, the coyotes will just get into it."

"Put some gas in it," Al grunts, absorbed in something on his workbench. "I'm not a millionaire."

In the same vague way he's always heard rumors that God lives in heaven, Jeremy has always known that his father lives in a place every bit as abstract and ineffable, called the LaFingous Institute, otherwise known as the loony bin, where he's been sequestered for most of the last twenty years. Jeremy's never been there before, so for the first time ever, he engages Al's sat-nav system, first locating the Institute on the map and then plotting a course to the outskirts of Bakersfield, just over an hour away. This proximity strikes Jeremy as odd; he's always thought of the distance between himself and his father as insurmountable. Real geography does not conform to his inner sense of topography, in which Wilkins occupies not a physical place but a whole other dimension, inaccessible to those who call themselves sane.

In reality, Wilkins lives in a complex of buildings of gentle architecture that manages to suggest everything will eventually be all right, with environmentally friendly landscaping that implies none of life's problems are really that major, and thoughtfully placed outdoor furniture giving the impression that the patients are cared for by a benevolent order of luminous beings with master's degrees in feng shui. Even the parking lot is peaceful. Instead of one vast plain of asphalt, it's broken up into emotionally manageable pods of perhaps twenty cars each. For this Jeremy is grateful; large parking lots are a major source of anxiety, and have in the past occasionally triggered panic attacks. Why, he doesn't know. Lola Linker suspects it has something to do with the day that's missing from his memory. She'd gone so far as to request a copy of the incident report of the explosion in which Jeremy was wounded, but the army refused, stating the need for operational security over the mental health of her client. That's just as well: Jeremy doesn't believe he could stand to read about what happened to himself and the others in the dispassionate tone in which army reports are written. Besides, he already knows how that story ends.

There's a reception area where Jeremy gives his name, and then, because he's unexpected, he has to have a conversation with no less a personage than the head of the place, a Dr. Somebody, who has an unruly mustache that makes him look like Groucho Marx. Dr. Groucho seems interested in knowing just who the hell he is, and then, once that's been established, what he wants. After Jeremy has answered this question as precisely as the doctor requires but as generally as he can manage, since he still isn't sure himself, the conversation shifts to a laundry list of behaviors that are frowned upon—gently, of course—and others that are encouraged, as if the staff would be standing around golf-clapping were he to perform well. Accusations, recriminations, probing questions, and anything remotely confrontational are best left at the door, the doctor explains. What clients appreciate most is a sense of connection with the world, of feeling loved, of knowing that they needn't feel shame for their condition. Jeremy agrees to all this readily, wishing meanwhile that he had someone like the doctor to run point for him in his own life. Once he's signed a release form of some sort, which he presumes absolves the loony bin's directors of responsibility in case one of the patients sticks a spork in his eye, he's shown to an Encounter Room, where he sits next to a spray of flowers that seems better suited to a funeral home, and waits.

Wilkins is shown in three or four minutes later by a middle-aged woman attendant who sits him down and then hovers by the door. Jeremy isn't sure what he was expecting, but it wasn't the complete lack of emotion he feels after seeing his father again after all this time. Then again, he's aware that there have been many moments in the last five years when he should have felt something and didn't. And many moments when he shouldn't have and did.

Wilkins has lost a great deal of weight since Jeremy saw him last, which was, according to his math, about fourteen years ago. He's as wispy as a puff of smoke, and he sports a trim goatee now. His hair is tucked into a neat ponytail, shorter than Jeremy remembers, which emphasizes his protuberant eyes. He looks much older than his fifty-one years. He wears a Victorian-looking bathrobe with deep, bulging pockets that sag under the weight of their contents.

Wilkins nods to Jeremy politely, as if they were merely waiting for the same dentist, then proceeds to unload his pockets onto the table next to his chair: a notepad, a variety of pens, a purplish crystal, a digital camera, a candle, and finally—and inevitably, Jeremy feels—a candleholder. Wilkins places the candle in the candleholder, then turns and looks over his shoulder expectantly. The attendant steps forward, produces a lighter, and lights it for him. Then she returns to the doorway, where she touches a rheostat and brings the lights down to four-star dining level.

"I hope you don't mind," says Wilkins. "If the lights are too bright, they can trigger a panic attack."

Oh great, thinks Jeremy. It's me from the future.

"No problem," he says. "How's it going . . . Wilk—uh, Da—uh, Wilkins?"

"Fine," Wilkins says. He clears his throat. "Jeremy. Son. My son. Fruit of my loins. Issue of my lineage, heir to the leadership of the tribe. Before we begin, I'd like to ask you a question. Are you on Facebook?" He holds up the camera and clicks a picture of Jeremy, then puts the camera down and takes up his pen and notepad, waiting. When Jeremy doesn't answer right away, mostly because he's already weirded out, Wilkins arches his eyebrows. "This is an artistic project," he explains. "I'm a conceptual artist. Do you know what that is?"

"You . . . take pictures of people?"

"I challenge paradigms. I create new spaces within existing perceptual frameworks. Also, I shatter conventions."

"Oh," says Jeremy. "You shatter conventions. Like . . . the Elks Lodge?"

"Like societal conventions."

"Ah. Gotcha."

"You look just like your mother," says Wilkins.

"Really? So, I'm in your project?"

"Only with your consent. In this particular work, I take a picture of people's faces at the precise moment I say the word *Facebook*. Then I get the staff to print it out, and I glue it into a book. Get it? It's a face book about Facebook."

"Ah . . . yeah, I get it."

"Words change people's faces, you see. This is an observation I've made. *Republican. Lunar. Amniotic fluid.* I say these things and they appear in your features, or rather the residue of them does. It's like a slide show. Really quite amazing. Underneath your picture, I'll put what you say as a caption. So, are you on it?"

"Yeah, I'm on Facebook," says Jeremy. "Although I don't really go on it that much."

Wilkins notes this down. Then he closes his notebook in satisfaction. "Everyone always says the same thing: they have a Facebook account but they don't really go on it much. But I suspect they're not being entirely honest. I think Facebook is a little bit embarrassing for people. Do you agree?"

"You could be right about that," says Jeremy.

"A very diplomatic reply. I suppose they probably explained to you that you're not supposed to upset me. They say that to everyone. They weren't singling you out."

"I figured that," Jeremy says. "I didn't come here to upset you, though."

Wilkins shrugs. "I don't get upset like I used to. To be honest, and this is something I was hoping I would get the chance to say to you someday, I regret a great deal of my past behavior. I have no excuse, except that I did too many drugs when I was younger. I took an awful lot of LSD. Way, way, way too much.

That's the source of most of my problems. To use the vernacular, I fried my brain."

"Sorry to hear that."

"Don't be. I was exploring my own limitations, probing the edges of my own particular cosmology. I was my own conceptual art piece. But I fell off the pedestal on which I'd installed myself, and I broke on the floor. Shattered into a million pieces. You were actually conceived while I was tripping. Did you know that?"

"No," Jeremy says, imagining a psychedelic sperm seducing Rita's egg with groovy patter, "I didn't know that."

"No, I don't see how you could. Again, I have to apologize. I was an incredibly self-indulgent person in those days. But that's something you probably would have figured out by now."

Jeremy has no idea how to answer this, since affirming it might violate the terms of peacefulness under which he's allowed here, so he merely nods.

"My very presence here is a form of self-indulgence, in fact," Wilkins goes on. "I'm committed, but voluntarily so. I think your mother might find that amusing, in a sick sort of way, because she always used to tell me I had a problem with commitment. Well . . . not anymore." He spreads his arms expansively, smiling. "Anyway. I haven't seen you in a long time, and to be truthful, I hadn't ever expected to see you again. I can't handle going out, and I just assumed you wouldn't want to come here, so this really is a very pleasant surprise."

"You sound completely normal," Jeremy says before he can stop himself. He half expects the attendant to whisk him out for this violation, but she doesn't react.

Wilkins smiles again. "In here, I am. If I went out, though, I wouldn't be. I haven't left this place in well over twenty years, except for that one rather abortive attempt when I signed myself out and went to your eleventh birthday party. But you were quite a young boy when I went away. If I hadn't gone to your party,

I'm sure you probably wouldn't even remember me. It must have been hard for you, growing up without a father."

Jeremy remembers that birthday party clearly. Abortive is a charitable way to describe it. Wilkins had appeared out of nowhere, uninvited, his presence unnerving everyone—most of all Rita. His birthday present to Jeremy had been a rock. Not a particularly pretty or interesting rock, just a rock like you might find anywhere, but which for Wilkins apparently had some sort of symbolic significance. He'd tried for several minutes to explain it to Jeremy, with no success. Then he'd wrapped himself in a bedsheet and spent the afternoon in a corner, glowering at the other partygoers, all boys who were tripping balls on sugar and making tremendous amounts of noise. When they'd asked who Wilkins was, Jeremy had pretended not to know. The highlight of the party was when the police arrived. It transpired that they had been called by Al, and they led Wilkins away, sobbing. Jeremy had been very popular after that, because no one else had ever had a police birthday party before.

"It's okay," Jeremy says. "Hardly anybody has fathers anymore."

"Sad but true. You're not angry?"

"I guess I would be, except that so much other shi—stuff . . . has happened that . . . well, it's all relative, you know?"

"So you didn't come here for a confrontation?"

"A confrontation? No. Why would I do that?"

"You know. Son accuses father of being a bad father. Of being absent, abusive, egocentric. All of which I'm guilty of. Father repents, begs forgiveness. Father and son hug. Emotional string music on the soundtrack. The audience sniffles and goes home feeling redeemed."

Maybe in some other, forgotten era of his life, Jeremy has harbored such thoughts. Maybe there was a time when he was angry at his father for not being a father. But all this is so far in the past that he doesn't even remember it. It all ceased to matter a long time ago.

"No, I didn't come here for anything like that," Jeremy says.

"Do you remember much of me?" Wilkins asks.

"Not a lot. A few things here and there." In fact, several images come to mind, but he can't tell whether he really remembers them or whether they're from the album of snapshots he discovered once under his mother's bed, and to which he returned many times over the course of three or four years, until she realized he'd found it and hid it somewhere else. In other families, they hid porn or drugs; in his, they hid memories. "I do remember something about a motel," he goes on, wondering if this is the right tack to take.

"Really? A motel?"

"Yeah. Well, I don't exactly have a memory of it. But something happened yesterday that kind of reminded me of something, I couldn't say exactly what. And Mom told me that you and I were in a motel for a while when I was little."

"And you've come to ask me why," says Wilkins. He relaxes in his chair, nodding. "A perfectly valid question."

"Did you really kidnap me?"

"Ah . . . well, words," Wilkins says, laughing helplessly. "Kidnap. Rescue. Does it really matter what I call it? The law made its decision, so I guess they're the arbiter here. They say I kidnapped you, and I was clearly out of my head, so I guess that's what I did. But I didn't think of it as a kidnapping because you are my own son, and I was trying to save you. Kidnappers, you see, they're into ransom or beheadings or whatever sick shit goes through their heads. The last thing I ever would have wanted to do was hurt you, Jeremy. I was trying to protect you, in fact."

"From . . ."

"From your mother's family," Wilkins explains. "I have to beg your pardon in advance. I feel certain this conversation is going to bring on a panic attack. We probably have about two minutes before it starts. I'll try to control myself as long as possible, but then I'll have to leave."

The attendant has definitely heard this. She squares her shoulders and lifts her chin, ready for anything.

"Sorry," says Jeremy. "I get them too, sometimes. Panic attacks. So I know just how you feel."

"You do?" Wilkins appears interested. "What are they like?"

"I dunno. They're kind of like . . . well, they always start with this weird feeling, like, 'I can't believe this is happening to me right now.' Sometimes I don't even know what starts them. All of a sudden I feel like I'm—"

"In the third person?" Wilkins interrupts.

Jeremy nods. "Yeah. Like that. Like I'm watching the whole thing. This weird kind of detachment. Like I've been—"

"Cast adrift, so to speak?" Wilkins says. "Yanked out of your body?"

Jeremy nods again. "Yeah."

"Yeah," says Wilkins. "That's how it is for me too."

"Wow. And then does your face get really hot?"

"Hotter than a two-dollar pistol on Saturday night," says Wilkins. "Hyperventilation. You get that too?"

"Oh, yeah. And sometimes I get these headaches. They're bad, like . . . my brain is being sliced in half or something."

Wilkins frowns. "Headaches?"

"The worst thing, though," Jeremy goes on, wrapped up in an odd sense of camaraderie now, "is that I never know what's going to set them off. Like, sometimes it's loud noises, or bad thoughts. But other times it's something completely random. I can even think myself into one if I want. They stopped happening for a while. But they're coming back. I had a bad one just yesterday."

"Why?"

"I've got a bit of a situation at work." Suddenly he feels the need to minimize it. "Nothing major. I'll deal with it okay."

"What do you do for a living?"

"I'm a teacher."

"Ah, a teacher. Very good." Wilkins nods. "College?"

"High school."

"Interesting. My father was a high school teacher. You never met him, or my mother. They both died when I was young."

"I think I remember Mom saying something about that."

"Yes, your mother is full of all kinds of theories as to why I'm crazy. That was one of her favorites—that I'm an orphan. Maybe she's right. I was just about fourteen. They each got cancer, and they went within a year of each other. That would destabilize most people, I imagine. I was sent to live with my uncle in San Francisco. That's where I was still living when I met your mother." Wilkins removes a pack of cigarettes from his bathrobe and lights one on the candle. "Smoke?"

"I quit after I got out of the army," Jeremy says.

"Yes, I heard you were in the army. And you went to Afghanistan."

"Yeah. How do you know all this?"

"I communicate with your mother once every few years, although I'm sure she never told you that. You know, your entire face just changed when I said the word *Afghanistan*," Wilkins says

Jeremy doesn't say anything to that. Wilkins leans forward.

"Jeremy," he says. "The reason I kidnapped you, or rescued you, whatever, is because I knew that if I didn't, if I failed to protect you, that you would end up in the military. And you know what? I did fail, and I was right."

Jeremy leans forward. "What? How did you know that?" Is everyone psychic but him?

"Simple. Because of that asshole Al."

"What do you mean?"

"After your mom and I broke up, when you were still pretty small, and she'd moved back home, he was raising you as if you were his. And I knew how that was going to turn out. Al and his rah-rah belligerence. Al and his sheer thickheadedness. His stupid, pro-American, fuck-everyone-else, kill-'em-all-and-let-God-sort-'em-out attitude. I was afraid that if he got his claws into you, you'd turn out to be some kind of ignorant redneck, just like him."

"Well . . . Al isn't a redneck," Jeremy objects, thinking of pickup-driving bruncles and NASCAR-themed pig roasts. "Not technically, I mean."

"Figuratively speaking, his neck is as red as Mars," says Wilkins, sitting back and tapping his ashes into the base of the candlestick. "Mars, the god of war. Mars is Al's personal deity. He believed passionately in Vietnam. Any war America was involved in was a good war, by definition. And that's what I was trying to save you from. He hated me from the minute he saw me because I had long hair. What kind of criterion is that for judging someone? It makes no sense. But to him I was a threat. I threatened everything he believed in, every made-up tenet of that mockery of masculinity he so deeply cherishes. Okay, I admit I have my flaws. But being a murderer isn't one of them."

Jeremy looks down. He can hear Wilkins breathing.

"How was it for you over there?" Wilkins asks.

Jeremy shrugs. "Okay, I guess. Not great. No worse than it was for anyone else."

"Were you in combat?"

I'm a mothahfuckin' killah, yeah, a loony with a gun.

"Yes," says Jeremy.

"I'm sorry. I don't mean to bring up bad memories. I'm sure you struggle enough already as it is. And you were wounded? I heard about this too. I was very sorry to hear it. I don't pray, but I prayed that day. Human instinct."

Jeremy nods.

"How did it happen?"

"I don't remember," Jeremy says. "I mean, I sort of know from what they told me later. A bomb went off right next to our Hummer. It was one of the old ones—no armor on the bottom.

We shouldn't even have been driving it. But I don't have any memory of it. I'm missing a whole chunk of memories. From that day and the day before. They said the explosion caused that. All I know is, one minute I'm minding my own business, and the next thing I know, I wake up in a hospital in Germany. I was in a coma for a while. They told me I would never walk again. But then they operated, and they put my spine back together. I guess I just got lucky."

"That's horrible. See, Jeremy, here's where my real regrets come in. I regret that I was such a weak father to you. If I hadn't been so crazy, I would have come up with an actual plan. I wouldn't have been so stupid as to think that simply taking you away from them would have made you safe. Children need structure. They need people they can depend on. I should have had the presence of mind to start over somewhere else, to change our names and get a job and start a new life, so that you would not have believed that the army was a viable option. Then that never would have happened to you. I blame myself."

"It was my best choice."

"The army is never the best choice," Wilkins says. "It's the worst possible choice that exists. You're a peon in a corporation whose business is death. The army protects the interests of the insane plutocracy that rules this country. They have the money, so they make the rules. And they brainwash you with so-called patriotism. Don't ever fool yourself into thinking this is a democracy."

Wilkins, thinks Jeremy, is starting to sound a lot like Rico. Rico tried to talk him out of joining the army too. He'd forgotten that until just now.

"Why did you join, anyway?"

"I dunno," says Jeremy. "I guess at first I believed it was the right thing. I wanted to help the country out. And I believed in what we were doing there. We were really helping people, you know, clearing the Taliban out so normal people could live. And the army would pay for college. I didn't have any money of my own. There weren't any good jobs. I thought it would be an adventure."

"And was it an adventure?"

"Yeah, at first. The people were amazing. They were really grateful, and I got a good feeling from helping them. But after a while it became like this camping trip to hell. Our captain got killed, and we got a replacement. And he was . . . different. That was when things got bad. I tried to get out. I mean, it was insane. We were living in dirt. We had no showers. Shitty food. We came close to running out of ammo. It was like they'd just dropped us there and forgotten about us. A chopper would show up when someone got hurt or killed and take them away. That was when it used to hit me the worst," he says, remembering now the thundering silence in the wake of the transport birds, how their rotors would echo in his head hours after they were gone, nothing to do but stare at the walls and wait for something to happen. The endless bickering of the platoon. Woot pacing up and down, riling them, ranting madly. I chase them raghead niggahs down, I shoot they ass fo' fun. Life as a fobbit. "I started cracking up. But they said they would yank my benefits. And my new CO threatened to kill me."

"Did you report that?"

"Are you kidding? Report it to who? We were a million miles from anywhere. He was crazy. We were all crazy."

"Small wonder," says Wilkins. "That's what happens to human beings when they're thrown into an inhuman situation. Are you getting therapy?"

"I was, for a while."

"Good. So you don't have to worry you're going to end up in a place like this."

"It doesn't seem so bad here," Jeremy says.

"It's not. The staff are kind and well trained. The other people, the patients, are hard to take sometimes. But I'm actually getting a lot of work done."

"What kind of work?"

"I read, I write, I think," says Wilkins. "I create conceptual art. I contribute to the economy by helping provide jobs for people like Mrs. Slobodka here." He indicates the woman at the door with a backwards nod of his head. "I even trade stocks. That's how I pay for this place. You're going to inherit them. Some good ones. You won't be wealthy, but it will help. I bought some Google, some Apple. I believe in technology, even though I'm not allowed to use it. But I don't mind that. The news sets me off. It's very stressful. Can I ask you something?"

"Sure."

"Why did you come today? Was it just to ask me about the motel?"

"I guess I was curious," Jeremy says. "After what Mom told me, I wanted to know more. I just wanted to know what you did with me after you took me. Where we went."

"Mostly, we just watched TV while I tried to keep from having a nervous breakdown," Wilkins says. "I stopped taking my meds, which was a mistake. I need structure too, which I guess makes me something of a child myself. I did take you to an amusement park."

"You did? Which one?"

"Magic Mountain. We had a lot of fun. We couldn't go on the bigger rides, of course. You were too short. Not that I regretted that. There was a roller coaster that went upside down six times. Talk about panic attacks. You begged me to ride it, but we stuck to the little-kid stuff, which suited me just fine. I bought you popcorn and cotton candy. It was a good time. That was one day I felt like we were a normal father and son. The only day, in fact. I wish we'd had more days like that."

"Me too, I guess," says Jeremy.

"Does Al still drink?"

"No. He quit a long time ago."

"Thank God for that. The man has powerful demons. Booze doesn't help. How's Helen?"

"She died just a few weeks ago," says Jeremy.

"What a shame. I always liked her. She didn't like me much, but she was a lot more accepting than Al. What did she die of?"

"She just stopped breathing in her sleep. They said it was apnea."

"My condolences," says Wilkins. "Rita must be taking it hard. Did she ever remarry?"

"No."

"What does she do for a living these days?"

"She's a waitress at the Coffee Mug," Jeremy says.

"A waitress? Still? My God. She should have gone to school. I always thought she would. Woman has a brilliant mind, you know."

"She does?" Jeremy's never heard his mother described in this way before. It sounds as if Wilkins is talking about someone else.

"Oh yes. That was what attracted me to her in the first place. She's a great analyzer. She should have gone into business."

"Why didn't she?" Jeremy asks.

Wilkins shrugs. "Probably because she was never encouraged to. I hope you don't mind me saying this, Jeremy, but it's a very damaged family you come from. And a lot of it has to do with the very thing I was trying to protect you from: that military mindset I spoke of. Al's demons. Has he ever talked to you about the war?"

"Never."

"Two veterans living in the same house, and never discussing the source of their greatest pain. How sad."

"Yeah. I guess."

Wilkins sighs. "Well, it's been great seeing you, Jeremy. I think I probably ought to get back to my room now. I don't get a lot of stimulation, and this conversation has given me enough to think about for a long time. It's easy for me to overdo it. I should have a nap. But I hope you come back and see me again. You can anytime, you know."

"Okay," says Jeremy. "I just . . ."

Wilkins waits, peering at him over his bifocals. "Yes, I can see there's something else on your mind. Go ahead. Whatever it is. Ask me."

"It's just—I wondered if you ever think the way I do. Like . . . what the point of everything is. If we're all just going to die, I mean. Do you ever think that way? Like, we do all kinds of horrible shit to each other, and when you're alive, you think you're going to be alive forever, until one day you realize that isn't true, and that it just doesn't fucking matter. You ever think like that?"

Wilkins doesn't answer. He just listens, and so Jeremy goes on.

"All these people, billions of them. All the people who've ever lived. Most of us, you know, we're just going to die without ever doing anything that important, and no one will ever even remember that we were here. No one. And I guess what I wonder is why no one ever stops to think about that kind of stuff before they do something. Even something big, like building a skyscraper or starting a new country or something. Or starting a war. Or even fighting in one," he says, realizing that maybe only now is he getting to the point of what he's trying to say. "You go into it thinking there's some big reason behind it, but there isn't. It's just the same damn thing over and over again. So many people get hurt and die, but eventually so much time passes even their suffering doesn't matter anymore. It's like they never existed. It all just gets wiped out, like . . ."

"Like a sand dune," says Wilkins.

"Yeah."

"Yes. I have thought about these things."

"Yeah? Well . . . what's the answer?"

"I can't really tell you," Wilkins says. He looks up at the ceiling, as if the words he must choose are stored there. "Partly because I'm not really sure how to frame the question. I know that humanity relies upon a few people to help move them forward. A few special people, who see things the way you do. People who ask the right questions. For every person who has a great idea, there are millions more who will scream that you're ruining everything, you're crazy, you're making things worse. So we kind of march in place, until finally a change takes hold and suddenly we've moved an inch forward. In one sense the answer is you're right, nothing does matter, at least not outside the moment it happens in. But the moment is everything. Nothing else exists besides right now. And you are asking the right questions, Jeremy, because when you think like this, you start looking at things in a new way, a more careful way. I wish I could tell you definitively how to ease your pain and make you feel better about things. But all I can tell you is we are moving forward, little by little. Don't give up on the human race just yet, Jeremy. People do a lot of beautiful things too."

Mrs. Slobodka clears her throat. Wilkins stands. Jeremy does too, and then Wilkins holds out a hand. They shake, his father's hand a bony bird. Wilkins puts his belongings back into his pockets, blows out the candle, which he leaves smoking on the table, and turns toward the door. Then he turns back.

"Jeremy, are you really interested in the pursuit of truth?"

"Uh . . . sure. I guess."

"When you see Al again, there are two words you should say to him. *My Lai.*"

"What? You lie?"

"No. Not 'me lie.'" Wilkins takes his notepad from his pocket again and writes on it. Then he rips out the sheet of paper and hands it to Jeremy. He looks at it. On the paper is scrawled: *MY LAI.*

"Ask him about that," Wilkins says. "If you want to know, that is. If you don't, don't. Just be aware it's kind of a Pandora's box. Once it's out, it can never go back in."

"What does it mean?"

"Look it up. It's a place in Vietnam. A village. He'll know what it means. Just be prepared for the fact that it won't be a very pleasant conversation. Not nearly as pleasant as this one has been." He shuffles a few more steps in the direction of Mrs. Slobodka, then turns again. "Good luck with everything, Jeremy, and thanks. Come see me again sometime," Wilkins says, and then he and Mrs. Slobodka disappear through the doorway.

He delays going home for as long as possible. When he finally can't put it off anymore, he feigns having work to do in the basement. Rita has made dinner and left it out on the counter. She's gone to Sam's. Jeremy eats alone, in the basement. Tomorrow, he's remembered, is an assembly schedule. The goddamn dedication ceremony. He knew there was something he was particularly fearing, but he'd forced it to the back of his mind. At least there will be shortened classes. Thank God.

"Jermy," comes Henry's voice from the top of the stairs. "Will you hang out with me?"

"Leave me alone, Henry," says Jeremy. "I'm not feeling well."

"Can I hang out with you?"

"No, Henry. Leave me alone, I said."

"Are we still friends?"

"Yes, Henry. We're still friends."

"Am I still cool?"

"Yes, you're still cool."

"Are you still really tired from the war?"

"Henry," says Jeremy, "leave me alone."

"Okay," says Henry.

Jeremy sleeps. Because the fact is, even though he's been home for five years, he is still really tired from the war.

8

MONDAY MORNING, the day of the dedication ceremony, Jeremy is awakened as usual by his alarm. His back is worst in the mornings. He's learned to set the buzzer twenty minutes early so he can work himself into a sitting position without rushing. When he feels that he and his spine have once again come to an understanding—a negotiation that must be held anew each day—he gets up and pees in the utility sink. Then he fills his electric kettle. After the water boils, he pops a largish bud into a teapot and pours boiling water over it, steeps it for several minutes, and sips it slowly. He can't smoke before class or someone will smell it on him. He's never really liked the taste of marijuana smoke anyway. It burns his throat and glues up his tongue, and he has to drink gallons of water afterward. The tea was an idea given to him by Rico, his savior, without whom he would surely be addicted to Vicodin, or OxyContin, or some damn thing. It tastes like hay-flavored water, but it's better than a tear-inducing, five-minute-long coughing fit. And with a little honey, it's not bad at all.

He hears the front door open and close, then footsteps overhead. Rita has returned from her latest romp with the beturbaned Sam Singh. What kind of weirdness do they get up to over there? He's never allowed himself to wonder, or rather he forces these thoughts from his head whenever they arise. Nor has he stopped to ponder just what she sees in him. Not that Sam isn't without his good points. By his mother's standards, he's a real find. Owns his own business. Doesn't drink or take drugs. Isn't locked up in a loony bin. That last quality is a real plus.

He goes upstairs and sits at the table while his mother makes his breakfast.

"Are you going to wear your uniform today?" she asks.

Jeremy snorts. "Hell, no."

He doesn't mention that he's secretly tried it on and found that it no longer fits around the middle; it appears that the appetite-enhancing effects of the dope are sneaking up on him. At first, this had been a good thing. The medications he used to be on killed his desire to eat, and his weight had dropped to dangerous levels. When he'd left the hospital the first time, he weighed only 110 pounds. But he's pudging up now, edging closer to 160 than he'd like to admit. No matter. Nothing a few thousand sit-ups wouldn't fix. Unfortunately, he cannot do sit-ups with his back in its current condition. Maybe one of those electric belts would do the trick, the kind that shocks your stomach muscles all day long. He must look into getting one. He makes a mental note of it, and hopes his short-term memory will retain it somehow.

"I just thought it might be nice to look your best," Rita says.

"It's not about me anyway," Jeremy observes. "It's about Thomas."

"Poor Thomas."

"Poor everyone," says Jeremy.

She shoots him a sidewise look. "You sure you're up for this today?"

"Why wouldn't I be?"

"I just thought it might stir stuff up for you. You know. More attacks."

"Naw," says Jeremy, forcing a show of bravado, though it occurs to him that maybe she's right. What if he dissolves into a quivering mess in front of the entire school? That would be a disaster he'd never live down. "I'll be fine," he says.

"If you say so. I have to go to work. Can you get Henry his breakfast? I'm in a hurry."

"Why can't Al do it?" says Jeremy.

Rita sighs.

An hour later, he's rolling in Al's Saturn through the mean streets of Elysium, smelling the powdery dust and the acrid tang of creosote bushes through the air vents. It's only 7:10 a.m., but already he must turn the air-conditioning on if he's to tolerate sitting in the car. Heat like this makes a person take things minute by minute. At this rate it's going to be a hell of a long day. An endless series of minutes, stretching to the horizon, each one filled with pain and accidie and frustration—and heat—punctuated only by a government-subsidized cafeteria lunch, then the prospect of lying in bed and staring at the ceiling for a few hours before falling asleep again. In between, teenagers. A crowd of people looking at him all big-eyed. Someone will undoubtedly call him a hero, thank him for his service, pump his hand, grow misty, ask more stupid questions, tell him they want their kids to grow up to be like him. Fuck them all. Thank you for your service is something you say to a waiter. To a soldier you don't say anything, because unless you were there with him, there's really nothing you can say. And if you were there with him, that's probably the last thing you'd want to talk about.

Suddenly Jeremy realizes that he would like very much to get out of this ceremony. But how? He has no options, really. He's to be one of the guests of honor. This is blatantly unfair. You should have a choice about these things. Maybe a fake injury is the way to go. He's sorely tempted to swing the nose of the car into the wall of the Kozy Kart, the Lebanese-owned convenience store he happens to be passing at that moment. Not hard enough to hurt himself—maybe just so he can spend the morning in the emergency room getting checked out. But if he went to the ER, he would have to see other people who were sick or hurt. That might bring on another attack. And he might hurt someone else, such as Kazar, the lonely guy from Beirut who is always on duty behind the cash register, or his grandmother, with whom he lives. And hurting people is something he's promised himself he's never going to do again.

Then, he says to himself, you shouldn't have pushed Jenn.

But she was trying to kiss me.

Think about that for a minute, you fuck. A kiss. What's a kiss?

Something nice.

And you gave her back something shitty.

Yeah, but I'm a teacher and she's a student.

Who gives a fuck? Babies are dead and limbs are blown off and entire villages are laid waste and your panties are in a twist because some girl tried to kiss you.

I'm a fuckup.

Yeah. You're a fuckup.

After he arrives in the parking lot, it takes him a few moments to work up the breath to swing his legs out of the car. He heads through the doors of the place that by the end of the day will officially be named Thomas Sarty Memorial High School and checks his mailbox. There's another handwritten note. You'd think people had never heard of email.

Come see me first thing so we can talk about today.
Peter Porteus.

He files this in the trash can. No one else is here yet except Jesús, the custodian, whose wheeled bin he can hear rolling along somewhere on the open campus, echoing from the sixties-era brick walls with a sound remarkably like that of mechanized armor. He heads out the back door of the building and into the Quad, outside again. There are few hallways in a desert high school. Everything is open to the sky, so that the students' minds may know no limits.

Jeremy attended high school here, and every time he unlocks his classroom he has the sense that either his childhood was a bad dream or his adulthood is, but he can't tell which. The nostalgia the so-called friends on his Facebook list seem to feel for those days is a complete puzzlement. High school for him was neither a bad time nor a good one; it was just a time, a stretch he did, a sentence he finished to the satisfaction of his jailers. In comparison with what had come after, it had faded quickly into insignificance. Now, as he steps into the same room he once entered as a student for lessons that scarcely sunk in, he wonders yet again at the timelessness of buildings and rooms, how one moment he passes over the grimy linoleum in his Converse All Stars, his head full of thoughts that seem fluffy and inconsequential now even though he can't even remember what they were, and the next moment he treads upon them in his admittedly shoddy but still far more adult loafers, seven or more years behind him, his burden made heavier by the knowledge that seven years hence the contents of his mind in this moment will seem just as ridiculous. And there is nothing timeless about buildings at all; they are as temporary as anything else, destructible and flammable, although by tacit agreement everyone seems to concur that it would be better not to think or talk about such things. Someday this building will be gone and everyone in it will be long dead, and none of it will matter in the slightest. There is only this moment, in which he sets his steaming mug on the black stone of the demonstration table, in which he picks up the dry erase marker from the tray, in which he uncaps it with a pop like a bottle of champagne and begins to write.

He writes the date on the board, followed by the half-assed lesson plan he came up with in his head on the way over here.

Jeremy's knowledge of physics is largely limited to the principle of what goes up must come down. His nights for the past month have consisted of lots of Internet cramming sessions, and in addition to every other thing that's wrong with him, he's also developed an advanced case of impostor syndrome. At any moment he expects a tap on the shoulder from someone informing him that there's been a terrible mistake, that he actually has no business in a classroom, and if he leaves quietly, right away, they're willing to just pretend the whole thing never happened.

Which would, he thinks, be a vast relief. Almost as sweet as waking up last night and finding himself at home, and not back in the old schoolhouse they'd used as their post. Imagine that. Soldiers stationed right here in paradise, shitting into blast holes in the linoleum floor, sleeping in corners of classrooms, the windows taped up and boarded over, Porteus's office turned into a command base, a fifty-cal set up on the roof behind a pile of sandbags. These things happen, in other parts of the world. They can happen here too. He would like to make people aware of this somehow, but no one will believe him. Among the American people, or at least the American people he knows, there is a tacit belief that shit happens to people in other parts of the world simply because they did not have the good fortune to be born in America. That people who live in mud houses and ride donkeys and wear long dresses even if they are men are somehow not real people. He'd once believed this himself, but now he knows it not to be true. War had once been just as inconceivable to the people of Afghanistan as it is now to the people of Elysium. This is one of the things he knows best, but the things he knows best are things that no one else wants to hear.

They're doing a unit on Force equals Mass times Acceleration. So he tries to think of some examples. That's easy. A fifty-caliber round slams into a human body with a force that is equal to its mass of 94.99 grams multiplied by its incredible velocity of about three thousand feet per second, which is too hard to do in his head but is certainly enough to separate a head from a neck, or a lower torso from an upper torso. Or a mother from a child.

He closes his eyes until that one goes away. There are images, like that one, which he does not consider to be actual memories. Real memories live and breathe and even have motion and emotion, as if they were actually made of cells rather than flashes of electricity; but this image, the sight of a dead mother clutching a dead child, exists instead in some kind of frozen state. It flicks on at odd moments like a spotlight that holds him in its steady eye, daring him to gaze directly at it. He doesn't know who shot that woman. Maybe it was him. It was surely a mistake. He'd come upon her after a bad fight, just as the baby was breathing its last. The mother was already dead. The top of her dress had been torn away by the force of the round, and he had seen her breast, long and floppy and gray, drops of milk still beading on the nipple. And he had screamed for the medic. But his voice made no sound. It just came out as a rush of forced air.

No, no, no. No, no, no.

Not today. Please. Not today.

It's possible that he stands there for several minutes, arm upraised, the dry erase marker poised in his hand. He doesn't know. He tends to lose time, like those people who say they've been abducted by aliens. At least these episodes seem to occur only when he's alone, when he has nothing to distract him from his own thoughts. He wonders if he looks like Henry does during those petit mal seizures he used to get, when he simply stared off into space as if he were listening to some secret voice. If this were to happen during class, the students could ping spitballs off his forehead and he'd never notice.

But when he hears other people coming into the building, he snaps out of it. He grabs his mug and locks the classroom door.

Then he heads back to the admin building for another cup of joe, and to see what the principal wants.

Porteus is a chubby, argent-haired man who, like all school officials, is more politician than educator and who seems to regard parents, students, and teachers alike as pesky obstacles to his ambition. At least he seems to genuinely like Jeremy. He's regaled him on many occasions with closed-door tales of his own days in the army, which he'd apparently spent driving around Cold War–era Europe in a convertible full of German chippies. Most of these stories ended with some subvariety of "and my dick was so hard I thought it would explode."

Jeremy finds Porteus at his desk, humming. So he's happy about something. Standing astride his day planner is a fuzzy new Elysium Trojan, the mascot of the football team, wearing a felt helmet and holding a flaccid cloth spear. Against the wall is a box of more Trojans, their eyes pleading helplessly with Jeremy to set them free.

"Hey, Merkin," says Porteus. "Check this guy out. The new fundraiser. Got twenty bucks?"

Jeremy makes a show of patting his pockets. "Nope," he says.

"Well, hit up the ATM and you can buy one at lunch, maybe. The cheerleaders will be selling them. It would be great if our faculty would show some support."

"Twenty bucks for that?"

"I know, great deal, right? Hey, I thought you were gonna wear your uniform."

"It's at the cleaners," says Jeremy.

"You didn't tell them you needed it for today?"

"They lost it, actually. It musta slipped behind something."

"Too bad. It would have made a great impression."

"I'm sorry," says Jeremy. "What's the drill for today, anyway, sir?"

"I love it when you call me sir. It adds a certain air of decorum to this place that is sadly lacking." Porteus checks his watch. "The Superintendent is in the men's room taking a shit right now. And I got the Senator arriving in an hour. We start when he gets here. He'll be late."

"The Senator? You mean Commander Quickly?"

"Yeah, that's right."

"I used to watch Commander Quickly," says Jeremy. He's amazed to discover that he feels a jolt of excitement at the prospect of meeting his old childhood idol. "He did the voices for all his puppets. And he used to fall into a big puddle every episode."

"Right, that was his gag. Jesus, you're that young?"

"I guess so," Jeremy says.

"Well, this is a big opportunity for him. Show support for the troops, plus look good on education. Fuckin' sweet. A doubleheader. He wants a picture with you. That's why I was really hoping you'd be in your uniform."

"Commander Quickly wants a picture with me."

"Look, do me a favor and don't call him Commander Quickly to his face, okay?"

Jeremy would like to grab Porteus by his lapels with his left hand and bring his right fist at great velocity into the man's nose. Suppose his fist weighs a pound and a half. Suppose he accelerates this mass at thirty miles an hour. But instead he says, "Don't worry, sir, I wouldn't do that."

"You, ah, don't remember the name of the cleaners, do you?" Porteus asks, hopeful. "I could call them and ask them to look again. Pretty hard to imagine they could lose something like a whole uniform."

"No," says Jeremy. "I think they actually went out of business."

"Really," says Porteus, his tone growing dry. "I wonder why."

"They, uh . . . got in trouble for something."

"Hmm. Any idea what?"

"Money laundering," Jeremy says, and then he promptly wishes he could detach his own tongue until such time as he can be trusted to use it.

"Really," says Porteus. "A dry cleaner got in trouble for money laundering."

"I know, it's ironic, right?" says Jeremy.

"Hey, fellas," says a voice behind him, and Porteus rises. Jeremy does too, as quickly as his fused vertebrae will allow, and he turns to see Superintendent Gonzalez, a wee man of Latin aspect, sporting a toothpick-thin mustache and wearing a beautiful bespoke three-piece suit. A streamer of toilet paper adorns the heel of his left shoe and trails two feet behind. Gonzalez holds out his hand. Jeremy shakes with him. Dry and warm. So the dandified little fucktard didn't even bother washing. "Thought you might be in uniform today, soldier," Gonzalez says to Jeremy.

"So did I," says Porteus. "Apparently it was stolen by money launderers."

"They didn't steal it, exactly," Jeremy mumbles.

"The Senator will be disappointed," says Gonzalez. "He was hoping for a picture with you with all your medals and stuff. Seeing as how this other guy—what's his name?"

"Who?" said Porteus.

"The guy who's getting the school named after him."

"Sarty. Thomas Sarty," says Porteus.

"Yeah, him. Seeing how he's dead. So you gotta be our hero for the day," says Gonzalez.

"I'm not a hero," says Jeremy, for perhaps the nine hundredth time in his life. And neither was Thomas, he thinks. Thomas Sarty had certainly not been heroic when Jeremy knew him, which was only in passing. He was a few years older than Jeremy, which meant that the sum total of their interaction was that he occasionally elbowed Jeremy out of the way in the lunch line. Jeremy was given to understand that his status had not changed much, hero-wise, in later years. He'd been killed in a jeep accident in Iraq, which was, Jeremy thought, the perfect way for someone as hapless as him to die: the victim of someone else's stupidity. But he's the only citizen of Elysium to have been killed in uniform in a recent news cycle, and the town needs someone to canonize.

"Sure you are," says Porteus absently. "You're all heroes."

"Every last one of you," says Gonzalez, as he checks his iPhone.

Students have begun filing past the window of the office, which looks out over the Quad. They're a lot younger-looking these days, Jeremy's noticed. This year's crop of freshmen are so small and timid that he cannot believe a fifth-grade teacher somewhere isn't wringing her hands in agony, wondering where her class has gone. Only the wispy mustaches of the boys and the blossoming bosoms of the girls are proof that they are in fact in the right place. Then a trio of women who look as if they've just left a nightclub clack by in tight skirts and makeup, expertly balancing on high heels, their perfume permeating the window, which is open just a crack. These are seniors, a different animal altogether. Everyone has been told to dress up for the day. Jeremy sees one boy in a tie run up to another boy in a tie and point at himself in amazement, probably saying something like, Look, I'm wearing a tie. Every time he sees the student body from the perspective of Porteus's window, he has the sensation that he's visiting some kind of adolescent wildlife exhibit, safe behind glass, while the dangerous beasts circulate in their native element.

"If those skirts were any higher, you could smell their pussies," says Gonzalez dreamily.

"Ha-ha!" laughs Porteus, far too loud. "You're totally joking, of course."

"Mr. Porteus, the Senator is here," says Mrs. Bekins, sticking her head in the door.

At that moment, in walks Commander Quickly, a tall, smooth-featured man with gleaming hair that has miraculously gotten darker in the years since Jeremy last tuned into his show. He's followed by what appear to be aides and security personnel. Only now does Jeremy remember that Commander Quickly has revealed himself in recent years to be a staunch conservative. The more liberal bloggers, like Rico, hate his guts; they pillory him every chance they get. But something strange is happening. He finds, staring at the Commander, that he cannot bring himself to feel the resentment he knows he ought to feel, the vile loathing he experiences when reading about his plans to put more people in jail for possession of marijuana, to cut funding for schools, or to start new wars in far-off countries. Instead, he feels a vague but growing sensation that he would like to cuddle up with the Commander and rest his head on his chest. Wait a minute. What the hell is happening?

"Senator, it's a pleasure to see you again," says Superintendent Gonzalez.

"Hiya, Senator," says Porteus.

"Hey, what's up, guys," says Commander Quickly. "Got some shitwipe on your shoe there, Gonzo. So, who's who here?"

Gonzalez looks down and does a funny sort of sidestep until the toilet paper comes loose from his heel. Then he looks at Jeremy—accusingly, Jeremy thinks at first, but then he realizes he's only going to be introduced.

"Senator, give the glad hand to a real American hero," says Gonzalez. "One of our fine teachers here in Elysium, as well as a former soldier. Jimmy . . ." He turns to Porteus, expectant.

"Jeremy Merkin," says Porteus.

"A hero in the fight against terror," says Gonzalez.

"Excellent. Outstanding. With a résumé like that, you oughta run for office," says Commander Quickly, shaking hands with Jeremy. The charisma evaporates. Jeremy can feel the beneficial bacteria on his own skin curdle at his sulfurous touch. At least he'll have killed off Gonzalez's E. coli, Jeremy thinks. "Did you get a lot of those bastards?"

For a moment Jeremy has no idea which bastards the Commander is talking about. Then he realizes he must mean terrorists. Commander Quickly likes to talk about terrorists a lot. Jeremy did not see any actual terrorists while he was in Afghanistan. He saw a lot of different kinds of people, and some of them were not very nice, and some of them wanted to kill him, though by this standard Jeremy supposes this made him a terrorist too. But most of them were just people. Not much different from the people one sees in California every day, if one discounts superficial things such as clothing, language, or religion. He can see Porteus's anxious intake of breath. He realizes that the principal is afraid of what he might say. Don't worry, fat man, thinks Jeremy. I know how to play this game.

"Yeah, sure," he says. "Lots of them."

Porteus beams.

"Wonderful, wonderful," says Commander Quickly. "Well, what say we get this show on the road? I've got about fifteen minutes." He looks at his watch, then looks at Porteus, who appears about to faint.

"Fifteen minutes?" he says. "I think we were planning on holding the ceremony at—"

"I'm going to Sacramento by chopper in like half an hour," the Commander says. "It's gonna land on your football field, matter of fact. So we need to kind of get cracking here."

"Sure, sure, no problem. We can move things along," says Gonzalez. "The Senator is here, right? That's all that matters." He spots the PA system on a wheeled cart in the corner and goes over to it. "Let's see if I still know how to work one of these. Not that I ever did. When I was a principal, I always had my secretary do it."

"You want a hand?" asks Porteus.

"No, no, I can do it," says Gonzalez. He begins flicking switches. Feedback threatens the hearing of an entire generation of Elysians. Porteus dives past Jeremy and swims through the air to Gonzalez's side. He kills the screeching and hands the microphone to Gonzalez.

"Now hear this, now hear this," says Gonzalez. "This is Superintendent Gonzalez. All students and faculty will report to the Quadrangle for the rededication ceremony. That means right now. Everybody. Let's go. The Senator is here."

"Well, that sounded authoritative," Porteus says brightly, flicking the system off. "Normally I try to throw a 'please' or two in there. Let's give them a few minutes to gather, shall we?"

"What is there, like a cornerstone or something?" Commander Quickly asks. "Am I smashing a bottle of champagne over something? Unveiling a new sign?"

"No champagne, ha-ha, what a shame, and no sign yet either, Senator," says Porteus. "We've got one on back-order. It was supposed to be here last week, but they said it might be another month. It's because of the, uh—" He sneezes his way through something that sounds like budget cuts. "We're just dedicating today. And the boy's parents are coming."

"Whose parents?"

"The young man we're renaming the school for. A former student. He was killed in action."

If riding in a jeep can be called action, Jeremy thinks.

"Ah," says the Commander. "Right. His parents. I bet they're super, super sad about that."

There is a moment of silence in the office.

"Because they raised him and everything," the Commander adds. "Like their own son."

"He was their own son," says Jeremy.

"That's what I mean," says Commander Quickly.

"Yes, the Senator is absolutely right," Porteus says. "They are super, super sad."

"They sure are," says Gonzalez, checking his phone again.

"And so are we," says Porteus.

"No doubt," says the Commander, looking appropriately somber. Then, spying the box of Trojans against the wall, he brightens. "Look at those cute little guys. Hey, anyone wanna see a trick?"

"Sure!" says Gonzalez, far too brightly.

The Senator clears his throat and twists his lips. "Hey, guys, let us out of here!" he says in a high-pitched voice that sounds, almost, as if it's coming from the box. "What did we do wrong, anyway? Come on, guys, have a heart!"

Despite himself, Jeremy feels his innards melting with love for the Commander. Then he clears his head. Porteus and Gonzalez are laughing. Jeremy forces himself to smile.

"Geez, I'm rusty. All right, enough with the gags. Where's the media?" the Commander asks.

"Pulling up now," says Porteus, looking again out the window. A portion of the parking lot is visible from here, and Jeremy can see that two TV vans have just arrived. A couple of techies in neon sneakers hop out and begin uncoiling cables, followed by a brace of anchors in pressed clothing, a man and a woman hatched from the same test tube, hair Commander-perfect. Through the window he can see that students and faculty have begun drifting toward a more or less central location in the Quad. Jeremy scans them. There's no sign of Jenn. He wonders if she's still in the motel room.

"Well, let's go," says Porteus, as a bewildered-looking couple appears in the Quadrangle, clutching each other's arms. Thomas Sarty's parents.

It's been some time since Jeremy's stood at attention. Actually, it's been some time since he's tried to stand for any length of time. Even when he's teaching, he moves constantly from whiteboard to stool to desk. He can rarely stay in any position for long, except supine. Now, as he tries to pull his shoulders back, he's fighting a bellow of discomfort.

". . . decorated for bravery and courage under fire," he hears Porteus say. He's talking about Jeremy. When he was a boy, he'd thought the phrase "under fire" meant something like dashing under a campfire, the way one does the limbo. He could not for the life of him understand why anyone would want to do that. Now that he has a true understanding of the phrase, he thinks his original explanation would have been a sounder practice. People shooting pieces of metal at each other through long tubes— what an insane thing to do. Sophisticated monkeys without an ounce of sense.

Porteus introduces the Superintendent. The Superintendent makes a speech that is interrupted by a sonic boom, close enough that they can all feel it in their chests. No one bats an eye except for Commander Quickly, who, unlike the boom-wise residents of Elysium, has not developed sonic smarts. He looks around, wild-eyed, and appears ready to dive under the nearest protective object. The students titter at his consternation. Jeremy practices Lola Linker's trick: remember, it's not a big gun, it's just sound waves. Gonzalez finishes his speech and introduces the Commander. The Commander goes over to the parents of Thomas Sarty and says a few words to them, shaking their hands with both of his, three pumps and a shoulder touch for Dad, four pumps and a lingering hold for Mom, before proceeding to the microphone.

"It's days like this that I'm proud to be an American," he says. "Actually, that's every day. Because America is great because of young men like Thomas, who laid down his life to help keep our country great and keep it safe from terror." He waits for the applause that dribbles in after a moment. "They're everywhere. In our airports, on our highways, in our railroads, in the various liberal educational institutions all over the country. They have to be rooted out and destroyed at home, just like in Afghanistan and Iraq and France and everywhere else. We have to look under every bed, behind every curtain, inside every closet. You don't know where they're gonna be. Why, we even have some of them in our very own government." There are plenty of nods of agreement, two or three groans of commiseration. "But never you fear, we're gonna get them all in the end. And thanks to young men like Thomas, we are one step closer to doing just that."

"Rapist!" someone yells.

The word rings out clearly, timed to fall between the Commander's own words. It's so incongruous that no one appears to hear it. At least, no one reacts, except for the Commander's security team, who are suddenly sniffing the air. They begin to move unsubtly toward the rear of the crowd, touching their ears. The Commander himself is unperturbed. Perhaps, Jeremy thinks, he's used to this kind of thing. He wonders whom Commander Quickly raped, and when. He doesn't recall having heard about this before. When the Internet gets hold of this, it will be big. He looks at the news anchors, who are poised next to their cameramen. Incredibly, they too appear not to have noticed. At least, there has been no alteration in the wattage of their smiles.

"So we are here today to rededicate this fine place of learning to PFC Thomas Sarty, Elysium High Class of 2000," the Commander says. "And here to assist me with the dedication of the stone is our own hero, Lance Corporal Jeremy Merkin. Keep on making heroes, Elysium! How many of 'em did you get again, Jeremy? Ha-ha! No, he's a modest guy. Doesn't like to talk about himself. Atta boy, son." He shakes a friendly fist at Jeremy. The crowd titters. Jeremy swears that just for a moment he can hear Smarty's voice in his head, egging him on to do something stupid and rebellious. Just what that would be, he can't make out. But the spirit of Smarty has finally been awakened.

"Rapist!" the yeller yells again, closer this time.

Then there is a disturbance in the crowd, and a man pushes himself to the front. He's tall, potbellied, hair pulled back in a ponytail. He wears an olive drab jacket with military patches all over it. On his head is a baseball cap with another patch of some sort. A veteran, and he wants everyone to know it. Just another guy whose life broke the day he first saw combat and who hasn't been able to pick up the pieces again. The security men have already zeroed in on him, but they aren't quick enough with the hand one of them claps over his mouth, and the word escapes yet again. Finally, the cameras swing toward him.

"That son of a bitch raped my daughter! My baby girl!" the man screams, shaking free of the hand over his mouth, pointing. Not at Commander Quickly. At Jeremy. "JEREMY MERKIN RAPED MY DAUGHTER!" he screams.

Time has really been doing some weird things lately. Jeremy can feel each instant ticking past him like the distance markers on a highway. Yet he seems to be getting no closer to any kind of destination. He will exist like this forever, suspended in front of a crowd of perhaps four hundred people and two TV cameras, all of them gawking at him, and also at Jennifer's father, who is still screaming, and is now being hauled away by four burly men in suits.

"Jesus Christ of America," mutters Porteus, to Jeremy's left.

"What the fuck?" murmurs the Superintendent, to Jeremy's right.

Both of them turn to look at Jeremy. He holds up his hands to show his helplessness and lack of understanding, his mouth working but nothing coming out. They turn away, disgusted. Porteus looks at him once more, in disbelief. In the distance, he hears the sound of an incoming chopper. Apaches, come to strafe the Quad? No. Commander Quickly's ride is here.

"Nothing happened!" Jeremy croaks.

"Oh, Mother of God," says Porteus.

Commander Quickly is standing directly in front of him, and he steps backwards two paces and turns to make an utterance over his shoulder, his lips twisting again.

"I like you, buddy, so let me give you a word of advice," he whispers, throwing his voice into Jeremy's ear. "Deny everything. Even after they prove it. Keep denying it no matter what. Deny, deny, deny." He winks, and then he steps away from Jeremy as if he's erupted in plague boils.

Which, Jeremy supposes, he has, in a manner of speaking.

"Let's go," says the Commander to his minions.

All of them exude from the scene in a puff of vapor, heading for the football field, where the chopper is now landing. A mighty swirl of dust erupts skyward. Skirts and ties begin to flap in the rotor wash like landed fish. The Superintendent heads briskly toward the admin building, his phone out, thumbs flying. The student body remains, some of them laughing in shock, others in mockery, a few silent in stunned disbelief, and a few looking around as if they are wondering where the pitchforks and torches are kept. No one can hear anything over the noise of the blades. The anchors have set their sights on Jeremy and are approaching. He tenses, then immediately regrets it as the muscles in his back seize.

"Everyone go back to class," Porteus bellows. "Resume normal scheduling. Merkin! My office, now." Then he trails after the Superintendent.

Jeremy looks up and watches the helicopter as it begins to peel away from the earth. Here's one big difference between his current self and his eighteen-year-old self: at eighteen, he could have made it from here to there in time to grab onto one of the landing struts and cling to the chopper as it rises, ass first, and heads for the horizon. And that would have been the last anyone saw of him.

9

AL WAKES MONDAY MORNING with a sense of purpose: today is the day. Not the day he does the actual deed, but the day he will finally confront the tasks that must be accomplished beforehand. For last night he dreamed of Helen, standing by the bank of a river, and he could tell that she was calling him home. He's not much for interpreting dreams, but it's the first time Helen has come to him since she passed, and he knows what that means. It's time to get ready.

Halfway through his morning coffee, he remembers how he saw Helen standing on the bank of a wide, slow-moving river, looking into the water, a lamb at her side. He'd tried calling to her, but she couldn't hear him. She looked young, much younger than when he'd first met her—just a little girl, really. He hadn't known her then; he hadn't met Helen until she was sixteen. Now that was a woman. They didn't make them like her anymore. In those days, her fulsome beauty had hinted at an awesome procreative power. Large farm-girl breasts as ripe as watermelons, broad hips, a nice smackable ass. In ancient times, men had sculpted statues of bodies like hers and worshiped them as fertility symbols. It was 1961, the year he turned twenty, and although Al had already been drafted—there was a draft then, people today tended to forget that, though if they brought it back it would be the best damn thing that could possibly happen to this republic of lazy fat asses—they planned on farming when he got out in another year, or maybe in another four years if he decided to re-up. In those days that were made blissful by the fact that they were too young to know much of anything, they'd giggled over the possibility of having a dozen children, two dozen even. Consumed by the happy promise of boundless reproduction.

That was before his father's garlic farm had failed. His parents went into bankruptcy, dashing Al's hopes of having a farm to inherit, and this was also before the military had providentially held out the promise of a war to fight in, which meant a steady paycheck. There were few other choices. Helen's older brothers got the farm she was raised on—and promptly lost it as a result of their endless feuding. There were no jobs then, not for boys with no farms and no education.

It was also before the two children who'd died, the one who came between Rita and Jeanie and the one who came after Jeanie. He still didn't know whether it was appropriate to think of them as children or not. Helen had insisted on carrying them to term, even though she knew ahead of time they wouldn't make it. Medical technology had advanced by then to the point where they could predict your misery before you began to live it. The babies deserved to know what it was like to live inside her womb, she said. She could love them that much. If they were to leave this life knowing only that one thing, then that would be enough.

After the second baby died, Al had his balls snipped. He suspected his sperm had been fouled by Agent Orange. He did not blame the government. He would never be one of those whiny professional victims who tried to cash in. Life dealt hard knocks to everybody. He blamed the Vietcong, for making the use of Agent Orange necessary. Those little fuckers were still lashing out at him. He never told Helen about his vasectomy. He'd said he was going in to have a hernia repaired. Of course, she knew anyway. She had to. They had simply never discussed it, just as they had simply never discussed many other things.

In the privacy of his room, he calls his lawyer and schedules an appointment. He needs to find out just what must be done to give the house over to Rita. He also wants to make out a new will, he tells the shyster, to designate Jeremy as the new beneficiary of his life insurance policy. He hopes this sounds reasonable enough, considering the recent death of his wife. Al is aware that he's going to have to make his own death look like an accident or the insurance won't pay out; he knows this much from watching television. He's unused to deception on this scale. He's convinced the lawyer can hear the lies dripping from his voice. But if the lawyer suspects anything, he doesn't let on. What would he care? As long as he gets paid, it's all the same to him. That is why lawyers exist: to charge hourly fees for deconstructing the tangled legal mechanisms they themselves contrived.

Then there's the matter of Helen's hearts. These have been plaguing him, but now he knows what he should do. First, he must take an inventory. He will count, catalog, and organize them. Then he'll talk to Jeremy about putting them up for sale on the Internet. This, he's now sure, is what Helen would have wanted. It's the very reason she made them, after all. The hearts were intended to be dispersed into the world. They were coded messages. What did they say? Perhaps that there was more to life than deformed children in the womb and alcoholic husbands who lashed out in their sleep. Never mind that Al had always grumbled when she asked him to saw her another batch at his garage workbench, a paint-and-glue-stained, tool-strewn plain that was the last place in the house he could truly call his. And never mind, too, that he'd considered odious those weekly trips to the craft fairs of Kern County and regions beyond, where other middle-aged women converged with the sound of a thousand cooing pigeons over acres of cheeseball trinkets. There was no escaping craft fairs. They were his punishment. She made him drive her to every single one. Helen hated driving, believed it was a man's job, while her task was to fret aloud over missed turns and imaginary timetables, and to shriek in alarm if a truck turned five hundred yards ahead of them. Once they'd arrived, she would order him to cart the boxes in, while she fussed over her pink plastic tablecloth and arranged each heart in a precise location based on criteria known only to her. There was the weak coffee in foam cups, the plastic trays of soggy danishes, and cookies that made his head pound with glucose and despair. There was also the knowledge that it would be hours before this purgatory had been called to a close and he could go back to his automatically adjustable lounger and his beautiful new fifty-two-inch flat-screen television. Women have always exhausted Al—the energy they devoted to mindless details, the money they would spend on useless things. He had once suggested to Helen, in one of his cruder moments, that if you packaged dog diarrhea properly, put it in a curvaceous pink bottle, and wrapped a bow around it and gave it a cute name, some woman would buy it. He was trying to be funny, but the acid in her glare imparted the information that she was not one bit amused.

It's been a long time since Al has felt this clear about anything. He's realized that if he doesn't have any more answers than he had when he went to sleep, at least he knows what the next step is: eBay. This is the solution he's emerged with from the depths of his unconsciousness, like a diver holding aloft a prize lobster.

If Jeremy were here, and if Al were feeling up to braving his eye-rolling sighs, he could ask him just how this eBay thing works. He's perused the site himself many a time, fascinated by the sheer variety of items for sale. But he's never actually bought anything, not daring to trust his credit card to cyberspace, which, according to *Time* magazine, is populated with perverts and con men; and he's certainly never sold anything either. Yet he knows that one must take a picture of the thing one wishes to sell and put it on the site somehow, so people can see what they're buying. So the first thing he must do is photograph the hearts. This is how you eat an elephant: one bite at a time.

He carts every shoe box of hearts he can find into the garage, where he removes them one by one and lays them out on newspapers. He separates them first according to whether or not they are finished; those that have not yet been painted or adorned with scrolls go back into a box. The rest, exactly one hundred of them, lie twinkling on the floor. In recent months Helen, undergoing another artistic metamorphosis, had begun using a new kind of paint. It has sparkles in it, or glitter, or ground-up fairy shit or some damn thing, and now the hearts catch the light and shine in a way that Al finds tawdry but which had delighted her.

There's a digital camera somewhere in the house, but that belongs to Rita and he dares not touch it. Instead, he goes for the Sony he'd bought to demonstrate to Helen once and for all that she snored, an antique now, so large that he must hoist it onto one shoulder. Maybe Jeremy knows a way to put videos on eBay.

He'd intended to use this camera often, but once he'd made his case to Helen with video evidence, it had sat untouched. This made it a rare extravagance. The category of Equipment was a sacred one, encompassing everything from the smallest screwdriver to the Saturn, perhaps even the house itself; and one of the key tenets of Equipment was that it must be used often enough to justify its purchase. He'd planned on videotaping Jeremy's future star performances on the football team, but to his eternal disappointment Jeremy had turned out to disdain football; he only wanted to play video games with that fat little Mexican. He could have videotaped Henry, he supposed, but who wanted to watch movies of a retarded kid? That would just be depressing. Never once did he look at Henry without imagining how he might have turned out if that cord hadn't been wrapped around his neck. Besides, Rita was the photographer of the family. At least he'd packed the Sony away properly in its original box and molded foam bed. The top of the box was dusty, but that was the only way in which time had ravaged it.

Inside the camera, Al finds the original videocassette he'd used to record Helen, over two decades ago. He knows her snoring will not still be on it; mortified, she'd forced him to erase it, he remembers. He wishes now he hadn't. He would pay good money to hear her snore one more time. He plugs the camera in and is gratified to hear it whir into life. Those Japs made a good machine, for which he supposed they could thank the billions of Yankee dollars that had flooded their country like water into a rice paddy after they'd made it necessary to nuke them into submission. They all did the same thing, the Japs, the Koreans, the Chinks: we kicked their asses, and then we sent them all our manufacturing jobs. Soon enough it will be Vietnam's turn, he supposes, but he will be dead by the time that happens.

After a full minute of struggle, he deduces how to make the thing record. He points it at the hearts and pans over them. Suddenly it occurs to him that he ought to provide some narration, for he wants people to really understand what they're looking at. He clears his throat and begins.

"This is Alvin Merkin speaking. The date is September 5, 2011, and I'm standing in my garage in my house on Jacaranda Street in Elysium, California, U.S.A. We've resided here since 1988. I retired from the Edmonston Pumping Plant in 2002, where I worked for thirty-three years, mostly as a supervisor." How much should he say about himself? As little as possible, he decides. The people viewing this on the Internet are not buying him, after all. Nevertheless, he feels they might appreciate some context, so he swivels the camera to look down the driveway, treating them to a view of the front yard and the house across the street. People are always interested to see what America looks like.

"There is the home of Mr. Richard Belton, one of our neighbors," he says. "Mr. Belton is employed by the State of California. He commutes to Sacramento three times a week. That is an acacia tree in our front yard. I didn't plant it. It was already here when we moved in. As you can see, the weather today is clear, as usual. The temperature is approximately ninety-five degrees. That's Fahrenheit," he adds, for the benefit of his European viewers. "We are not expecting any precipitation today."

Enough background. He returns to the hearts, which glitter at him in the slant of sunlight that comes in the open garage door.

"The items of interest here are several dozen hearts that were manufactured by my late wife, Mrs. Helen Merkin, who passed away last month at the age of sixty-six. Helen and I were married for forty-seven years. We met when she was still a high school student and I was a private in the U.S. Army, where I served my country proudly for almost ten years. Our fathers had done some business together and that was how we became acquainted. We courted for two years, and were married in 1964. Helen always enjoyed her crafts even then. It was a hobby, you might say. Even back in those days, she was always making decorations of one sort or another."

A memory comes to him, and he decides to share it.

"When I first met her, she used to knit all kinds of doll clothes. Little shirts and pants and skirts and whatnot. Quite skilled at it. I'd forgotten all about those. Then she got into picture frames, and after that it was Christmas ornaments. She used to paint them herself and give them away. After that, she went through a scrapbooking phase. We have a whole box of those inside." He debates getting out the scrapbooks to show the camera, but decides against it; he's not even sure what's in them. "I would estimate that she commenced making hearts in about 1995. So she had achieved quite a high level of skill. You wouldn't know it to look at them, but each one of these things takes quite a bit of work. I would say that she spent at least half an hour on each one.

"The hearts are made of high-quality balsa wood, which I procured at our local hardware store and cut out for her on my jigsaw." Al swings the camera around to show the jigsaw in question; no doubt his male viewers will enjoy seeing it. "I utilize a Black & Decker. It gives a good cut. I've maintained it well, of course, as I do all my equipment. I replace the blades every year. The moving parts are sealed with factory lubrication, so I haven't had to get involved in taking those apart. All in all, I find it was well worth the price, which I believe was around two hundred dollars some years ago, if I remember correctly."

Back to the hearts. "Anyway, these hearts were then painted with a red glittery paint and decorated with hand-lettered scrolls. Helen did all that. She had a pretty steady hand. She was often a vendor at craft sales throughout the region. If you live in Kern County and you ever went to a craft fair, chances were you saw Helen there at her table. She didn't do it for the money, of course, just for the pure enjoyment of it. If someone wanted a heart but didn't have any money left, she would just give them one, especially at the end of the day when she was packing up. She was happy to see them find a home, that's all. They do brighten up a place. Why, you ought to see the inside of our house. Hearts everywhere. You can hang them on your walls, you can hang them on your Christmas tree. Some people have even put them on their front doors. Others display them in the living room. They are a very versatile item. The price is three dollars and fifty cents each. But," he says, in a flash of entrepreneurial inspiration, "if someone was interested in purchasing the entire lot, I would be willing to arrange a discount."

That's all he needs to say, he supposes, but it still feels incomplete somehow. He clears his throat and goes on, still aiming the camera at the hearts.

"Helen was quite a woman. She put all her time and energy into her crafts, when she wasn't taking care of Henry. That's our grandson, who was born mentally retarded. You may not know it, but it actually takes a lot of talent to make these hearts. I guess they were sort of a reflection of the way Helen felt about the world." Al pauses. He feels himself growing flushed in the face, and he presses on to distract himself. "She was good with her hands that way. Always had a lot of patience for fine detail. She also enjoyed baking quite a bit. She made cookies, cakes, and pies, and whenever possible she tried to use fresh fruit in season. It's easy for us to obtain a lot of fresh produce here in California.

"I would have to say," he goes on, unsure now but forging ahead, "that Helen's most outstanding quality was the amount of care she showed in everything she did. And she did everything for her family. She didn't think about herself very much. If she had spare time on her hands, which wasn't often, she would always try to use it to make the house look a little nicer, or to do something for one of the grandkids. We have another grandson, Jeremy, who is twenty-five this year. He also served in the army. He was wounded quite badly in Afghanistan, but I'm happy to report that he's made a good recovery so far. I remember the day we found out he'd been hurt—"

Al checks himself here, for a catch has appeared in his throat. He disguises it as a cough.

"—Helen was just beside herself. She didn't eat, didn't sleep. She just sat by the phone for days and days. You couldn't get her to take so much as a sip of water. 'Al,' she said, 'I just don't know what I'd do if we lost that boy.' Those were her exact words. We raised Jeremy too, you see, because he has no father to speak of, and his mother was working a lot. When Helen wasn't waiting by the phone, she was praying in her bedroom. I'm not a religious man myself, but one of the great things about this country is our freedom of religion. You can decide for yourself whether you want to get involved in that or not. No one is holding a goddamn gun to your head.

"Anyway," he goes on, "Helen passed away, as I say, just over a month ago. The date was August 3, 2011. She died in her sleep, with no warning. I was the one who—"

This time there's no coughing his way through it. Al hiccups, tries to catch his breath, and decides finally that enough is enough. He looks frantically for the off button on the camera, but when he can't find it, he yanks the cord from the outlet, violating his own long-standing rule by failing to use a proper grip on the plug. Then he removes the cassette and packs the Sony away in its box again.

He watches it on the VCR in the living room, embarrassed and yet proud somehow. He's appalled at the way his hand shakes, at how his world is reduced to grainy footage in washed-out color, but he thinks that Helen would have enjoyed his testimonial. He hadn't intended it to be that kind of thing, but now that it's turned out that way, he feels pleased. Maybe Jeremy will know how to cut out the irrelevant segments. He doesn't want his customers to feel like they're dealing with an emotional fool. That kind of messiness does not inspire confidence in one's business dealings.

The next step is to figure out how to get this onto the computer somehow. For this, he'll definitely need Jeremy's help. Al doesn't pretend to understand computers; they have no moving parts, for one thing, and for another, he's embarrassed to admit that he never believed they would become even slightly useful. He's amazed at how everything these days is computers this and computers that. In *Time* magazine, he'd read that the average teenager carries more technology in his pocket than there was in the command module of the first moon lander. And still all they do is take drugs and have sex. America, he thinks, is wasted on the wrong people.

But he does know how to surf the Internet, and suddenly an idea occurs to him. You can find out just about anything these days, and there is no need for him to rack his brain any longer. He opens up a browser window and navigates his way to Google, where he types in: *how to put video from a sony camera circa 1991 onto the computer fairly easily.*

The results are disappointing; they don't make much sense. It's rare that the Internet lets him down. Maybe his search terms need to be refined. But he's weary, suddenly. He will turn the damn thing off, maybe take a nap or something.

Then another idea occurs to him. If you can look up things about video cameras, maybe he can solve another problem.

He opens a new page on Google and types in: *ways to commit suicide.* This time, the Internet works like it's supposed to. Just as he expected, there is a plethora of methods. But he's shocked at the number of people who seem to have devoted a great deal of energy to this topic. With almost seven billion people on the planet, it stands to reason that a certain percentage of them would be thinking about it, the same way he is. But who would go to the trouble of writing how-to websites? Attention seekers and sick puppies, he decides. No one who was really serious. If you're going to do it, you don't go around talking about it to the whole damn world. You just do it.

Al is uneasy now. He doesn't care to be associated with these macabre types. He's had a good life, except for some parts, and he will be sorry to leave it, but when he goes, it won't be a tragedy. He's seventy years old. Even though the time has gone by in a blink, it was just about long enough to be considered full.

He would have liked to squeeze another ten or twenty years out of it, but it would appear that this is a selfish desire that will only end up destroying everyone. If he doesn't off himself soon, he'll just end up spinning his wheels in some nursing home, eating up what's left of his material wealth while he drools into a bib and soils his adult undergarment, otherwise known as a diaper, and he'll have nothing to leave to anyone. Despite his distaste, he bookmarks the page so that he can come back to it later.

Then he remembers the camera, and the film that needs to somehow get onto the Internet. Thinking about it, he grows tired again. Jeremy will have to do that part for him.

He checks his watch. It's 9:18. Jeremy won't be home for another six hours.

Wait a minute. 9:18. Why isn't Henry out of bed yet? He's always up by now.

Al tromps down the hallway. Henry's door is closed. He opens it. The bed is empty.

"Henry?" he calls anyway. Maybe the kid is playing one of his hiding games. But it's been a long time since he was small enough to fit under the bed. He kneels anyway, gasping for breath, and looks. Nothing there. He's not in the closet either. Al leaves the room and circumambulates the entire house, calling his name in every room. He examines the backyard, then the front. He looks up and down the street. Then he goes to the head of the basement stairs.

"Henry?" he calls.

There is, of course, no answer. Henry never goes into the basement. He's afraid of spiders.

Al descends the quivering timbers of the stairway anyway, holding carefully to the railing; the last thing he wants to do is fall and break a hip. He blinks until his eyes adjust to the gloom enough to find the light switch. How Jeremy lives down here like a cavefish is beyond his comprehension. Maybe now that he finally has a degree and a job, he'll get himself an apartment or a house somewhere. And a car, so Al can have his goddamn Saturn back. It's high time he started thinking about getting married and raising a family of his own, instead of existing in this eternal postbellum adolescence.

Clearly there's no one here, but it's been a while since Al investigated his own basement. He feels a proprietary need to find out what goes on down here. He sees Jeremy's unmade bed; the clothes lying on the floor; his laptop, the screen open, busily whirring as it completes some invisible task. There's a plastic box of some kind of plant matter on the table next to the bed. Al picks it up and smells it. The odor is rich and grassy, and after a moment he realizes that it must be marijuana. *Cannabis sativa.* Well, supposedly Jeremy has a prescription for it, but how you can just go out and buy something that the government has plainly said is illegal is beyond him. If he needs medication, for God's sake, he can just take pills like everyone else.

Al takes the box upstairs and dumps the contents into the toilet. He has to flush four times before the last remnants, finally waterlogged, are carried away. The plastic box he drops in the garbage.

Legality restored, Al remembers that there is a more serious problem. Henry's not supposed to leave the house on his own.

He heads back into the kitchen and opens the cupboard door that has the phone numbers taped inside. He'll call Rita. Al knows just where she is, and just what they're doing, she and her swarthy little boyfriend. He dials her cell number.

"Hello?" Rita says.

"Is Henry with you in that Hindu sex palace?" Al demands.

"What? What do you mean, is Henry with me?" Rita asks.

"I believe the question is fairly straightforward," Al tells her. "Henry is not here. Therefore, I am calling to ask if he's with you."

"No, he's not with me. Is he gone?"

"That is typically what 'not here' means," says Al.

"Dad . . . what are you talking about? How can he just be gone? Did he leave? Did he go with someone?"

"I don't know. I just went to go wake him up and he wasn't in his bed. And I can't find him anywhere."

"Oh my God," says Rita. "Okay. Hold on. I'm coming home right now."

"Should I call the police?" says Al. But she's already disconnected.

Al depresses the button for a moment, then releases it. When he has a dial tone again, he dials 911. They'll respond quickly, he thinks with satisfaction. Not like in some countries, where the cops are all so corrupt you have to bribe them to do everything.

10

PORTEUS hadn't called it getting fired. The phrase he used was "extended leave of absence." It was a very short conversation.

"You're innocent until proven guilty, of course," Porteus had said, "except in cases like this, where you're just guilty. That's the way the board will see it. I have to let you go, Merkin. Can't have you around with this hanging over your head. Too disruptive. There's a procedure for it. There'll be a meeting of the board, too. They'll be the ones to decide officially about your job. But I can tell you right now that they won't care what you say. Once you're accused of something like this, that's it. I've seen it happen before. I tried to warn you," he added. "Didn't I tell you not to touch the goddamn students?"

"I didn't touch her," Jeremy said.

"Sure, okay," said Porteus affably. "Uh-huh."

"I'm serious. I will admit that I was in a motel room with her. But I didn't rape her."

"Then why does she say you did?"

"She didn't say anything," Jeremy pointed out. "It was her father who said it. And she told me herself he's nuts."

"What the hell were you doing in that motel room?"

"She needed help."

"Help with what? Her physics homework?" Porteus asked. "Don't tell me, I don't want to know. You shouldn't even be talking to me. I've got two pieces of advice for you, Merkin: number one, shut your piehole, and number two, get a lawyer. Now I gotta find someone to sub for you. You know any good physics subs?"

"No, sir. Do you know any lawyers?"

"Touché," said Porteus. "Well, take care, Merkin. Don't call us, and we won't call you. Deal?"

There was no point in telling Porteus the truth. He had no proof of his innocence, and Porteus cared only about covering his ass, the eternal concern of people in official capacities. He probably hoped to become superintendent one day himself. Now the worm of anguish that had been wriggling in Jeremy's intestines is replaced by a sense of numbness as he makes it to the parking lot and gets back in the Saturn, especially after he sees that the TV vans are gone. Public humiliation is a new one for him. At least there's no sign of Jenn's father, though he moves carefully between the cars, ready to react in case he's lurking behind one of them, fresh accusations in his mouth or a tire iron in his hand.

He can't go home. He needs to think, and if the open desert doesn't bring him peace, at least it will grant him solitude. So he spins the Saturn past the lake that Ouranakis had installed in the center of town, and which has since festered like an open sewer, riddled with stinking, nearly sentient algal life forms roughly the size and shape of sea serpents, and which is supplemented on a weekly basis by the volunteer fire department with yet more water stolen from the Indians of Mexico. The billboard painting of Elysium-as-paradise still stands, the happy drunk Greek revived every year by the real estate agents who show the same devotion to the late Ouranakis that Japanese holdouts once did to their emperor. And every year, the same asshole hits it up with the spray paint. Jeremy wishes he knew who it was; he'd

like to shake his hand. A fountain blares greenish liquid skyward, spreading droplets of water with the texture of pudding,
and probably scattering heinous microscopic life forms into the
Elysian air. Jeremy holds his breath until the fountain is safely
in his rearview mirror.

He travels next through the dead perimeter of town, where
the houses have never been built, aimless in his confusion. The
digital thermometer on the dashboard has reached ninety-eight.
He stops here, at the edge of Ouranakis's ambition. Tumbleweeds in the grip of the Santa Anas blow across where the road
used to be. The desert has encroached upon another imaginary
block, tendrils of gray dirt creeping in, drifting and duning over
the blank slabs of cement, incomplete pieces of plumbing jut-
ting skyward like tibias. He stares out across the expanse at the
broken jawline of hills in the distance.

As a boy, he'd often wandered through the desert, sometimes
stumbling across the odd relics that accumulated in this rust-free
zone. Nothing ever decomposed out there; there wasn't enough
moisture. Ancient flivvers and jalopies lay in gullies where they'd
been dumped by teenaged joyriders now in retirement homes.
Once he'd found an actual aerial bomb, which Al had explained
was a dummy, probably dropped by training crews during World
War II as they practiced for the destruction of Germany or Japan.
Another time he'd found an entire house, not much more than
a shack really, but still fascinating to his twelve-year-old self,
weathered gray and scarcely standing, held together only by the
electrostatic forces of its own decay. Inside was an old metal bed
frame, beer cans that had lost their labels, a bent fork, an iron
that was really made of iron, a page of a newspaper from 1948,
and a relatively modern tampon applicator. This last item he'd
prodded carefully with one toe, wondering what tales it could
tell. He'd considered setting fire to the place, just for the thrill
of watching it burn. But with no one there to egg him on, he'd
chickened out. He'd never been able to locate that shack again.

It was a kind of Californian Brigadoon, he supposed, appearing only once a year in the haze of heat.

The desert doesn't bring him the peace he seeks. He turns the car around and heads back into town. He passes the Kozy Kart, thinks about going in to kill some time, but he knows it will only be staffed by the overworked Kazar, who will fix him with his heartsick eyes and voice his wish that someone would play soccer with him. Only he doesn't call it soccer, he calls it football.

His phone rings. It's Rita. He answers.

Jeremy pulls up in the driveway of the house on Jacaranda Drive. Inside, he finds Al sitting alone in the living room, staring morosely at Henry's empty chair. Henry's blinders sit, a lifeless bat, on the cushion, which bears the permanent indentation of his rear end. This detail brings into Jeremy's mind the ludicrous thought that perhaps the police know how to dust for ass prints. He's always been good in sudden emergencies. It's these long, slow, drawn-out ones that render him a moron.

"Why aren't you at work?" Al says as he walks through the door.

"Something happened," says Jeremy.

"I'll say something happened. All hell's broken loose," Al says.

"I know. Mom called me."

Jeremy passes through the living room and straight down the hall to Henry's bedroom, feeling the need to confirm his absence for himself. Helen had tidied Henry's room once a day, but here Rita has drawn a line that she will not cross: Henry can learn to clean his own room. The consequence of this is that it's slowly begun reverting to some primordial state, as if Henry is attempting to re-create the chthonic muck from which humanity emerged.

Jeremy wades through a layer of dirty clothes, half expecting to be bitten on the toes by some new kind of life form. Reluctantly he pulls back the sheets on the bed, hoping for a clue. Somebody really needs to do the boy's laundry, he realizes. He opens the closet, just in case the whole thing is one big, elaborate hoax and Henry is hiding in there, giggling into his hands. But Henry doesn't stage hoaxes. It's beyond his capabilities. The smell of something rotting attracts the attention of Jeremy's nostrils. He roots around until he finds an empty potato chip bag. Inside is an apple core, fuzzy with mold, and some mildewed crumbs. He holds this item between thumb and forefinger and takes it to the kitchen, where he deposits it in the garbage can. Then he goes back out into the living room.

"Where's Mom?" he asks Al.

"Out looking for Henry with her swami," Al says. "The cops have already come and gone."

"Which cops?" Jeremy asks.

"The state police. They looked all over the house. Now they're looking all over the county."

"Did they go into the basement?" Jeremy asks, alarmed.

"Why? Got something to hide?" Al throws him a sidelong glance. "Don't worry, I threw out your illegal substances before they got here."

"You what?"

"That's right. My house, my rules. You want to snort cocaine or inject dope or whatever it is you do down there, you can go do it somewhere else. It's about time you got your own place anyway. You're old enough to be on your own. When I was your age—"

"Jesus Christ, I can't believe you sometimes," says Jeremy, running his hands through his hair. That had been very fine pot. But he will have to save this argument for another time. "You didn't hear him leave?"

"I didn't hear anything," says Al. "I've already played twenty questions with California's finest. By the time I looked in his room, he was long gone."

Jeremy thinks back to his search-and-rescue training. You started in the place where the missing person was last seen, and you worked outward in an ever-growing circle. So he looks in the garage, making a mental note to ask George why Helen's heart collection is spread all over the floor, but knowing this is just another Post-it Note that will slide off the refrigerator door of his short-term memory and never be seen again. Then he goes into the backyard and checks the shed. He's not there—not in the three-foot-tall Joshua tree, which is the sole piece of vegetation back there; not camouflaged against the long-dead lawn like an obese brown chameleon; not sitting on the roof watching the drama caused by his absence unfold.

He goes back into the living room and stares at the chair some more. Something is missing, something besides Henry, that is, but he can't put his finger on it.

"Satisfied?" asks Al. "What do you think, we just didn't notice him somewhere?"

"We need to go door to door," Jeremy says. "Ask all the neighbors."

"Your mother and the police already did that. Nobody saw him. They were all too busy watching TV. An alien spacecraft could have abducted him in broad daylight and no one woulda noticed."

"Do they think someone took him?"

"Who would take Henry?" says Al. "Seriously. Who the hell would want him?"

"There's all kinds of sick fucks out there," Jeremy says, examining the front door for signs of having been forced. He notices something suspicious. "What's this gouge here in the frame?"

"You made that when we carried the dining room table in nine years ago. The cops asked me about that too."

"I'm going out again," says Jeremy.

"Where?"

"Where do you think? To look."

"Yeah, but where?"

"I don't know. Anywhere. I can't just sit around here waiting."

"Hold on," says Al. He gets to his feet and begins scanning the area for his shoes. "I'm coming with you."

"I thought you wanted to stay here in case he came back."

"I'll leave the door open," says Al. "He can just let himself in. No need to worry about crime in this neighborhood, since everyone is of a satisfactory skin color."

"I'll be in the car," Jeremy says. "And your shoes are probably in the goddamn closet, where they always are."

He stomps back out to the driveway and gets in the driver's seat of the Saturn. The Santa Anas roar down the street, scouring the pavement. The whole town leans to the east. If everyone just picked up and left, in a hundred years Elysium would be sandblasted into nothing. There's no way Henry would have taken himself for a walk in this wind. He hates weather of any sort.

Al comes out a moment later, shod, and motions him out from behind the wheel. "I'm driving," he says.

"You? You can't drive for shit," Jeremy says.

"I am commandeering this vehicle as is my right under the law of the State of California," says Al. "Plus, I have the keys." He holds them up and dangles them.

Jeremy gets out, walks around the car, and gets into the passenger seat, stifling a wave of pain as he does so. Al gets into the driver's side, groaning as he lifts first one leg then the other.

"Well, we're quite a pair," says Al. "I'm better off than you are, though. By the time you're my age, you won't even be able to get out of bed."

"Thank you very much," Jeremy mumbles.

"What?"

"Is your hearing going?"

"What?"

"I SAID, IS YOUR HEARING GOING?"

"No, my hearing is not going," Al says. "You don't have to shout."

"You wouldn't even have heard him leave the house," Jeremy says.

"Don't blame me for this," Al tells him. "Your mother already tried that, and I wasn't having any of it. Boy has a mind of his own, even if it is only half a mind. I can't watch him every minute. If he's gonna take off, he's gonna take off."

"Henry doesn't take off," Jeremy says. Because taking off would require motivation, determination, purpose, fortitude. And Henry doesn't possess any of those things.

Al starts the car and backs out, neatly missing the mailbox with his side mirror by a margin of half an inch. He drives at the speed of a crawling toddler to the four-way stop at the corner, which is devoid of other cars. Here he puts on his right-hand blinker and waits.

"Grandpa, you can go," says Jeremy.

"The law states you must come to a complete stop for a full three seconds," Al says. "Traffic laws exist for a reason, you know."

"I could walk faster than this."

"No, you couldn't. Where are we going, anyway?"

"Drive around our block. Then go down through the dead neighborhood. Maybe he's down there."

"And what the hell would he be doing there?"

"Who knows?"

"I told him a million times to stay out of there," Al says. "Nobody listens, nobody takes heed. Everyone just does whatever the hell they want. And that's the definition of chaos."

They cruise around the block, then around four blocks, then around eight blocks. Then they go through the uninhabited, undomiciled streets. Jeremy knows that in about five seconds Al is going to say something derogatory about Ouranakis. Tumbleweeds blow in the gathering wind, and a dust devil heads up the street, passing through their car like a being from another plane. There's not a living soul in evidence.

"That goddamn sneaky little Greek," says Al.

They stop at the border of the desert. Jeremy gets out and squints at the hills.

"We need a helicopter," he says as he gets back in. "Someone could be lost out there for a year and you'd never find him on foot."

"They said they'll launch an outdoor search tomorrow. They have to wait twenty-four hours for that."

"What the hell for?"

"Policy," says Al.

"Don't they know he's retarded?"

"Sure, they know. But he's functioning, and he's legally an adult. They said he has the right to leave the house if he wants to."

"What the fuck," says Jeremy, "is wrong with those assholes?"

"Don't ask me."

"Let's go by the lake."

"A sound plan," says Al. "If he fell in there, he's no doubt bobbing around like a seal. Lord knows he's in no danger of drowning, with all that blubber on him."

They drive around the lake, but Henry is not there.

"How many hours since he left the house?"

"I have no idea," Al says.

It's now nearing noon. If he's walking, he could be anywhere within, say, five miles, Jeremy thinks. But why would he do that? He wouldn't just take himself for a walk. Henry doesn't ever go anywhere. He doesn't know anyone. His entire life has been spent in the house, anchored to Helen.

They go next to the Kozy Kart, where Jeremy gets out again and interviews Kazar, but Kazar hasn't seen Henry. He gets back in the car. He can see Rico's house from here, and outside it he spots Rita's Escort, parked in the street. Then he sees Rita and Sam, standing in the driveway and talking to Elizabeta.

"Aha," says Al. "Let's stop here and gather intelligence." He rolls down his window. Rita and Elizabeta approach. Sam remains at a wary distance from Al, though he catches Jeremy's eye and waves. Jeremy waves back.

"There you are," Rita says to Jeremy through the window.

"What are you doing here, Mom?"

"I was just asking Elizabeta if she has anything to tell us," Rita says.

"You mean if she sees anything in her crystal ball," Al says. "I hope you didn't cross her palm with any silver."

Elizabeta appears on Jeremy's side of the car. "I need to talk to you," she whispers, and she motions him out. Jeremy follows her to stand by the trunk of the Saturn.

"What is it?" he says.

"Yeremy, I never see anything like this. You got hundreds of people following you. More coming all the time."

Jeremy swallows. He is not going to start believing this shit, he thinks. But Elizabeta believes it. And it's the conviction in her eyes that spooks him more than anything. She's looking at them now, a horde of shades crowding up behind him on the street. At any moment her head is going to start spinning around on her neck and she'll be puking green.

"Well? What do they say?"

"They talk about Henry."

"What about him? Do they know where he is?"

"Of course they know. They the spirits."

Jeremy waits.

"But they not going to tell," says Elizabeta.

"Right," says Jeremy. "Of course not. Why should they?"

"They want you to follow him."

"They do, huh?"

"Yes. You don't believe?"

"Elizabeta," says Jeremy, "in my world, when you want someone to follow someone else, you tell them where that person has gone. It makes it a whole lot easier."

"Spirit world don't work that way."

"I've noticed."

"Yeremy, I think he all right. He is protected. But something big is coming. Something very big."

"For Henry?"

"For Henry, you, everyone in your family. Henry is gonna take you somewhere. You gotta go."

"Jesus Christ," says Jeremy, running his hands through his hair. "Fine. I'll go. Where?"

"I don' know, cariño, I'm sorry. You go see your father like I tell you?"

"Yeah."

"Good," says Elizabeta, nodding. "That gonna help."

"Help with what? Finding Henry? He doesn't have anything to do with him."

"Is all part of the same thing," Elizabeta says. "You don't see right now, but is all connected. Like a . . . a net that a spider make."

"A web."

"Yes. Like that."

"Are we gonna find him today?"

"Is not the finding that's important. Is the looking. Have faith, Yeremy. Okay? I know you don't believe. But have faith anyway."

"I'd believe whatever worked, at this point," Jeremy says.

"Sometime that is enough," says Elizabeta.

He gets back in the car.

"Jeremy," says Rita, leaning in the window and talking past Al. "Another cop came by as I was leaving. He wanted to talk with you."

"Who was it?"

"A sheriff's deputy. Moon, his name was."

So this is how it starts, Jeremy thinks. No sneaking around in the dark of night to jump him as he sleeps, no spontaneous traffic stops to find a planted gun or bag of heroin in his car. Just a visit to his mother in broad daylight. The message could not have been more clear if he'd had it delivered by singing telegram.

"What happened at school today?" Rita asks.

"I don't want to talk about it," Jeremy says.

"Well, you're the only one who isn't. Didn't I tell you that girl would be nothing but trouble?"

"She's not the problem," says Jeremy. "It's her crazy father."

"What are you talking about?" says Al.

"Never mind. If he comes by again, tell him you don't know where I am," says Jeremy. "I left town. You understand? That's what you tell him. And don't let him in the house."

"What on earth is going to happen?" says Rita.

"Never mind, Mom. I'll handle it. We have to keep looking. He might still be close. Let's go," he says to Al. "See you back at the house, Mom."

Al starts easing the car forward, but Rita stays in the window, clearing her throat.

"I won't be home tonight," she says.

Al stops the car again. It lurches. Jeremy winces.

"What the hell do you mean you won't be home tonight?" Al says.

"I'm staying at Sam's."

"What for?"

"What do you mean, what for? Because that's where I'm staying tonight, that's all."

"This is a hell of a time to pick for a vacation," Al says.

"It's not a vacation," says Rita. "It's a liberation. You're both entirely capable of taking care of yourselves. And I've got enough on my mind right now."

"At a time like this, this is what you think of?" Al asks. "Are you kidding me? Your place is at home with your family. Not lollygagging around with that pillowhead. Your mother would be ashamed."

"Mom is not here," says Rita flatly.

"Don't I know it," says Al. "That's everyone's excuse these days. You're just gonna end up washing his bathrobes for him, you know." He indicates Sam with a nod of his head. "You know how those people treat their women. Not an ounce of respect. You want liberation, stick with your own kind. He's just gonna make you into some kinda slave."

"I would smack you for that," says Rita, "but my wrist is sore from carrying other people's dishes all day. Jeremy, call me later. You and I need to talk."

"Talk about what?"

"I think you know damn well what," she says, and backs away from the car.

Al pulls away again, muttering misogynist incantations under his breath.

They drive down every street in town, stopping the only pedestrians they see, a pair of speed-walking women clutching miniature dumbbells, arms pumping. They haven't seen Henry either.

"Aren't you that teacher?" one of them says.

"I heard they arrested you," says the other.

"Keep driving," Jeremy says to Al.

They head out into the back roads that wind through the desert, marked with ATV tracks and littered with the leavings of beer parties and piles of disemboweled trash bags.

"What the hell did she mean, arrest you?" asks Al.

"There was a misunderstanding."

"Sounds like a big misunderstanding. Did you diddle one of those little harlots that prances around town in practically nothing? Tattoos halfway down their asses? Rings in their noses?"

"I didn't diddle anyone."

"Can't say I would blame you," Al says. "The way they dress these days. They're all asking for a good diddling."

"You're an old pervert," Jeremy says.

"Ha. I'm a man, same as you. At least I think so, anyway. When was the last time you got yourself a piece of tail?" When Jeremy doesn't answer, Al nods with self-satisfaction. "Thought so."

Jeremy feels his mood sinking with the sun as it wends its way toward the horizon, the earth and sky reddening, the shadows cartoonish in the way they run from the hills and the Joshua trees. Henry was never here. So where is he? All sorts of visions he'd rather not have come flitting through his mind. Henry bound and gagged in the trunk of someone's car. Dead on the side of the road somewhere. Lost and scared in the middle of the desert, wandering deeper and deeper into the wilderness and closer to certain doom. If he is out there somewhere, he won't last through tomorrow. The sun is still brutal at this time of year, and after a lifetime of sitting indoors munching on grape Popsicles, he is in no kind of physical condition. If he got lost or broke his ankle or something, he would just lie there until the sun dried him up, or until the coyotes found him and pulled him apart like a stuffed toy. Jeremy scans the horizon for the whirling vortex of buzzards and vultures that would tell him something Henry-sized had gone out into the desert and died. He sees nothing but contrails: passenger planes, fighter jets, test missiles. The world above is far more active than the world below.

"I had a full tank of gas in this thing when you left yesterday, by the way," says Al, whose concerns are always firmly rooted in what is in front of his nose. "Didn't I tell you to put gas in it? Where the hell did you go, anyway?"

"I went up to Bakersfield."

"Bakersfield? The hell for?"

"To see Wilkins."

"Wilkins? Are you serious? Why?"

"I just felt like it," Jeremy says, enjoying the shock on Al's face. As a child, he was scared of Al's temper. Now it merely amuses him.

"You just felt like heading up to see the crazy man who abandoned you and your mother?"

"He's not crazy," says Jeremy. "He might have been once, but he isn't anymore."

"I guess you and I have different definitions of crazy."

"I guess we have different definitions of a lot of things," says Jeremy.

An unlikely bolt of lightning shoots from his short-term memory in that moment, an idea that holds up its hand and jumps up and down. Oh yeah. He reaches for his wallet and removes the piece of paper on which Wilkins wrote the mysterious words. He opens it up and shows it to Al.

"This mean anything to you?" he asks.

They're on a dirt road now, under the upturned bowl of the endless sky. Al glances at the paper. Then he stomps on the brakes. The car skids to a halt, sending up a dust cloud in front of them. The dust is rendered in apocalyptic hues by the setting sun before it's whisked away by the wind.

"Where the hell did that come from?" Al says.

"Wilkins gave it to me. He said you'd know what it meant. He said it was a village in Vietnam."

"I know what the hell it is," Al says. He yanks the paper out of Jeremy's hand, crumples it, and throws it out the window.

"Hey," says Jeremy. "What's up with that?"

"Nothing is up with that."

"Well? What's it mean?"

"Never you mind," Al says.

"No, I want to know. It means something."

Al gives him a long, piercing look of a kind utterly unlike any he's ever given Jeremy before. He ceases to be his grandfather, and becomes instead a hawk-nosed old man with cold, rheumy eyes and thin, tight-set lips who looks capable of anything. Jeremy knows that face. He's seen it in the mirror, minus the decay of years, in his worst moments. Like the time he'd made the mistake of dropping a tab of acid when he was on a seventy-two-hour pass in Abu Dhabi. Someone had told him it would reprogram his mind, and he was stupid enough to believe them, because his mind was in desperate need of reprogramming. They hadn't told him it would also open the doors to the universe, allowing in every gibbering demon and wing-flapping incubus that had been lurking on the other side of his awareness. After that experience, getting back to the war had been almost a relief.

"It's not something I care to discuss," says Al.

"Fine," says Jeremy. "I'll look it up."

He takes his smartphone out of his pocket and calls up a browser window. He keys in the words with his thumbs.

"What are you doing?" says Al.

"'My Lai,'" Jeremy reads out loud. "'Site of a massacre of between three hundred and five hundred villagers in Viet—'"

Al grabs the phone out of his hand and throws that out the window too.

"Hey!" Jeremy says. "That thing is expensive!" He scrabbles at the door handle, but Al guns the engine and the car races ahead. "Stop!" he shouts. "Go back! I need my phone!"

Al drives on.

"Stop, I said!" says Jeremy. "Stop, or I swear to God I'll knock your ass out right now!"

Al slams on the brakes again. The car skids sideways, nearly leaving the road.

"You threaten your own grandfather," he says, his voice shaking. "You take drugs in my house, you speak disrespectfully, and now you threaten to hit me. You have no decency left in you, if you ever had any to begin with."

"Why did you throw my goddamn phone out the window?"

"Go ahead, if you want it so bad," Al says. "Go back and get it yourself."

"What the hell's gotten into you?" Jeremy asks him. "You're acting crazy!"

"If loving your country is crazy, then I'm as loony as your goddamn father," Al says. "Lock me up and throw away the key. Go on. Go get it."

Jeremy stares at him a moment longer. Then he gets out and begins the trek back up the road. He's made it about fifty yards when he hears a car door slam.

"I already answered for this!" Al shouts after him, his voice dwarfed by the wind. "I answered to the brass, I answered to Congress, and I'll answer to whoever's waiting for me on the other side when it's my time! I don't have to answer to you! You of all people, Jeremy!"

Jeremy turns to look at him again. Al is standing next to the car, arms akimbo, as if he's expecting a gunfight.

"Me of all people?" Jeremy yells. "The hell's that supposed to mean?"

"You're a soldier too!" Al shouts. "You should understand!"

Jeremy understands nothing. He turns again and keeps walking up the road. He spots the phone after another hundred yards, which feel to his spine as if they've been deducted from the lifetime total of yards he's allowed to walk. He bends down and picks it up, a maneuver he must break down into half a dozen steps, breathing carefully before each one. It's dusty but unharmed. Titanium case. Worth the extra money.

The screen is still up. He continues reading. It's a long article, but he's a fast reader. He doesn't hear the car creep up behind him until it's already there, the bumper inches away from his legs.

Al leans out the window. "Well?" he calls. "Satisfied?"

"You were here?" Jeremy asks, holding up the phone. It displays a picture of a row of dead villagers. All women and children, their faces still wearing their last expressions of disbelief and terror. "You did this?"

"I asked if you were satisfied," Al says.

"And I asked if you were there," Jeremy says.

"Yes, I was there. Any other questions?"

"Five hundred people?"

"That's one estimate. I didn't bother to count."

"Did you . . . do any shooting?"

"Did I do any shooting? I was a soldier in the army of the United States of America, same as you were," Al says.

"You weren't the same kind of soldier I was," Jeremy says.

"Oh, no? I guess you're right. We were different in those days. Deployed twice as long. No cell phones. No emails home. And a casualty rate ten times higher than anything you know about."

"That's not what I mean," says Jeremy. He looks at the phone again. "It says here women and children."

"And old people," says Al. "You left out the old people."

"Grandpa . . . what happened?"

"You of all people," says Al. "You should understand."

"Why do you keep saying that? What is there to understand about this?"

"You mean to tell me you really don't know."

"I don't understand how you can even ask me that," says Jeremy. "You think this is the kind of thing I was doing over there? This? Seriously? Just walking into villages and cutting down every person that moved?"

"That's what a war is like sometimes," Al says. "Do I really need to explain this?"

"Maybe you do."

"They were the enemy," Al says. "You know as well as I do, the enemy doesn't wear a uniform anymore. He doesn't carry a flag announcing himself. He wears regular clothes. Hides among regular people. Sometimes he isn't even a he. Sometimes he's not even an adult. There were plenty of kids. We found guns and bombs on them later. Maybe you think we should have just let them kill us. Would that have been the right thing to do?"

"Yeah, but kids eating breakfast?" Jeremy says. "Women? Old people? Babies?"

"It was a VC village. Women and old people provide comfort to the enemy," says Al. "And babies grow up into soldiers."

"Oh my God. I think I'm gonna be sick."

"Yeah, go ahead, lose your lunch," says Al. "That's what you liberals always do when you come face to face with reality."

Jeremy wants to say what Smarty would say: There is no single reality. All reality is subjective. Instead, he bends over, heaving. Nothing comes up but a long thread of spit that for the moment it hangs there feels like the only thing connecting him to this time and place. He's surprised at himself. He'd never gotten sick when he was confronted with these things in real life. Maybe it was because even the worst things he'd seen done to civilians—to people, he corrects himself, for the term *civilian* had often been uttered in the same way one might say that useless and annoying object—were accidental. This thing had been done on purpose. And without apology. By his own grandfather, among others.

The roiling in his stomach dies down. He straightens up and begins walking in the direction of the main road.

"You plan on walking all the way home?" Al says after him.

Jeremy doesn't answer. Al drives up alongside.

"You'll never make it," he says through the window. "Look at you. You'll be lucky if you get home before midnight, at this rate. Get in the car."

"Fuck you, Al," Jeremy says. "I don't want anything to do with you."

"What was that? What did you just say to your own grandfather?"

Jeremy stops. So does Al.

"Fuck," he says, "you. I'm not going home. I don't have a home. I don't live with you anymore."

"Don't be a drama queen, Jeremy. Let me tell you something: if you'd been there, you would have done the same thing."

"I was there, and I did not do the same thing."

"Oh, really? You were in Vietnam? That's funny, I seem to remember you weren't born yet."

"You know what I mean," says Jeremy. "I mean I was in the same situation. And what you did was the last thing I would have done. Not even the last thing. It wasn't even on the list of things I would do."

"It had to happen. I don't say I'm proud of it. But I didn't start that war. I just got sent to go fight it. Do you have any idea what that part of the world would look like now if we hadn't gone in?"

"I guess it would look pretty much what it looks like now, since we lost Vietnam," says Jeremy. "The Communists won. Didn't you get the memo?"

"We didn't lose anything!" Al roars. "A million men. That's how many VC we got. I'd call that a resounding success."

"A million dead people is not a success."

"It is if they belong to the other side," says Al.

"Go away, Al." Jeremy starts walking again. "Go far away from me. Wilkins was right about you."

Al pulls up next to him again in the car, matching his pace. "That little cock-nibbler? What did he say?"

"He said a lot of things," says Jeremy.

"Such as?"

"Such as you're . . . Never mind. What do you care what he thinks?"

"I want to know what he said."

"He said he tried to rescue me from you, and his one big regret was that he couldn't. And now I know what he meant."

"Rescue you? I raised you. If it wasn't for me and your grandmother, you and Rita would have been out on the street. I rescued you, Jeremy. Not him."

"Maybe I would have been better off on the street. I would have been better off never joining the goddamn army, that's for sure."

"I'm gonna pretend you didn't say that."

"You just go on pretending."

"So you didn't have to kill anybody yourself?" Al asks. "You just went over there and handed out candy and pro-democracy pamphlets, dug a few wells, that kind of thing? That's all there was to it?"

"I never killed anyone who wasn't shooting at me," says Jeremy. "I would never have killed a noncombatant. I never even thought about it. Only a fucking lunatic would do something like that."

"Bullshit. There are some people who just deserve to be killed. The planet is better off without them."

"And you call Wilkins crazy," says Jeremy.

He stops again. So does Al.

"How could you? How could you do it? What kind of a person are you, anyway? How could you think that was right? Here's a clue, Al, okay? When you find yourself pointing a gun at women and children, that's how you know you're on the wrong side."

Al says nothing. He looks at Jeremy for a moment then looks over the steering wheel, gripping it tight.

"Are you sorry, at least?" Jeremy asks.

"What?"

"I said, are you sorry? That's what I want to know."

"That's a hell of a question," says Al.

"It's the only question."

"Why should I be sorry for taking action to protect my brothers? That's all we were doing, Jeremy. Jesus. Every army since the beginning of time has done the same thing. That's what war is. It's even in the Bible. How can you not understand that?"

"You don't believe in the Bible."

"I don't believe the God parts, but I believe the parts where stuff happened. The Israelites slaying the enemies of God, right down to the firstborn sons. These are the kinds of things that happen. This is what people do."

"Just get away from me."

"Get in the car," says Al.

"No."

"You have no right to judge. No one does."

Jeremy bends over close, works up a mouthful of saliva, and sprays it in Al's face.

Al jerks backwards as if he's been shot. He gives Jeremy another long, cold stare. But says nothing. He simply reaches into the glove compartment and removes a box of tissues. He wipes his face clean.

Then he takes off, the car tires popping on the road.

Jeremy stands for a time, bracing himself against the wind. He watches the dust cloud left in Al's wake blow away and be replaced by another dust cloud. There's dust everywhere now. He was born into dust, and he went away to fight in dust, and when he came back, the dust was waiting for him. Just once, he thinks, I'd like to live somewhere where there's no goddamn dust.

He walks toward the main road. And as he walks, out of nowhere, he remembers once again the little girl in the yellow shalwar kameez.

The kids were the best part of Afghanistan. When they first got to their base in Helmand, it was just a deserted village. Everyone had gone away to escape the Taliban, and walking through that place was like walking through the dead streets in his own neighborhood. Only it was worse, because you could see traces of lives. You could see that people used to be happy here, and then their happiness had been stolen. Everyone had just gotten up and left—like the Anasazi, as Smarty had once explained to him. And that had been an excuse for another history lesson from the biggest brain in the platoon.

But a dozen major firefights later, the area was clear, and the people came back. You saw them when you went on patrol, and the bigger kids and the braver little ones would come running out, smiling and shouting the one English word they knew: Chocolate! Chocolate! Salaam, you would say, and you would dig into your pockets and bring out whatever treat you'd managed to scrounge from the mess. You would break the chocolate into pieces so that everyone got a bite. Then the kids would race around madly on their imported American sugar highs, democracy in action, future consumers in training. You should throw Big Macs, Smarty had observed once. Because no country with a McDonald's in it has ever attacked the United States. Their parents would watch from their doorways, watchful and wary but relieved to see you, because they didn't like the Taliban any more than you did. They didn't like the Americans either, and half of them were probably Taliban themselves, or at least made the occasional contribution to the cause. But at least now they had a little bit of their lives back.

Jeremy liked the people of Afghanistan, but he liked the kids best, and of all the kids, he felt pulled the strongest toward the scared ones who hung back, eyes wide, afraid of him. He would get down on one knee and swing his gun around on his back. He would take off his helmet and set it on the ground, so they could see he was human, that he had a face and eyes and ears just like everyone else. Kids would try on his helmet and race around, bumping into each other and laughing. This was against procedure. But fuck procedure.

Out of all those kids, just one keeps coming back to him: the girl in the yellow shalwar kameez. He'd seen her squatting against a wall, looking at him. She couldn't have been more than two. She was so small he could have fit three of her in his pack. She seemed to be all eyeballs. She sucked on two fingers, just watching him. He'd only seen her once, but she'd stuck in his mind after that. He'd looked for her again whenever they passed through, but he hadn't ever seen her again.

Then that village had been overrun once more, and the next time they came through there, the people had repeated their vanishing act. There were bullets singing over the soldiers' heads and mortars thumping in the hills. That was the day they'd lost Collins, whose vest had failed to protect him from the bullet that managed to find its way under his arm and turn his chest into something that resembled hamburger so closely Jeremy was never able to eat hamburgers again. When he next passed the spot where he'd seen the little girl, he was running, clutching his M16 and following the evasive pattern that had been beaten into him in training: up, run, he's seen me, dive. Five meters at a time. There were moments when he felt it was his destiny to cross the entire nation of Afghanistan in this way. In the midst of everything, he remembered the girl in the yellow shalwar kameez, and he wondered what had happened to her. The Taliban killed people who talked to the Americans. They didn't care who they were. They would kill children just as easily as they would a grown man. He was glad then that she'd ignored his beckoning finger. He'd asked himself this many times: what kind of person would kill a child? The kind of people who would do that deserved the worst punishment you could think of. Not death. Death was a gift. There were plenty of things worse than death, and he had lived through some of them.

It was on that same road that the IED had gone off, not far from that spot. Maybe outside her very house. April 7, 2007. The day that was lost to him.

There were a lot of children killed in My Lai, he thinks. In the brief glimpse of the picture on his phone he'd seen their limbs intertwined with those of their parents and grandparents as they lay in the ditch. He wishes he'd never gone to see Wilkins. He wishes he didn't know these things about Al. But he knows them now and he can't unknow them.

That little girl from the village would be seven or eight now, if she is still alive. She would have grown up in war, and so had her parents, and so had her ancestors, all the way back to the time of the first British invasion—seven or eight generations of war woven into their DNA. There were three wars with the British, then civil war, and then the Soviets had come and gone. They'd scarcely had time to breathe before the Taliban arose, and then the Americans had come, accompanied by the British for yet another encore performance. The history of that country was a history of bloody clusterfucks. It was no place for little girls. So he was nothing more than another soldier to her. Just another man with a gun. She would never remember him. And maybe she wouldn't even distinguish between him and the bad guys. Maybe he came back to her in her nightmares. Maybe he was the bad guy.

When it's all over there, I'm going back, he says to himself.

This is surprising. He doesn't know where this thought comes from, but he knows it as surely as he knows anything.

When things over there have finally calmed down, I'll go back to that village and I'll find that little girl. I won't say anything to her. She won't know me. But it won't matter. And if I don't find her, maybe I can at least find some of the other kids I used to give candy to. By then they'll be grown-ups, maybe, with kids of their own. You grew up fast over there. You were married and had kids before you were even out of your teens. Maybe I won't say a word to any of them. I won't ask anyone if they remember me, because they won't want to remember anything about the war. And neither will I. Maybe it will be enough for me to just see them living their lives. So I can know the whole damn thing happened for a reason. And so I can know that somewhere, something good happened in the world, and that I was a part of it.

But suddenly he discovers he can't remember the name of the village. Why is that? He's only said it out loud a thousand times in his life. As recently as a week ago, he knew it. Now it's as if he never knew it at all. Something funny. Started with an N. Or maybe a W. Fuck. How could he forget something so simple?

When he arrives back at the road that leads to town, he stops, just breathing and thinking. It's growing dark. He can see Highway 58 from here. The traffic zooms by, kicking up yet more dust. He finds a small rise to sit against and gathers his arms around himself, watching the road. The night is growing cool. During the day you can wither like a sponge in an oven and at night you can die of hypothermia. The high desert is a place not only of extreme temperatures but of extreme irony. He shivers as he watches the traffic. He will have to get home somehow, but for now he just sits.

There are lots of commercial trucks, a few cars, and then a convoy of unmarked flatbeds bearing large, mysterious loads under black tarps, moving slow and ominous, with troop transports ahead and behind. Missile parts, probably. Headed for Edwards. Inside the trucks would be men with automatic weapons, huddled, waiting for an attack that will never come, not here. The children of Afghanistan had grown up in war and the children of Elysium had grown up amidst the preparations for it. They were on opposite ends of the same assembly line.

The sky is rent by a flight of planes, three of them. From their blunt noses he can see they're Warthogs. Not fighters. Tank destroyers. There have been plenty of times in the past when he's been very glad to see them. He waits, half expecting to hear the whump of their missiles or the farting of their cannons, but their ruckus passes with nothing happening, because this is a land of peace.

"Henry!" he yells. He has no expectation that Henry will answer. But he yells his name several times. His voice is lost in the wind and the sound of the traffic on the road.

He thinks back to Henry's empty chair. Something had seemed to him to be missing then. It's been working away in his mind, but it's taken him this long to make the connection.

It's Smitty. Henry always left Smitty on the chair, except when he took him to bed. But Smitty wasn't there. And he wasn't in his bed either. Wherever Henry is, he's taken Smitty with him.

So Henry hadn't been abducted. He'd left on purpose. Henry was going somewhere.

He pulls out his phone again and calls Rico.

11

THAT MORNING, Henry had made his way to the Kozy
Kart at 6:54, having waited up all night, his Ninja Turtle
backpack loaded with those things he deemed essential for
a trip to New York, New York: his magic rocks, his toothbrush,
the Picture Bible, and Smitty, his one-eyed teddy bear. He'd
briefly considered taking along the urn that contains Helen's
ashes, because he had the vague notion that it was still inhabited by her spirit, and he thought she might be interested in the
sights and sounds of a long bus ride—though how long it really
was, he had no idea. Also, he was afraid Nanny might be bored
just sitting on the credenza all the time, watching her family
go about their business. But in the end he left it, because he
knew the disappearance of such a venerated object would be the
source of a great deal of trouble. It did not occur to him that his
own disappearance might have a much greater effect.

Henry knew where to catch the bus because he often saw it
picking up and dropping off passengers there. He did not know
that it went to New York; he merely assumed it. On his way to
the Kozy Kart, he kept a close eye out for red cars, which would
have been a sign to him that trouble was near. One day, while
Jeremy was in Afghanistan and Rita was asleep on the couch,
Henry had dared to wander out of the house and into the dead

neighborhood, and a gang of boys in a red car had chased him until he cried. This morning he saw no red cars. This meant it was going to be a good day.

In his pocket was a fat wad of cash he'd taken from Al's dresser. He knew where Al kept it because he often used to hide in Al's closet whenever bad feelings overtook him, and he'd seen him stash it there. For his size, Henry could be remarkably hard to see when he chose to disappear. In fact, he believed he could make himself completely invisible at will; for in his own mind, Henry was very small, scarcely larger than a baby.

At the Kozy Kart, an exhausted-looking woman in a head scarf slumped on one elbow. She bestirred herself upon the ringing of the bell that announced Henry's arrival, but once she saw who it was, her exhaustion doubled. Her previous conversations with Henry had not gone well. None of her conversations in America had gone well. English was a struggle and a trial for this woman, who had been born sixty years earlier into a part of the world that appeared little different from a thousand years ago, and who through various accidents of marriage and politics had found herself launched into a strange alternate universe called America. She found America nearly impossible to describe. In her youth there had been flocks of goats, groves of fig and olive trees, and large gatherings of family that she still remembered fondly; people were connected by heartstrings you could practically twang with your fingers. Here, there were satellite televisions and cell phones and computers, all wondrous things her ancestors could never have imagined, but people were too busy pressing buttons and looking at screens to talk to each other. It was a strange time to be alive.

This woman's previous interactions with Henry had been the most confusing of her entire American existence, all twelve years of it. She steeled herself for yet another nonsensical encounter. It was obvious he wasn't right in the head, but all the same it was often she who came away feeling like the stupid one.

"I wanna go to New York New York," Henry announced. He took the wad of cash out of his pocket and pushed it toward her.

The woman in the head scarf looked thoughtfully at the money. She picked it up and counted it. There was over a thousand dollars, mostly worn twenties. She sighed again. Thievery was the furthest thing from her mind; her religion prohibited it, just as it prohibited taking advantage of the feebleminded. Her main hope was to get through this latest episode with Henry with a minimum of headache. And her main fear was that the large slow one had somehow stolen this money and was now trying to involve her in his crime. If her grandson, Kazar, were here, he could deal with him. But Kazar had worked all night, and he was asleep upstairs.

"What?" she said.

"New York New York," said Henry. "To see my mother."

"Mother?"

"I wanna see my mother," Henry said. "Her name is Jeanie Rae."

"No mother," said the woman. "Mother not here."

"She's in New York New York. I wanna go see her. On the bus. Jermy says you can take a bus to New York."

"Ah," said the woman. "You wanna ticket."

"I wanna ticket," said Henry. "How much does it cost?"

"You want one way?"

"Huh?"

"You come back?" she said.

"Maybe," said Henry. "Maybe I'll stay there forever. Daboo and Jermy can come visit me. My mother lives in a tall tall building with trees on the roof."

The woman sighed. "Yes? You come back? Or you not come back?" Fervently she prayed that the latter would be the case.

"I dunno," said Henry.

At such moments, the woman in the head scarf relied on her faith in the infinite mercy of God. If she left such matters up to Him, she knew that He would guide her hand in making the right decision. A one-way ticket it would be.

She peeled off a handful of twenties and pushed the rest back at him. Then she printed out a ticket and gave him that too.

"For driver," she said. "You give."

"Lady," said Henry, "are you beloved of the Lord?"

"What?"

"The Lord. Like in the Picture Bible. Are you beloved unto His holy bosom?"

The woman sighed. "I dunno," she said. "Maybe tomorrow."

"The Lord is coming with me on this bus ride. He told me so Hisself. He said, Henry, we are going on a long-ass bus ride here, and you're gonna have to keep it together. You are eighteen now and you are a man. That means no more crying and no more being a baby."

"Is good," said the woman in the head scarf, nodding.

"Okay," Henry said, and then he helped himself to a grape Popsicle, took his money and his ticket, jammed both in his pocket, and left.

There, thought the woman in the head scarf. That wasn't so bad. She was so glad to see him gone that she didn't even object to his lifting of the Popsicle.

When the bus arrived and Henry got on, he realized there were several passengers already aboard, none of whom he knew. This made him nervous. A memory of his short-lived school career came to him. Remembering that the safest place on a bus was in the front, he sat behind the driver, next to a diminutive, elderly black man with fluffy gray hair. Henry had never sat next to a black person before. He found himself staring at the man's arm as it lay lightly on the armrest. It was fascinating to him that people could be different colors, but like someone who is seeing a celebrity in the flesh for the first time, he also disbelieved that the man was real.

The elderly man took one look at Henry and said, "Son, are you traveling by yourself?"

Henry didn't answer him because he was not supposed to talk to strangers. This rule had been impressed upon him by all his family members repeatedly. Strangers were bad. They might steal him, and he would never be seen again.

But there was a conflict in Henry's mind between this directive and his belief that all old people were good. The only old people he'd ever known, Helen and Al, had been nice to him, and he could not believe that all old people weren't nice. The elderly man repeated his question, so Henry nodded.

"Where are you goin'?" he asked Henry.

"Blackfella, I am going to New York New York to visit my mother Jeanie Rae. That is where she lives," said Henry.

The elderly gentleman patted him on the arm. "That's fine. You and me are going to have an adventure. This bus is going over the desert and over the mountains and across the prairies, and then we'll be in New York. Yessirree. I am going to see my daughter who I haven't seen in three years. Praise God."

Henry pricked up his ears at this ejaculation. "Praise God," he said.

The bus had already started moving. The elderly man leaned his head against the window. Henry marveled that his bushy hair seemed to provide him with a natural pillow; it was a great advantage, he thought. He was still nervous about all the strangers on the bus, so he concentrated on making himself as small as possible.

He watched out the window as familiar landmarks zipped by. There was the school he used to attend, where Jeremy was a teacher now; there was the rock museum, with its display cases of glittering geodes; there was the hardware store, and the restaurant where his aunt Rita worked; and finally the borax mill. But very soon the bus had passed out of the world Henry knew, and then he had the feeling that he was adrift in deep space, far from anything that was known. Homesickness gripped him; and something else gripped him too. He needed to go to the bathroom.

Henry's educational career had been brief, but one of the things he remembered quite well was that you had to put your hand up if you wanted to go to the washroom. Forever afterward, he'd associated this convention with all official places, including churches, post offices, and now buses. It seemed entirely logical to him that if he held his hand up, the bus driver would call on him, he would announce his need, and the driver would pull over somewhere.

Yet he hesitated, for he also had bad memories of other kids making fun of the way he spoke. Henry harbored the hope that he might be able to hold it until they got to New York. It couldn't be much farther now, he believed; he'd already traveled well beyond the dimensions of his existence, and it was hard to fathom that the country just kept going.

Soon, however, the need became urgent, so up went his hand. He waited and waited for the driver to notice him, but he didn't. This was not unexpected; Henry had noticed that people in official capacities had a tendency to overlook him. That was all right. He was a patient fellow. The elderly gentleman next to him was still asleep.

Finally Henry could hold it no more. He'd thought this was going to be a good day, but he realized now he'd been fooling himself. The world was a cold, hard place, and it was about to become much more uncomfortable. His urine dripped audibly onto the floor.

At this point his seatmate woke up.

"Son," he said, "did you just go to the washroom in your pants? 'Cause I can feel something wet here."

"Yes, blackfella," Henry said. "I was waiting for the driver to call on me so I could ask him to stop and let me go to the washroom, but he never did. I'm sorry."

"Driver," said the elderly gentleman, "when is the next stop?"

"Just a few minutes," said the driver.

"Well, this here young man is on his own and he don't know about washrooms in buses. He just had himself a accident. He's a special case, if you know what I mean."

"Well, I didn't know anything about it," said the bus driver. He looked at Henry in the mirror. "Nobody said anything to me about a special case traveling on his own. I can't be looking out for every special case who comes on here, can I. It's not part of my job derscribtion."

"No," said the elderly gentleman, "but a little Christian mercy would go a long way in a case like this. This young fella is all on his own and he's goin' all the way to New York."

The bus driver looked at Henry again in the mirror. Henry looked away. He had a dreadful feeling that he was about to be punished. Maybe he'd be kicked off the bus altogether. Maybe he'd never be allowed to go to New York and see his mother.

Soon the bus stopped at a shopping center and everybody got out. Then it was just Henry, the elderly gentleman, and the bus driver. The driver got up and said, "Come on back here with me, son. I got something to show you."

He took Henry to the back of the bus and showed him a little door that opened up. Inside, there was a washroom. Henry could scarcely believe his eyes.

"You never been on a bus before, have you, kid," the bus driver said.

"No, sir," said Henry.

"Well, next time you think you got to go to the washroom, you don't have to wait for me to tell you to go. You just get up and come back here and go anytime you want. It's just like a washroom at home except smaller. You follow me?"

"Yes, sir," Henry said.

"Mind you sit down even when you got to piddle, because if this bus hits a bump, you can go ass over teakettle. Did you bring any other clothes with you?"

"No, sir."

"You don't have any other clothes in that backpack you're wearing?"

"No, sir," Henry said. "I just have Smitty and my magic rocks."

"Now listen," said the driver. "How in the hell do you expect to get by going all the way to New York without any change of clothes or anything? It's a three-day ride. You're not gonna be smelling too good by the time we get there. You gotta get yourself some new clothes. You got any money, or were you planning on winning the lottery?"

Henry showed him his money, slightly damp now, but the driver made him put it back.

"Don't just go showing your money to anyone who asks. You have to be careful. People will steal from you, specially given you're simple. There are some folks out there on the lookout for simple ones just like you, and when they find you, it's like a free-for-all. Jesus Christ, boy. What is your name?"

"Henry Eustace Merkin the First," Henry told him.

"Well, Henry Eustace Merkin the First. This is a shopping center, and inside of it they sell clothes. I think you best go and buy yourself some new pants and a couple of shirts. And some jockey shorts. Maybe your friend there can help you out with that. You understand?"

"I am not allowed to buy things. Nanny or Daboo always does that. Or Jermy."

"Son, you don't have much of a choice at this point. Now you go on with your friend and see if you can't clean yourself up a little," the bus driver said.

Henry returned to the elderly gentleman and said, "Blackfella, would you take me in that shopping center there and help me buy some new clothes?"

"Listen, young man," said the elderly gentleman, "I know you don't mean nothing by it, but you best stop calling me blackfella. My name is Mr. Jenkins."

"All right, Mr. Jenkins," Henry said. "My name is Henry and I need some new pants."

Mr. Jenkins's shoulders began to hop up and down, and tears leaked down his cheeks.

"Mr. Jenkins, are you crying?" Henry said.

"No, son, I am not crying. I am laughing."

"Oh, you've got happy tears."

"Lord bless you, boy," Mr. Jenkins said, "you are something else."

They ride all that day and through the night. When Henry awakes, the sun is coming up and they are in a place that looks vastly different from California.

Mr. Jenkins wakes up too. "This here looks like Colorado," he says. "We must be right smack in the middle of it by now. After that we come to Nebraska."

"Is that so," Henry says.

"Henry, have you ever been to Nebraska before?"

"No, Mr. Jenkins. I pretty much never been anywhere."

"Well," Mr. Jenkins says, "I have been there, and I have been to lots of other places too. I been all over North America in my wanderin' days. I was born in the South. That was seventy years ago. I guess you never been to the South, have you, Henry?"

"No, sir."

"Well, I was born in Georgia in nineteen fawty-one. And if you know anything about history, you will know that Georgia in nineteen fawty-one was no place to be a black person. You know anything about that, Henry?"

"About what?" Henry says.

"Oh, you know. Jim Crow and all that."

"I don't know anybody named Jim."

"Lord bless you, Henry, Jim Crow is not a person. It's what they called the laws back then that said a colored person could not use the same bathroom as white people or the same drinking fountain, and you had to sit in the back of the bus. You see here where you and I are sitting side by side in the front of the bus?"

"Yes, I see that," Henry says.

"Well, in those days, until I was twenty-three years old, you could not do such a thing. I would have gone to jail for what we are doing right here and now."

"Have mercy," Henry says.

"And then later, I went away to Vietnam, and when I came back, Jim Crow was gone. But they did not get rid of the hate. Do you know about Vietnam?"

Now here is something Henry knows all about. "Vietnam is nothing but a big hot hole of ess-aitch-eye-tee where all the whores have the clap and the beer tastes like piss."

Mr. Jenkins looks at Henry in surprise. "Well, that's about right, but I wonder how come you knew that. I wonder if you even know what the clap is."

"Daboo was there," Henry says. "He got tattoos. He got one of a dragon and he got another one of a snake and a knife."

"Who's this Daboo fella you're talking about?"

"Daboo. Daboo and Nanny."

"Is he your daddy?"

"He is my grandad," Henry says.

"Is he the one taught you how to say that about Vietnam?"

"Well, I heard him say it plenty of times."

"I see. Well, how about we change the subject, on account of this might not be a fitting thing for us to discuss. Let me tell you about my daughter. She's living in New York and she been there since she finished college. She is thirty-eight years old now, and she's married and got two little ones."

"That's nice," Henry says.

"Well, it certainly is, Henry. But I wish I was going under better circumstances. My daughter is mighty sick."

"Uh-oh."

"Yes, as a matter of fact this is probably the last time I am going to see her alive. She has the cancer all through her. They opened her up two weeks ago to take out her appendix and they found out she was just full of it. Everywhere. No point in trying to help her, they said. It's too late. So they just closed her back up, and now I'm coming down to see her. I sold my house and I sold my 2003 Cadillac and I cashed in my accounts and here I come. It don't matter to me. I don't need none a that for myself. It was all for my little girl anyway. I was just gonna give it to her when I die. I saw my daughter come into this world and now it looks like I'm gonna see her leave it too. The Lord's will be done. It's a mighty hard thing, Henry, for a parent to have to watch their child die. It's a mighty awful horrible thing. It's against the natural order of things."

"What's that mean?" Henry asks.

"It means like how the old are suppose to die and make way for the young. You know. And how parents are suppose to watch their children grow and increase their place in the world."

"Maybe the Lord will take care of her," Henry says.

Mr. Jenkins brightens. "Yes, of course He will. For the Lord heals all wounds and taketh away all pain. And I know I will see my daughter on the other side."

"Mr. Jenkins, you know, I talk with the Lord a lot. I can ask Him to help your daughter for you."

Mr. Jenkins dabs at his eyes with a tissue. "God bless you, boy, you have such a simple good heart. I wish there was more people like you in the world."

"Mr. Jenkins," Henry says, "that's a nice thing of you to say. But there is not anyone else like me in this world. I do not have any peers. I am special."

12

MORNING brings Jeremy a bad wake-up. He's jostled out of sleep by a vision of something amorphous descending over him, a dark, poisonous cloud that cuts off air, light, and sound. It's unlike anything he's ever experienced, and at the same time it's familiar to him from previous dreams. Or nightmares.

When he was younger, he loved to read about older wars, back in the days when being a soldier meant glory and honor and clutching your shoulder as you fell, grimacing, on the playground, urging your buddies to go on without you to the base under the jungle gym while you bravely held off the enemy as they advanced from the swings. Later, in the middle of his real war, he would think about those childhood games, and he realized that as boys they'd been training themselves for war the same way wrestling kittens are training themselves to hunt. But their games had nothing to do with the real thing, because in games you were devoid of fear. You couldn't practice being afraid; and once you became afraid enough, you could never shake it. It sank into your bones, and there it stayed.

When he was a kid, he knew all about foxholes and Stukas, trenches and gas; and of all the ways he imagined being killed, gas terrified him the most. He'd been grateful that the Taliban didn't seem to have any gas, even though the Americans had trained for it just in case, learning how to fit those awkward masks over their faces that made it impossible to see or breathe. And it's of gas he's been dreaming tonight. When he wakes up, he's choking, his eyes and throat swelling up and his lungs burning like twin Hindenburgs, and he believes, for an insane moment, that the year is 1917 and he's in France. The truth is always the last thing to occur to him in the morning. He hyperventilates himself into wakefulness, and he feels around, as he hasn't done for some time, for the comfort of his gun.

Then he hears Rico snoring gently on his mountainous mess of a bed, and the soothing trickle of the fountain where Columbine the betta lives. He remembers he no longer has a gun to be responsible for. It had been drummed into him from the first day he was issued a weapon that the worst thing he could do was lose it, and it strikes him once again as patently unfair that the army never taught him how to let go of his gun, emotionally speaking, once they took it back. What was he supposed to do, just forget about it? They should have been allowed a grieving period for their lost arms. Once, in the hospital in Germany, he'd asked if they could give him one—not a loaded one, maybe just a training dummy—so he could clutch its familiar outlines and at least have the illusion that he would be able to defend himself when the hajjis came pouring in the window. Even a wooden gun would have been better than nothing. They'd told him he was delusional, and they tried to prescribe him psych meds. But he was not delusional. He just thought it wasn't right that they should take his gun away. Nobody needed the love of a gun more than a wounded man who lay helpless in bed.

He struggles upright and tries to remember why he's here. His conversation with Al comes back to him like a sick memory of a bad party, as if it was just another hazy keg-side argument. He thinks once again of the picture of the dead villagers lying in the ditch. He should have known better than to call that one up on the screen. Pictures are not just pictures to him; they are moments into which he can insert himself, as vivid as if he were there. Lola Linker had suggested that he suffers from the inability to block out stimuli. Low latent inhibition, she'd called it. So he could add this to his list of conditions. From that one picture, he can smell the rich smell of the blood in the heat, the flesh already starting to turn, the lingering odor of cordite, the burning roofs of the hooches his grandfather had helped torch. Yesterday was a day of catastrophes. No reason to believe today will be any different.

In his mouth is the gummy taste of stale pot smoke and morning breath. He turns his phone on and checks the screen. It's six-thirty in the morning. Rita's called three more times. She's left no messages. Then he sees he has another text.

U PREVERT U!!! R DED I KNO U R REDING THIS

He debates replying to this: Dear Mr. Moon, I believe there has been a misunderstanding. I'm not sure what the source of it is, so why don't we get together for coffee and a chat? No doubt we could clear everything up. Sincerely yours, Jeremy Merkin.

But instead, he just deletes it.

Then he goes upstairs. Elizabeta is awake, sitting at the kitchen table before her glowing laptop.

"Long time since you boys have a sleepover," she says.

"Yeah."

"This make me remember the old days. You stay up all night, playing those horrible shooting games."

Jeremy remembers those days too. During high school, he'd spent two or three nights a week in Rico's basement. Rita hadn't liked it. She was always asking him, what's wrong with our house? As if she didn't know. Well, maybe she didn't. But he couldn't bring himself to tell her even part of the truth: for one thing, Elizabeta was a much better cook. Rita let him get away with it because he kept his grades up. She thought Rico was a good influence. They would go back to his place after school and do their homework together, it was true, but little did she know that they would then smoke pot and play Call of Duty until they passed out, waking up just in time to do another bong hit and race to class. In their case, the term "high school" had an entirely different connotation. Even after he'd gotten his job at the Freezie Squeeze, when he looked forward to going home at the end of his shift, it was Rico's house he thought of, not his own. Elizabeta always left the door open for him, and there was always food on the stove or in the fridge. There were no harangues from Al to deal with, no lectures on early to bed and early to rise. And no Henry following him around the house like a ghost, always wanting to know what he was doing, if he could do it too, always sitting too close, always draped over the back of his chair, his hot, moist breath condensing on Jeremy's neck. A big sponge mop of need. And they weren't allowed to play Call of Duty at the Merkin residence, because the sound effects were too realistic. Everyone was afraid Al would have a flashback and start throwing grenades around the house.

Which is a concern that Jeremy understands perfectly now. It took him over a year to adjust to sonic booms again.

"Yeah, I don't play those anymore," says Jeremy.

"You are too grown-up," says Elizabeta.

But it isn't that. His children, if he ever has any, will not be allowed to play those games either. Because the fear is in his bones, and it will never leave.

Elizabeta makes him coffee Mexican-style, laced with cinnamon. He's conscious of having invaded some kind of morning ritual, and she's in her bathrobe, so he takes it into the living room and stands at the window. Rico probably stayed up all night again, communing with his invisible cyber-protectors and exposing the brutality of corrupt regimes around the world; he won't be up for hours. Jeremy drinks his coffee and wonders how this day is going to go. Right about now he should be getting ready for work, downing a cup of tea and getting in the shower. Automatically he wonders what his lesson plan for the day will be. Then he remembers he doesn't have to come up with one. That is a very fine feeling. At some point, maybe, he would have settled into life as a teacher. Years in the future. But he can't see his future now, and he feels gratitude for that too, because in three short weeks he'd discovered that there was nothing more depressing than knowing where he was going to be every morning for the rest of his career.

Then he thinks of Henry. He wonders where he spent the night. He wants to ask Elizabeta if the spirit world has told her anything new. But this is him being desperate, just grabbing at straws. There is no spirit world. Not for him, anyway.

As he's standing there, a Greyhound bus goes by. It squeaks and hisses to a halt at the corner, making its usual stop at Kazar's convenience store.

Jeremy watches it and thinks. He puts his cup down and walks outside. He sees the bus driver get off, a couple of packages under his arms, and go in the store. He's inside for perhaps two minutes. When he comes out again, a man carrying a suitcase is with him. The driver opens the luggage bay and puts the suitcase in. Then the two of them get on the bus and the bus turns around and passes Jeremy again. The sign on the front says BARSTOW AND EAST.

Jeremy stands there thinking some more. Then he walks down to the corner and goes into the store. Kazar's grandmother is at the counter, resting her chin on her hands. She wears a silk scarf on her head.

"*Salaam,*" Jeremy says.

"*Salaam aleikum,*" says the old woman, brightening at the sight of the only non-Arab Arabic speaker in Elysium. "*Kaifa haloka?*"

"*Jayed,*" says Jeremy. "You work morning?" He has to keep it simple. Her English is limited to the vocabulary of convenience store commerce. His Arabic is limited to asking questions about weapons caches and Taliban sightings. Get up. Stay down. Don't move. Hands up. None of these phrases apply here.

"Yes, morning," the old woman agrees. "And night."

"Kazar work morning?"

"No, no. Kazar sleep morning. I sleep daytime."

"What time you sleep?"

"I sleep ten o'clock."

"You work yesterday?"

"Yes, yes," she says.

"You sell ticket?" He points to the ratty Greyhound sticker on the counter. "Ticket," he says. "Big boy come, buy ticket." He holds his hand up to indicate someone tall. Then he holds his arms out in front of himself to indicate a belly.

"Ah," says the old woman. "Yes. The big slow one."

"He come here, buy ticket?"

"Yes, yes."

"What ticket?"

She spreads her arms, shrugging, palms up. She doesn't understand.

"Where he go?"

"Ah, where he go," says the woman. "New York."

"*Shokran jaleezan,*" says Jeremy.

"*Ma'a salaama, sadiqi,*" says the old woman.

He turns and leaves. The old woman had been asleep when he came by here with Al yesterday. She didn't know they were looking for Henry. She probably went upstairs and watched her Arabic satellite channel until it was time for her to work or cook or go to sleep. Her life is no different than anyone else's in this town, except she doesn't understand anything anyone is saying unless they want a pack of cigarettes or some lottery tickets. Or a bus ticket. That hadn't occurred to him yesterday. He could smack himself for that. He's wasted a whole day.

He goes back to Rico's house. Elizabeta is standing in the living room.

"Where did you go?" she asks. "I thought you left."

"I'm leaving now. Elizabeta, I need a big favor."

"What is it?"

"I need to take Rico's car."

Her eyes get big. "You want to drive Rico's car? Ha. I carry him in my body for nine month and I am not allow to take his car."

"He'll understand, once I explain it to him," Jeremy says. "Just tell him I had to go in a hurry. I'll call him later."

"Where you will go?"

"To find Henry. He took the bus. He's got a whole day's head start on me."

"Where he go?"

"He went to New York to see his mother."

"You going to leave, just like that? What about your yob?"

"Elizabeta," says Jeremy, "you're going to hear some things about me soon. None of them are true. And there's a bad cop after me. He has the wrong idea about me, and he's going to find me. And when he does, things will be bad. So I really need to get out of town for a while. You understand?"

Elizabeta knows all there is to know about bad cops. Bad cops are the reason she's a widow. She asks no further questions. She nods.

"You don't want breakfast?"

"There's no time. I have to go, right now. Can you find me his keys?"

She looks at him for a long moment. Then she goes into the kitchen and comes back with a key ring in her hand. She hands it to him.

"Yeremy," says Elizabeta.

She comes to him and puts her hand on his heart. The warm feeling pervades him again, spreading outward from his chest. She says nothing, only touches him, and he can see she's crying.

"Letting go is very hard," she says, and he knows she's not talking about the car. She sees something.

But he doesn't need to believe in that stuff anymore. Now he possesses a fact: Henry is on a bus headed east. Facts trump spirits any day. One fact dropped in a swimming pool of spirits will make them all disperse, like detergent in a sink full of greasy water.

Jeremy goes back to the store, and from the woman in the head scarf he buys a bottle of water, several bags of beef jerky, and some candy bars. Road trip food. As an afterthought he buys a large plastic bottle of ibuprofen and a smaller one of caffeine pills. He gets in Rico's car and then, as another afterthought, gets out again and opens the trunk. Rico is a pack rat; the trunk is a nest of random objects, and he's hoping one of those objects is a hat. He roots around through comic books, jumper cables, spare items of clothing, and an old pair of sneakers until he finds a baseball cap. He gets into the driver's seat again and pulls the cap down low over his eyes.

Then he drives to the Fortress of America Motel. He parks outside the office and goes in. Sam is standing behind the desk.

"Good morning, sir," Sam says. "How may I be of service?"

"Hi, Sam, it's me," says Jeremy, lifting the brim of his cap.

Sam stiffens. "Jeremy. I didn't recognize you in your head-wear."

"I need to see my mom."

"She's sleeping," says Sam. "She was up all night."

"Can you wake her up?"

Sam lifts an eyebrow. "May I ask what you are wanting?"

"I just want to talk to her, Sam," Jeremy says.

"I value my manhood too much to risk it. You are not here to tell her to come back?"

"You mean come back home?"

"Yes."

"Why would I do that? She just stayed over. It's not a secret."

"That is not what I mean, Jeremy," says Sam.

Jeremy leans against the counter. "Okay, Sam, then what do you mean?"

"I mean that your mother is going to live here with me from now on. This is what I am referring to. And she was anticipating some disagreement from you in this area. So I am prepared for argument. But I warn you in advance, I will not give in. I am very good at arguing. I was on the debating team at Oxford."

"You mean . . . she's moved out for good?"

"Yes, Jeremy, for good. For her own good. And I suggest you let her do this. Your mother is tired. Very tired. She has been taking care of too many people for too long. She needs someone to take care of her for a while now. And that someone is going to be myself."

"Oh," says Jeremy.

"She fell asleep only one hour ago, Jeremy. She had a big argument with your grandfather last night. He said horrible things to her. If I were you, I would just leave her alone. She was crying from midnight onwards. She was not consolable."

Goddamn that Al, Jeremy thinks. Is he bound and determined to destroy everything he touches in this life?

"Listen, Sam. Tell her I know where Henry went, and I'm going to get him. She shouldn't worry. But she needs to get hold of my aunt Jeanie right away. That part is very important. Okay? Tell her Henry is on his way there. Jeanie needs to be there to meet him. He left on the seven a.m. bus yesterday. Tell her to check the schedule and find out when he gets in. All right?"

Sam takes a pad of paper and notes all this down. Jeremy observes his slim brown hands, the neat line of his graying beard, the spotless maroon cloth of his turban. He wonders if Sam will take her back to India someday. He tries to picture Rita in a sari, with one of those red dots on her forehead. No, wait, those are Hindus. What's the difference? He has no idea. Would she have to become a Sikh to be with Sam? Or would he have to give up being a Sikh for her?

"Anything else, Jeremy?" says Sam.

"Make my mom happy, Sam," says Jeremy.

"I will greatly endeavor to do so. I am very relieved that you and I have not argued. I confess to you now I was somewhat anxious when I saw you walk in the door. I assumed you were here to tell her to get back home and return to her post in the kitchen, which in my opinion she has occupied for far too long."

"Sam, nobody held a gun to her head," Jeremy says. "But I'm not arguing with you. I'm glad. Just tell her I said that. Okay? I'm glad."

"May I offer you a complimentary continental breakfast, Jeremy?" With a sweep of his arm Sam indicates a table set against the wall, with pastries and coffee urns on it.

"I'll take it to go, Sam. Peace out, brother."

"Peace out to you too, my dude," says Sam, beaming. "I hope you find him."

On his way out of town, he sees a sheriff's car parked by the on-ramp. He pulls the cap down lower and slouches in his seat. He puts his turn signal on and keeps a careful eye on the speedometer. In the rearview mirror he sees a deputy sitting in the car, waiting. Maybe it's Lincoln. He can't tell. But Lincoln will not be looking for a lime green Honda Civic. He's looking for a white Saturn. He pays no attention as Jeremy drives by. Just another lowrider.

Right about now, his students will be talking:

Dude! Did you hear about Mr. Merkin? Yeah, he porked Jenn Moon in a motel. They're lovers. He's a total pervert. Holy shit, wasn't he some kind of war hero or something? Yeah, but you never can tell about people. Guess he's just another creep. And holy fuck, what a whore, I always could tell she was a slut, I shoulda banged 'er when I had the chance, ha-ha, too late now. Now her dad knows, yeah, I heard, he totally freaked out at school the other day, screaming rapist and shit, wow. And now Mr. Merkin is gone and Jenn is gone too. So they must be together. Yeah, I heard they ran away. Yeah, I heard they got married in Vegas. Yeah, I heard they got married in Mexico. No, guess what? He killed her and he's on the lam, the cops are looking for him. Dudes! You won't believe what I just heard. Mr. Merkin got killed in a shoot-out with the FBI.

No matter what direction it takes, the disillusionment of the children of Elysium will slide another notch lower. They will believe in nothing now. Not that they believed in anything in the first place. They believe in fast food and pirated movies and expensive sneakers and getting wasted on the weekends. The football games on Friday nights, the bored fights on Saturday nights. Who got into whose pants, who is a slut, and who is a stud. Who is a faggot and who is a dyke. Who is a stoner and who is a drunk. The temporary glory of senior year. He should know: this was his life, not very long ago.

But that is just one side of things. On the other there are the fundamentalist clans who populate the desert, the Mormons who make their kids get up at five every morning and do two hours of Bible study before they are even allowed to have breakfast, or the various sects of born-agains that are indistinguishable to Jeremy, and who get irate when you write *Xmas* instead of *Christmas* because it means you are crossing out Christ, and who lose their shit if you even mention evolution. There is no middle ground in Elysium, it seems; no one is just sort of anything. You have to be balls-to-the-wall one thing or another.

Like Al: he can't just be a Vietnam veteran, he has to be a fucking war criminal.

You have to hand it to those Mormons, though. Their kids are awfully polite. And they always have their homework done.

He watches the sheriff's car in his rearview mirror until it's out of sight. Even then, long after Elysium has receded behind him, he keeps glancing upward, expecting to see the whirling bubble-gum machine at any moment. He knows how this could go, too. Rico succeeded in scaring the shit out of him. *Holy balls, did you hear about Mr. Merkin? He got arrested and he committed suicide by stabbing himself twenty-seven times in the chest. He was in handcuffs at the time. No, I heard he kept ramming his own head against the wall even after he was unconscious. Broke his own skull and spilled his brains across the floor. Wow. Amazing. The cops say that's what happened, anyway. And we all know they wouldn't lie. They're there to protect us. If something happened to Jeremy Merkin, it was because he had it coming. I always thought there was something strange about him. I always knew he wasn't right.*

Rico won't be mad about his car, Jeremy realizes. He'll be glad Jeremy got out in time.

He keeps going. By noon he's across the Arizona line. He breathes a little easier, but not much.

Rita lives with Sam now, he thinks. That's weird to contemplate. In the space of a month, everything has turned upside down. Now what will happen? Say he brings Henry back to Elysium. Who will take care of him? Not Al, that's for sure. He can't even defrost a chicken. Rita wouldn't take Henry on at Sam's. And Henry can't take care of himself.

Which means it will be him, he realizes. He'll be in charge of Henry.

He pulls over to the side of the road and thinks about this for a while.

Maybe, he thinks, he should just go back home. Let nature take its course. The way you leave a baby bird on the ground when it falls out of its nest. The way he accepted his dog had gone out into the desert to die alone, because in the end, even after all the ball games and the treats and the way he'd taught him to sit and stay and come, his soft ears folding under his hand and his warm, wet tongue annoying but somehow flattering on his face, he really was nothing but a coyote after all, a wild animal, and his coyoteness had overpowered everything else about him. The way Henry's Henryness overpowered everything about Henry.

But home is a dangerous place now. His grandfather is a war criminal. Lincoln is looking for him. His reputation has been ruined.

He feels his phone buzz in his pocket. He takes it out and looks at the screen.

U ASSWHOLE, it says.

He turns the phone off, gets back on the highway, and keeps going.

The pain in his back is a second presence in the car, a malevolent shadow that keeps him awake as he passes through Arizona and into New Mexico, each mile a study in different shades of red. He continues pushing on through the rim of blackness that greets him on the border of Texas, until finally he gives in to the exhaustion of sixteen hours of driving. He gets a motel room just shy of Amarillo and collapses on the bed.

Maybe thirty or thirty-five more hours of driving like this and he can be in New York. He can get there at the same time as the bus, if he doesn't stop for too long. Between Amarillo and New York is a whole lot of white-knuckling, of talking to his pain aloud as if it were a hostage-taker who has to be placated. He might make it, if no headaches come. He thinks he feels one now, sneaking up on him from behind even though he's lying down, so he swallows another handful of ibuprofen. He wishes he hadn't taken so many caffeine pills. He wishes he had some pot. He'll never fall asleep. He feels as if he's still moving forward, into the interior universe that opens up for him whenever he closes his eyes. His thoughts are as unruly as a stadium of drunks. He's so tired it hurts.

He should have known immediately where Henry had gone. Now he's remembered their conversation about the Green Witch and how far away New York was. Jeanie lived in Greenwich Village. He really needs to do something about this short-term-memory business.

How long had it taken Henry to work that out? He'd been poring over Rita's address book at the dining room table, sounding out the words and numbers. Jeremy had forgotten Henry could actually read. By the time he left school, he could read as well as a slow first-grader. That was when he was fourteen. They were supposed to keep on teaching him at home. That hadn't happened. Henry could recite stories he'd memorized from the Picture Bible. Jeremy had always thought that was because Helen had read them aloud to him. But now he wonders. Maybe Henry has been reading the word of God all this time, in comic-book form. What better way to read a book like that? Jeremy thinks. He had loved the Picture Bible himself, back when he was little, until he realized there were people out there who would kill him for not believing in every word of it.

Somehow, he sleeps. He wakes early, though still later than he meant to. He doesn't shower or even brush his teeth. He gets a cup of coffee at a gas station and with it he washes down two more caffeine pills.

Then he spots a drugstore in a strip mall across the road. He goes inside and buys a pack of condoms, a thin plastic tube, some duct tape, and a hot water bottle. He returns to the gas station and gets the bathroom key from the attendant. Inside the bathroom, he makes a hole in the tip of one of the condoms. He runs the tube inside it and tapes it firmly in place. The other end he runs into the hot water bottle, and this he also tapes in place, so that nothing can splash out of it. He strips from the waist down and fits the condom over his johnson. He does his very best not to think about the fact that this is the first time he's ever worn a condom. Naturally, he fails, because telling himself not to think about something is a guaranteed way of putting it in the forefront of his mind. When Samantha Bayle, assistant manager of the Freezie Squeeze, had taught him the true meaning of double-dipping his sugar cone, they hadn't used any protection, which he realized later was kind of stupid. Well, really stupid. Things had been what you might call spontaneous.

And now is also not the time to think about the fact that he has not had sex since then. There were a couple of encounters with women while he was in the army, but those didn't really count as true scores, because money had changed hands. And besides, those had gone badly, very badly, practically worthy of a comedy film. These incidents, he finds, he has no trouble not thinking about. He'd forgotten them completely until this moment. What a strange thing it is, he thinks, the idea of hiring a woman to do things to you or let you do things to her. Almost as strange as men shooting pieces of metal at each other through long tubes.

When he was a boy, he'd always thought that things would start to make more sense to him as he got older, but this was not the case. If anything, they made less sense. There were days when the entire experience of being alive struck him as a bizarre, almost accidental state. His soul, if there was such a thing, inhabited a body that was made of substances ultimately no more durable than a cheese sandwich left out in the rain. Within this cheese sandwich there were processes taking place that meant he was alive and that he had the ability to think about the fact that he was alive. But if enough of those processes came to a halt, for example if his heart stopped beating or he ran out of blood or his spinal cord was severed, all of which had once very nearly happened, then he was no longer alive and he no longer inhabited the cheese sandwich. How could this possibly be? Of all the things that could potentially happen in a universe as large as this, why these things, in this way?

He recognizes this pattern of thought by now. It's a familiar cycle. Sometimes, when he's thinking like this, he feels himself to be on the verge of a great leap in understanding. But the leap never actually happens. Instead, he drowns in a whirlpool of confusing thoughts. And eventually he forgets about it, because being a cheese sandwich is time-consuming and distracting. Like now. Here he is in the men's room of a gas station in Texas, and the filthy tile floor is cool on his feet through his socks. This is what is real to a cheese sandwich. Thoughts of souls and existence and what it means that he inhabits this almost-ruined body and what will happen to him when he no longer inhabits it always fade in favor of the cool tile floors or the strange powdery sensation of latex on his manly bits, or whatever he happens to be feeling at the moment. A truly brilliant and awake person could maybe forget these things easily and spend all his time dwelling at the edge of his understanding, edging forward little by little. Smarty had been that kind of person. And yet he had embraced his cheese-sandwichness without feeling any apparent contradiction, either. This was the true mystery of Smarty: he had no trouble inhabiting both planes at once; he could move from one to the other without effort, whenever he pleased. Or he had been able to, anyway, before his period of being a cheese sandwich was brought to an end through the abrupt cessation of the biological processes that were taking place inside him.

It was all very strange.

He tapes the hot water bottle to his leg, making sure it sticks to his sock and not his leg hair. Then he puts his pants back on over his piss-bottle rig. Now he won't even have to stop to go to the bathroom.

Suddenly he remembers that his phone has been turned off all this time. He turns it on and sees that Rico has called him no fewer than two dozen times. He puts it back in his pocket, thinking that he will deal with Rico later, but at that moment it rings again. It's Rico again. He can't put it off, he thinks. He has to face the music.

"Hello?"

"Oh, hey, how's it going?" Rico asks.

"Fine," Jeremy says cautiously.

"That's great, man. Just wanted to check in, you know, because you stole my fucking car and all."

"Dude."

"Dude."

"Listen, I didn't have time to explain."

"Do you have time to explain now?" Rico's voice is high with fury. "Can you fit this into your schedule?"

"Bro, seriously. Just listen."

"Don't bro me, bro. I'm gonna fuck you up so hard you're gonna shit out your own teeth. Okay, bro?"

"Rico," says Jeremy. "Just shut up a minute. It was an emergency, okay?"

"Where the fuck are you? Tell me right now. I have friends at the Pentagon. I'm gonna call in a drone strike on your ass."

"Dude. Come on. Would I do this just to fuck with you? Would I do this if there wasn't a very good reason?"

Rico sighs. "No," he says.

"Right. So."

"Okay," Rico says. "Tell me what's going on."

"Didn't your mother tell you?"

"She said I should hear it from you."

"That is so your mom."

"Mexicans are a very noble people," says Rico. "We believe in a level of personal honesty that is unknown to you white-skinned motherfuckers. For example, no Mexican would have taken the car of another Mexican like this. It just wouldn't happen. It's inconceivable."

"I'm trying to tell you why."

"So start talking."

So Jeremy explains. Rico listens, breathing fatly into the phone.

"All right," says Rico when he's done. "Here's what you're gonna do. You're gonna treat that car like it was made of glass. You're gonna treat it like the last baby that will ever be born. If it has one dent in it—one little scratch, one speck of dust, anything— you're gonna pay to have it fixed. And even if it's not damaged in any way, you're gonna have it detailed. You're gonna have it serviced. Oil change, filters, everything. Shampoo the carpets. You're gonna lick the tires clean with your own tongue. *M'entiendes?*"

"*Yo te entiendo,*" says Jeremy.

"Don't speak Spanish to me, you cracker-ass motherfucker. Spanish is my language. Your accent is all fucked up. It's an insult to my ancestors, the way you speak Spanish."

"*Estoy muy feliz que tu entiendes,*" says Jeremy.

"Stop it. You're hurting my ears."

"You mad, bro?"

"Listen," says Rico. "Don't ask me that right now. I'm getting calmer. But you could easily rile me up again."

"Don't have a heart attack."

"I'm not gonna have a heart attack."

"I'm sorry."

"There are the words I was waiting to hear," says Rico. "It's amazing how long it took you to apologize. It would have been so simple to say that first."

"I'm sorry. Here's the I'm So Sorry Song. Won't you help and sing along?"

"There were probably easier ways for you to go about this. But I guess if you took the easy way, you wouldn't be Jeremy."

"We still friends?"

"Detailed. Serviced. Shampoo. Every fucking thing."

"I promise."

"You're a complete fuckup, and I hate your guts," Rico says.

Jeremy hangs up, vastly relieved that everything is okay between them.

He leaves Texas, and the journey ahead presses down like a weight on his shoulders. All through that day he limits himself to a mouthful of beef jerky every hour and two caffeine pills every two hours. He takes ibuprofen whenever the mood strikes him. He urinates into his homemade piss bottle. This takes some getting used to. At first it feels as if he's wetting his pants. But then he takes a childish delight in the warm stream running along his leg. He might wear one of these for the rest of his life, he thinks.

There is tired, and then there is bone tired, and then there is a fatigue that transcends psychology and makes you forget who you are. He remembers this feeling well. He had it all through basic. That was how they turned you into a soldier. This is the state he's in when he makes it to Columbus after another twenty hours. He doesn't even remember checking into the motel.

He's awakened only moments after falling asleep by the ringing of his cell phone. The curtains are drawn tight over the window. It's dark everywhere. He went to sleep without noticing his surroundings, and there is not so much as a night-light. He could be in Kathmandu. It rings forever before he finds it, hidden in one of his pockets.

"Hello?"

"Jeremy?" The voice is a whisper.

"Who is this?"

"It's me. Jenn."

Jeremy groans.

"Please don't hang up."

"Why shouldn't I?"

"Jeremy, I'm so sorry."

"Jenn. Do you know what your father did to me? In front of the entire school?"

"I know. I heard."

"I lost my job," says Jeremy. "Because of you. Someone was sending me these insane texts."

"That would be my dad," says Jenn. "He took my phone. I got it back, though."

"And your brother came to my house. He was looking for me. I had to leave town, Jenn."

"Jeremy, I feel really really bad. I never meant for any of this to happen."

"Why did he say all those things about me? What did you tell him?"

"I didn't tell him anything. I swear. I—I had to lie."

"You had to lie about me to save your own ass? Are you serious?"

"I didn't lie about you, Jeremy. He just assumed. He was spying on me. He saw you come out of the motel room. And also it was kind of based on some things I said."

"Well, what did you say?"

"I told him I was pregnant."

"Why in the hell would you tell him something like that?"

"He was gonna hit me. It was the only way I could get him to stop."

"Yeah, but why would you tell him that? Of all the things you could say?"

"Because I am."

She allows this to sink in.

"You're really pregnant?" Jeremy says.

"Yeah. Oops."

"Oh my God."

"I should have just let him hit me. That's when he freaked out. Started saying he was gonna kill whoever did this to me. He had to believe I was raped, because that's the only way he can imagine me getting knocked up. Not his little girl. You know what I mean?"

"So you told him I did it."

"No, no. I didn't say that. I didn't say it was you."

"Well, who did you say it was, then? Who is it?" A horrible thought comes to him. "Is it . . . your brother?"

"My brother? What on earth are you talking about?"

Jeremy feels in the darkness for the mattress underneath him, even though he's lying on it, just to make sure it's still there. Because if the mattress is still there, then the floor is still there, and so is the motel room, and so is the earth underneath it.

"What do you mean, what am I talking about?" he says. "All that stuff you told me in the motel room."

"Oh," says Jenn, "yeah. That stuff. I kinda made that up."

"You what?"

"I'm sorry, Jeremy. Sometimes I don't know what I'm talking about." She giggles. "I say these whacked-out things, and then later I'm like, whoa, did I really say that?"

"You're insane," Jeremy whispers.

"Jeremy! That's not very nice. Besides, I never came right out and said anything, did I?"

"So none of this really had to happen," Jeremy says.

"None of what?"

If she hadn't left him that note, he wouldn't have gone to the motel room. If he hadn't gone to the motel room, her father wouldn't have seen him there. If her father hadn't seen him there, he wouldn't have humiliated him at the ceremony. Jeremy would still have his job. Strangers power-walking on the streets would not know his name. A crazy policeman wouldn't be after him. Except now he sees that Lincoln isn't the crazy one after all. It's her. He should have guessed this, he thinks. After all he's been through, he's still a naive idiot.

"I gotta hang up now," he says.

"No, wait. Please. Talking to you makes me feel so much better, Jeremy."

"I can't help you," Jeremy says. "Don't ever call me again."

"Jeremy, I swear to God, if you abandon me now, I will make you regret it."

"How could I regret it any more than I already do?"

"I'm trying to make things right here, Jeremy! Please!"

"It's too late for that," Jeremy says, and hangs up.

He's desperate for more sleep, but again, just moments after drifting off, he's awakened once more, this time by the knife in his head. He rolls off the bed, flailing, and stumbles around the room. But the wielder of this knife seems to want him on his knees, so he obliges. When this is not quite enough, he collapses face forward onto the floor, feeling pinned, a butterfly in a collection. I cannot get any lower, he thinks. I can't abase myself anymore. This is the deepest bow I know how to make. I submit to your greatness, O headache. All things begin and end with you. You giveth and you taketh away—except you never really giveth anything. You taketh my sleep and my sanity and my peace of mind, and also you taketh away the last shreds of hope I might have that I survived. Because of you I can see that I haven't really gotten through this war yet. It's still up in the air as to how this is going to go.

He lies there and suffers through it, willing himself not to make a sound. It wouldn't matter if he did; there's no one there to hear him. But they'd practiced for this. Endurance training. How much pain can you take before you have to cry? It was a point of pride with them; they glorified those who could tolerate the greatest amount of discomfort or even agony without making a peep. The squad had spoken in awe of Jorgensen, whose leg had been blown off by an RPG one day and who'd lain there, stoic, until the shooting was over, and then calmly said, "Little help, guys?" Which was the understatement of the year. Of course, that was the shock taking over, and it was actually pretty stupid of him. As evidenced by the fact that he'd later died.

But for a long time Jorgensen lay there in the mud that was made of his blood and the dust without making a sound, because the enemy were so close you could practically smell the sheep shit on their dicks and he didn't want to give away their position. It was funny to see a person's leg just lying on the ground. Not funny as in a joke. Funny as in it removed one more support from the walls of your mind, walls you had always taken for granted and which you realized were not so hard to topple after all. His leg was a piece of meat. They were all meat. No different than the pallid slabs of plastic-wrapped flesh you bought in a supermarket and cooked for dinner. And though they did not discuss it, Jeremy knew that the squad had all felt the horror of cattle in the abattoir.

Afterward they'd asked each other the same question: how could he be in that kind of pain and not scream? Other guys howled like babies ripped from their mother's teat when they broke a finger or chipped a tooth or took a bullet in some part of themselves. Not Jorgensen. He was a Spitting Cobra among Spitting Cobras.

He can cry if he wants to. There's no one to hear him. But he doesn't, because he was a Spitting Cobra, and in the Spitting Cobras you don't cry, you just take it.

"Hooah," he whispers.

He lies there, thinking of Jorgensen and whispering hooah to himself like a crazy person, and he waits for it to end. This doesn't happen until late morning. It must be those damn caffeine pills, he thinks. When he can stand up again, he throws them away in the bathroom trash can.

He's tempted to push on, but he's weak on his legs. He's slept maybe only three or four hours. So he goes to the motel office and pays for another day, and then he returns to his room and collapses on the bed. It can't be helped. He won't be any use to Henry if he's smeared like a bug against a concrete barricade.

He sleeps until early evening. When he wakes, he waits to see if the knife is going to come again, but it doesn't. He struggles to his feet and thinks he might as well shower, now that so much of this day is gone. The hot water feels like liquid cocaine on his back muscles.

When he gets out, pink as a steamed ham, he turns his phone on, checks his screen, and sees a text from Rita: *I CANNOT GET MY SISTER TO ANSWER HER PHONE!!!*

He gets dressed and gets back in the car. He drives through the night, singing aloud to keep himself awake, pissing into his hot water bottle and watching the speedometer. The farther he gets from the craziness, the better. He passes through Ohio and across Pennsylvania, where he sees a black bear toddle across the highway and a row of Amish buggies parked outside a church. The world here is impossibly green.

The next time he sees the sun rise, it's behind a row of skyscrapers that glisten like the wet jawline of a slavering beast.

13

THE BUS is due to arrive at 11:05. At 10:30, he parks in the fourth story of a public garage, squeezing Rico's car into a space so tight that it would be easier to crawl out the window, if only his body were capable. If Rico could see this parking job, he thinks, he'd shit his pants. The potential for dinged doors and scratched paint is off the charts. But Jeremy doesn't care. His ass is furious with him, his back is threatening to go on strike. He may never stand erect again.

Out on the sidewalk, he realizes yellow lines have been zipping past in his periphery for so long that the world is still sliding by him. He shuts his eyes and stands still, waiting for the sensation of movement to cease. People eddy around him. Humanity is a river, he thinks, and I am a rock. If I stand here long enough, they'll just wear me away, and I'll disappear.

He walks into Penn Station, an ant creeping into a cathedral, and finds a men's room. In a stall, he reluctantly disengages himself from his piss bottle. He throws it into the trash, listening to its final sad slosh. Then he washes his hands, meanwhile regarding himself in the mirror: his eyes are egg whites poached in blood, rising out of kangaroo pouches. Then he finds the right gate, and he waits.

Up to this point, he hasn't allowed himself to imagine all the things that could have gone wrong on this bus trip. Now he realizes that if Henry is not on the bus, he's going to have to retrace his steps and turn the whole country upside down until he finds him. And if something happened to him, he is going to find out who did it, and he is going to put a large hurt on him. A hurt to end all hurts. He still knows how to prepare himself for battle. The worst part was the waiting. When it finally started, he was always fine. All he had to do was forget about ever going home.

This, he understands now, is the secret to getting through a war. Thoughts of home take a while to die. You have to forget that you're a person, and that you have a mother and a house and a dog and many other things besides. You have to leave all that. Detach yourself from it. Accept that you aren't going home again. Some guys couldn't do it, couldn't make the mental leap. Other guys did, and then found to their astonishment that they'd survived anyway. Those were the ones who were well and truly fucked. How did you return to a world you'd let go of? How did you come home and do things like get a job and get married and have kids when a handful of months earlier you were kicking in doors in a dusty little village and screaming in the faces of terrified families, threatening to kill all of them if they didn't tell you where the weapons were? The two worlds did not exist on the same plane. There was no point at which they intersected. The gap between them was so vast that not even the spark of memory could cross it.

Had he really managed to let go of his life? Maybe, sometimes. If he ever stopped to think about anything, he became desperately afraid. But if he stopped thinking and focused only on the task at hand, he found he could bring himself to do outrageous things. He could dash across exposed areas with bullets whizzing all around him and feel not fear but a thrill, for as long as he didn't get shot, it was the ultimate playground game, and it made his balls tingle with excitement. He could wait in hiding for hours for a hajji to pop into view like a deer, so he could experience the sublime satisfaction of sending a round into the front of his head and watching his brains come out the back. He liked to throw grenades and to watch them be thrown. He liked to scream taunts across a stretch of open ground and hear them scream back.

But afterward, he would dissolve. He would shake so hard he couldn't see straight. And every time this happened, it became harder to throw himself into it. Until finally he had nothing left, and he knew he really had no choice anymore but to die.

He didn't fear death. What he really feared, though he would never have admitted this to anyone, even Smarty, was getting hurt. And that was precisely what had happened. So there was no listening God. There was nothing in the world that was not so fragile it could be destroyed as easily as stomping on an egg. And there was simply nothing left to experience.

Thinking about all this is exhausting. He wants to lie down. He needs to drink some magic tea.

The bus is only an hour late. Henry gets off first, clutching Smitty in the crook of his arm. He looks utterly dumbfounded, his mouth hanging open, his eyes seeing nothing. He's a goldfish exposed to the air, a newborn hung by his feet. Jeremy knows that look. Seizure territory. He had that same expression the morning Al found Helen in her bed.

"Jermy?" Henry says, gaping. "Are you here?"

"Hiya, champ," Jeremy says. Henry hugs him in his awkward, bent-over way. Jeremy wrinkles his nose. The kid doesn't smell too good.

"How did you get here?" Henry asks.

"I drove, Henry."

"In a car?"

"Yes, in a car."

And then he can't help himself. The last three or four days have created a charge in him that now senses a point of contact, and it all tries to come out of him at once. He covers his eyes with his hand and tries to fight it, but it's like trying to hold back electricity. Henry strokes his head with one meaty paw.

"Why are you crying? Did you stub your toe?" he asks kindly.

Jeremy wipes his face with his hands. "No, you idiot, I did not stub my toe."

"Are you sad about something?"

"I'm not sad."

"Oh," says Henry. "Happy tears. Are you going to live with me and my mom?"

"Henry, we'll have to talk about that," Jeremy says. "What you did was very bad. You should never have left the house without telling anyone. You scared everyone. Everyone has been looking for you. And you—you don't even know what the hell I'm talking about, do you? You think you can just get on a bus and go wherever you want, and somehow things will just work out?"

He stops himself. There's really no point in getting mad at Henry. You can yell at him all you want and he'll just stand there without having the faintest idea why. And it is all the more maddening because it *has* worked out. His plan has succeeded because he had no plan. He simply did it. And here he is.

"I'm eighteen years old," says Henry.

"Who cares? What the fuck does that have to do with it? Everyone's been worried sick. The police were looking for you and everything."

"The police?"

"Yes, Henry. The police. They're very mad at you too."

"Am I going to jail?"

Jeremy sighs. What would they have done with Henry in other societies, in other times? Maybe he would have been made a shaman. Or maybe they would have kept him in a special hut, feeding him whatever he wanted, worshiping him and letting him make all their laws, until the signs became auspicious and they drowned him in a sacred lake. Or maybe he just would have occupied some lowly position, like shit carrier. But in this world he has no status. He's nothing. He's just Henry.

"No, Henry," he says. "You're not going to jail."

"I want to see my mom," says Henry.

"Yeah, well, she's not here."

"Where is she?"

"How the hell should I know? She was supposed to be here and she's not. I need to call her."

"Is this New York New York?" Henry looks around.

"Yes, Henry. This is New York."

"An aitch-ee-double-hockey-sticks of a town," Henry sings tunelessly.

"Sure is," says Jeremy.

"Where are the tall tall buildings? I saw them through the window."

"They're outside, Henry. This is a bus station."

"I want to see the buildings."

"We will. But there's a thing I gotta do first."

Henry insists on holding his hand. Jeremy takes him to a restaurant in the terminal and sits him down. Then he calls Rita.

"I've got him," he says.

"Thank God," says Rita. "Is Jeanie there?"

"No."

"Damn her. I've been leaving messages like crazy. She doesn't answer."

"Give me her address," says Jeremy. "She'll answer her doorbell, or I'll go in through the window."

"Hold on," says Rita, and she puts the phone down while he waits. Then she picks it back up and reads it off to him.

"Okay," says Jeremy. "I'm gonna go now."

But she's not ready to let him off the phone. "You talked to Sam, I guess," she says.

"Yeah."

"And he told you."

"Yeah."

"I was going to tell you myself. I just didn't know how to say it."

"It doesn't matter, Mom," says Jeremy. "It's fine."

"You sure?"

"Does it matter if I'm sure?"

"What do you mean?"

"I mean—" Suppose he told her it wasn't all right? That she had to leave Sam's and move back in? He could be cruel to her too. It would be easy. It always was.

"Never mind," he says. "I just want you to be happy."

"You know something?"

"What?"

"No one's ever said that to me before," she says.

He and Henry take a cab to Jeanie's place in Greenwich Village. It's a seven-story building, lots of apartments. Maybe as many people on this one block as in all of Elysium. He finds her name on the buzzer and presses the button. If she's not answering her phone, then maybe she isn't here. Maybe she's out of the country, in Rome or London or Milan on one of her goddamn modeling trips, flaunting her glamorous ass for the camera. But he hears a crackling sound, and then her disembodied voice comes to him like one of Elizabeta's spirits communicating through the ether.

"Yes?"

"Jeanie? Is that you?"

"Who is this?"

"It's Jeremy," he says. "And Henry."

"And Smitty," says Henry.

There's a long silence. He presses the buzzer again.

"Who the hell is this?" she says.

"Jeanie," says Jeremy, "open the mother*fucking* door."

He hadn't meant to say that. It just kind of slipped out. He's very tired.

"You said a bad word, Jermy," says Henry. "You should say sorry."

"Sorry," Jeremy says through clenched teeth.

After another long moment, the buzzer sounds. They climb three flights of stairs and find her standing in her doorway. She's dressed as if she's going out: black pants, black blouse, a black purse over her shoulder.

"Oh my God," she says. "It's really you. I thought someone was playing a joke on me."

"It's not a joke," says Jeremy. "Although it certainly feels like one."

"Mom," says Henry. "Mom. I totally found you, Mom." He hugs her. After a long moment, Jeanie hugs him back.

"Henry . . . what are you doing here?"

"Mom, I have some really really good news," says Henry. "I came to live with you! I will stay here and be your Henry. We don't have to be apart anymore."

"He ran away," Jeremy explains. "I followed him. And here we are. That's the CliffsNotes version of it. There's a longer version, but it's not much more exciting than that."

"Okay," says Jeanie. "I might need a few minutes to process this."

"No problem. Can we do the processing inside? I need to sit down for a while."

Jeanie sighs. "Sure. Come on in."

Henry badly needs a bath. Jeremy starts the water running and supervises his entry into the tub, which has a tendency to be overly splashy. The apartment is small, not much bigger than

Jeremy's basement, come to think of it, and is divided not into rooms but areas. While Henry is splashing around in the bathtub, Jeremy and Jeanie sit in the couch area. He stares at her face in the dim light and thinks, Jesus, she's so goddamn beautiful. She's the most beautiful woman I've ever known or even spoken to. Through some miracle or propitious alignment of her parts, she is a cheese sandwich that happens to conform very closely to our ideas of what a cheese sandwich is actually supposed to look like. That's why all the other cheese sandwiches are crazy about her. If she wasn't my aunt, I'd probably be in love with her. And yet there's something in her that's just not there.

"So I have some questions," she says.

"I have some questions too. Why didn't you answer your phone?" says Jeremy.

"I have two phones. One of them I answer and one of them I don't."

"Let me guess," Jeremy says. "The one you answer is the number we don't have. The number for important people, maybe?"

"Don't, Jer," says Jeanie. "Please don't be hard on me."

"Oh, I'm so sorry. We'll just go away again until you can get your shit together."

"Stop it. What does Henry mean, he's coming to live with me?"

"I think he means he's coming to live with you."

"But, Jeremy—he can't live with me. I'm not ready for this. I'm not even ready for a visit. It's the worst possible time. I need some kind of warning. Some notice. You know?"

"All right," says Jeremy. "We'll come back in another eighteen years. Henry will be thirty-six. He won't be any easier to take care of then, just so you know. It doesn't even matter how old he is. He's pretty much always going to be five."

"Jeremy, this is totally unfair. Totally."

"You really want to have that argument? You want to complain about what's not fair? Not fair is you sticking everyone else with your responsibility while you're doing whatever the hell it is you do here."

"What I do here is I try to make it," says Jeanie. "And I wasn't sticking anybody with anything."

"You left without even saying goodbye," Jeremy points out. "That was sneaky."

"Things were tense with Rita. And with Dad. He was barely speaking to me. I couldn't take one more minute in that house. And besides, I hate goodbyes. All that drama."

"So you bailed," says Jeremy.

"Yeah, okay, I bailed. I admit it. I'm sorry, Jeremy."

"Rita wanted to talk to you about Henry. You knew that, didn't you? That's the real reason you left. So you wouldn't have to deal. So you could come back to your cozy, exciting life here."

"My life is anything but cozy or exciting. And as far as Henry is concerned, I had a deal worked out with Mom."

"Nanny is no longer with us," Jeremy explains, as if to a child. "Which is something I thought you knew very well, considering you were at her memorial service."

"I hate the way you're talking to me right now."

"I don't care," says Jeremy. "I've about had it with you. And so has everyone else."

She should be getting mad at him, he thinks. If she were a normal person who felt normal things, that's what she'd be doing. But she isn't mad. Instead, Jeanie just stares off into space. It's like she's not even here. She's waiting for her beauty to save her, he realizes. She's waiting for him to say, Never mind, it's okay, you're so hot that the regular rules don't apply to you. But he is her nephew and he's immune to this about her. Which comes, he realizes, as a huge relief. When you don't want to have sex with a woman, she has no power over you.

"How is this going to work?" she says finally. "I'm never home. I can't even have a cat, Jeremy. I don't have time."

"I don't know how it's going to work," Jeremy says. "It's not my problem."

"You're just going to leave him here?"

"You got a better idea?"

"Yeah. Take him home."

"There is no more home," says Jeremy.

"What do you mean?"

"I mean, everything is over. New game now. New rules. Somebody hit the restart button and forgot to tell everyone else."

"You're being very strange, Jeremy."

"I'm sorry," he says. "I've been driving for three days. What I mean is, Rita has moved out. She's living with Sam now. And Al is . . . well, Al."

"What about you?"

"What about me?" says Jeremy. "I'm not going back to Elysium."

He hasn't planned to say this, nor has he even thought about it. But as the words come out, he realizes it's true. He'll find some way to get Rico's car back to him. Ship it home somehow. The fact is, home never existed in the first place. Not the way he'd imagined it and remembered it. It's taken him five years to realize this. And now the whole town will be talking about him and Jenn. He could go back and make everything right again, maybe. But what's the point?

"Where are you going, then?"

"I . . . don't know," says Jeremy. "I guess you could say I'm in transition."

"You mean you're moving out too?"

"Yeah. That's what I mean."

"Where will you go?"

"I have some ideas," Jeremy says, though in fact he has none. "I don't feel like talking about them yet."

"I thought you had a job."

"I did. I don't anymore. Long story."

"Jesus," says Jeanie. "I can't believe this is happening."

"He's your son, Jeanie."

"It's not that simple, Jeremy."

"Actually, it is. When the females of our species give birth to their young, they become what's called a mother."

"I was never Henry's mother."

"You didn't give birth to him?"

"Of course I did! But I didn't want to."

"It still happened. I know Henry was a mistake. But you have to deal with mistakes."

"He was more than a mistake," says Jeanie.

"What do you mean?"

Jeanie stares at him. "Jeremy, let me just tell you this. I left for his sake as much as mine. Henry was in danger."

"What do you mean, in danger?"

"It's kind of hard to explain."

"Try me," says Jeremy.

"He was in danger from me. When he was a baby, I mean. Mom found me one night, walking down the street with him in my arms. I was asleep. But I was headed for the lake. That was when we decided it would be better if I wasn't around him anymore. So she and I made a deal: I'd send her money, and she'd take care of Henry for me. It wasn't fair, what happened to me."

"Nothing is fair," says Jeremy.

"So you've noticed," Jeanie Rae says. She takes up her purse and begins searching through it. "I was raped, Jeremy. By someone I trusted. He told me it was God's will. He said that I would get pregnant and the child would be a child of the Lord. Fine, I said. Then the Lord can raise him."

"Who was it?"

"A preacher," Jeanie says. She gives up looking for whatever it was in her purse. "A minister. A blind man."

"Did you tell Nanny and Al?"

"Mom knew. She said never to tell Dad. Or he'd end up doing twenty years."

"I'm sorry to hear it," says Jeremy.

"Thanks. It was—"

"It was eighteen years ago," says Jeremy.

Jeanie Rae stares at him. "I know," she whispers.

"I want to get out now," calls Henry from the bathroom.

"Go get him out," says Jeremy.

At this suggestion, Jeanie looks horrified. "Are you serious?" she whispers. "He's a . . . a grown man."

"Yes, I know," says Jeremy. "I've gotten him out of the bath many a time myself."

"Have you heard nothing I've said?"

"Sure, I heard you. Something shitty happened, and Henry was the result. It sucks. Life isn't fair. I'm sorry. Go get your son out of the tub."

"I can't."

"Why not?"

"Because I . . . don't do penises," she says.

"What do you mean, you don't do penises?"

"I just think they're . . . weird. I can't deal with them."

She has a point there, Jeremy thinks. Penises are kind of weird. But he's not going to surrender an inch. He says, "Is this your way of telling me you're a lesbian?"

"I'm not a lesbian," Jeanie says. "I'm not anything."

"How can you not be anything? Everybody is something."

"Yeah, well, not me. I opted out of the whole sex thing a long time ago."

"I didn't realize you could do that."

"This is not a conversation I'm going to have with my baby nephew. I'm just telling you, I can't do this."

"You don't have to do anything. You just have to help him out and give him a towel."

"I cannot now, nor will I ever be able to, deal with seeing Henry naked," says Jeanie.

"I guess he's going to shrivel up like a prune, then. Or maybe he's going to drown. I'm not going to get him out."

"Please, Jeremy. We need to talk more about this. You can't just do this to me. Not like this. It's not fair."

"Nothing is fair," says Jeremy.

They hear more splashing. After a moment Henry appears in the couch area, naked.

"I was calling and calling and calling," he says, "and nobody came."

"Oh, sweet Jesus," says Jeanie, putting her face in her hands.

"Hey, look at that," Jeremy says. "He got himself out."

"Praise the Lord," says Henry.

Jeremy and Henry, clothed now and his head toweled dry, sit at the small table in what Jeremy assumes must pass for a dining room in this city. Smitty sits on Henry's lap, regarding them with Cyclopean calm. Jeanie Rae makes four sandwiches and sets them down. Then she sits and lights a cigarette while they eat.

"You mind putting that out?" says Jeremy. "It's kind of gross while we're eating."

"This is my apartment," says Jeanie. "I smoke."

"You'll have to quit. Henry's allergic."

"Since when?"

"Since now," says Jeremy.

She gives him a venomous look. Then she stabs the cigarette out.

Henry devours three of the sandwiches in the time it takes Jeremy to eat one. Then he begins to talk. He tells a long-winded story that features washrooms and restaurants and a blackfella named Mr. Jenkins.

"African-American, Henry," says Jeremy.

"What? What did you say, Jermy?"

"We don't say blackfella. We say African-American."

"We say Africa?"

"Yes."

Henry thinks about this carefully. "Mr. Jenkins was from Georgia. He was born in Georgia in nineteen fawty-one. And that was no place to be a black man." He chews his food, pondering his next point. "He was enemies with Jim Crow."

"What is he talking about?" says Jeanie.

"We'll never know," says Jeremy.

Jeremy watches Jeanie while Henry goes on. Her eyes are flat. She's somewhere else. Not even listening. Wrapped up in her own thoughts, her own problems. No doubt wondering how she's going to weasel out of this. She's always looked like that, he thinks. She's always had that veneer. He'd always thought it was just because she was beautiful, and beautiful women are impenetrable. Even when they're your aunt. But it's deeper than that. She has something wrong with her. Something deep that no one can touch.

He can't leave Henry here with her, he realizes. There's no way. Something terrible will happen. She'll forget him in a store or abandon him in a park or something. His legs duct-taped together like a puppy, so he can't run after her. Or she'll keep him in a closet and feed him once a week. If this place even has a closet.

"The Lord came unto me in the washroom," says Henry around his sandwich.

"Don't talk with your mouth full," says Jeremy.

Henry chews and swallows. "I like New York food." He sniffs. "I like New York air too. What do New York possicles taste like?"

"Like Popsicles anywhere else, I guess," says Jeanie.

"I wanna possicle," Henry says.

"Eat your sandwich," says Jeremy.

"The Lord tricked me and turned into the Devil," he says.

"Henry," says Jeremy, "did you bring your medicine with you?"

"What medicine?"

"The yellow pills. The ones you take in the morning at break-fast time."

"Nope."

To Jeanie, Jeremy says, "He'll need his prescription. They can fax it from the drugstore in Lancaster. He needs a refill. The sooner the better."

"Great," Jeanie says, her voice dull. "I'll get right on that."

"Listen, Jeanie," says Jeremy, and he's about to deliver another lecture when suddenly his back goes into a spasm. He pitches forward over the table, pounding it with the flat of his palm.

"What is it?" Jeanie says, alarmed.

"My back." In a supreme effort of self-control, he manages to say this without screaming. But Henry does the screaming for him.

"The Lord is giving Jermy a heart attack!" he shrieks.

"No, no," Jeremy says into the table. "Henry, I'm fine."

"Lord, stop it!" Henry shouts. He stands, knocking his chair over. "Stop it stop it stop it!"

"Shh, Henry," says Jeanie. "Shh. It's okay. He's not having a heart attack."

Henry begins to cry. He gasps and hiccups. Jeanie puts her arms around him. Her fingertips can't even meet. He leans into her, almost knocking her over.

"Oh, this is really sad," Henry sobs.

"Relax, Henry," says Jeanie. "I have to help Jeremy now. Okay?"

"Okay," says Henry, and he stops crying.

"Hey, look at that," Jeremy says. "You calmed him down."

"All right, Jeremy, let's get up," says Jeanie.

"I can't move," says Jeremy. His head is resting on his plate, pressed against the remains of his sandwich. Who was it who brought the head of John the Baptist to the king on a platter? Salome, he remembers. Another Picture Bible classic. What a wonderful family-oriented book.

"Come on. I'll help you."

"If I move, I'll die."

"You won't die. Come on. Just walk bent over. Crawl if you have to. You need to get out of that chair."

She helps him up and brings him into the sitting area. She shoves the coffee table out of the way and lowers him to the floor. He lies on his side, feeling as if he's been shot.

"Can you roll over on your stomach?" she says.

"No," Jeremy says.

"Try." So he tries, and fails. "Again," she says.

"Hooah," Jeremy says, and he makes it. She begins to tug at his shirt. "What are you doing?"

"I'm taking your shirt off."

"No," he says. "Don't."

"Why not?"

"I don't like people seeing me with my shirt off."

"It's okay, for heaven's sake. I'm your aunt."

"I know who you are. Don't."

"I'm a trained massage therapist. Think of me as a professional."

"When did you become a massage therapist?"

"I've had about a million jobs since I moved here," she says.

"I thought you were a model."

"I was. Once. That was a long time ago."

"What happened?"

"Nothing happened. It turns out there are a lot of other pretty girls in this city who wanted success worse than I did."

A cell phone begins to ring somewhere.

"Hold on," Jeanie says. "Don't move."

"No problem there," says Jeremy. "Is that the important phone or the family phone?"

"Shut up," Jeanie says, and takes her cell out of her purse. "Hello? Yeah, I know I'm late. Something's come up . . . Start without me, I guess . . . How should I know? Something's come up, I said. I'll get there when I get there. Yeah. Bye." She clicks her phone shut and puts it back in her purse. Then she resumes her position on the floor next to him. "You need a massage," she says. "Come on."

So he lets her pull his shirt up, because he's powerless not to. He can hear her sharp intake of breath.

"Oh my God," she says. She traces his spine with one finger. He can feel her touch only on the flesh that isn't covered in keloids.

"Yeah, see? That's why I don't like taking my shirt off. It's disgusting." He feels a hot tear splash somewhere on his lower back. "Stop it," he says.

"Jeremy, is that where the ragheads blowed you up?" asks Henry, solemn.

"Jesus, what did those animals do to you?" Jeanie says.

"Luckily, I don't remember," says Jeremy.

She rests her hands on his back. "Jeremy," she says, her voice broken.

"Jeanie, if you say one nice thing to me right now, I swear to God."

There's no need for him to finish that sentence. She gets a hold of herself and begins to work on his muscles. Her fingers are hot and sharp, her hands strong, and she kneads him like dough. She digs into him and finds something deep, and then she works it like there's no tomorrow. The pain is an animal gnawing at him with razor-sharp incisors.

"What the hell are you doing?" he grunts.

"You've got a huge knot back here. All kinds of stress. Like you've been carrying a heavy load for a long time."

"Have you met Henry?"

"The issues are in the tissues," says Jeanie. "The body is a mirror of the mind."

"It feels like you're ripping my liver out," Jeremy says.

"Good. That means it's working. Didn't they give you exercises to do when you were in therapy?"

"Yes."

"Are you doing them?"

"Sort of," he says. "When I remember."

"You have to do them. They're very important." She touches his right shoulder, where several words are written. "Jorgensen," she reads. "Cowbell. Squiddy. Rocks. What are these?"

"Names," says Jeremy.

"Friends?"

"Used to be." Back when I still had friends, he thinks. He hadn't ever thought to get Smarty's name added to the list. By the time he got out of the hospital, he couldn't bear the thought of anything else jabbing into his flesh.

"Oh, Jeremy," she says, as it dawns on her who they are. "I'm so sorry."

"Why? Did you kill them?"

"Can't a person say something nice to you?"

"No," he says.

She touches his left shoulder, where there's another, more subtle scar. "What was here? On this shoulder?"

"Another tattoo."

"I can see that. A tattoo of what?"

"Nothing. Never mind."

"They look like tally marks. Five of something. Five what? Five years?" She flicks his earlobe with her finger. "Five girlfriends?"

She's trying to make a joke, to cheer him up. He wonders if he should tell her the truth. Five was his official count. Unofficially, it might have been higher. You never really knew. They used to whisk their bodies away as soon as they fell. They knew how much pride Americans took in numbers. Uncanny how they could just meld into the hills.

"Never mind, Jeanie," Jeremy says. "I had it burned off. That means I don't have to talk about it anymore." Which is another lie, because it is burned into his brain forever.

"If only it was that easy," says Jeanie. So she knows he's lying.

But she doesn't ask him any more questions.

Jeremy stays on the floor. They order Chinese food. Henry panics over the soup but loves the egg rolls. Jeanie Rae is quiet. Jeremy is too tired to care. Soon it's time for bed. Henry gets the couch. Jeanie takes the floor. She insists that Jeremy use her bed. It smells of her hair and some kind of lotion. He lies there and, despite his extreme fatigue, doesn't sleep a wink. In the morning, before either of them are up, Jeremy dresses and eases out the front door.

14

JEREMY'S almost forgotten that he's been to New York once before this, back when he was still stationed at Fort Drum. He'd made a road trip along with three other guys, each of them with a pocketful of cash to fork over to bartenders and tuck into G-strings. Smarty came along on that particular trip too. But while Jeremy and the others, whose names he can't remember now, scattered their money in bars and strip clubs across the city, flaunting their uniforms and their fake IDs— they were just nineteen or twenty then, too young to drink legally, as if alcohol would corrupt their innocence when drill sergeants and grenade practice had failed to do so—Smarty had gone home to Queens to visit his parents. Smarty had laughed at them for being such rubes. Why pay to look at naked women, he said, when you can see them on the Internet for free? He did not seem to understand that they wanted also to experience the throb and hum of the city for themselves, that such a thing was strange and wonderful to them, that they were corn-fed small-town boys for whom the sight of one beautiful woman walking down the street was enough to talk about for days. Manhattan held no allure for Smarty. It was a playground in his backyard. For him, the real draw had been his mother's matzo ball soup.

There were two schools of thought on what went into the perfect matzo ball. There were those who liked them thick and dense, so that they sank to the bottom of the bowl, and there were those who liked them light and fluffy, so that they floated. Smarty and his family belonged to the latter camp: they were diehard floaters. It took real culinary talent to make a matzo ball that floated. Anybody could make a sinker. It was a serious matter. Wars had been fought over less.

"Like in that Jonathan Swift essay about eggs," Smarty had said to him. "You know the one I mean? The one about the war between the people who liked to crack their soft-boiled eggs on the big end, and the people who cracked them on the small end?"

"There was a war about that?" Jeremy had asked.

"Not really," Smarty said. "It was a satire. It was really about how wars get fought over stupid reasons."

"Oh," Jeremy said, and for the hundredth time he'd reflected on how he would never, if he lived ten lifetimes in a library, know as many things as Smarty.

Smarty had tried to get Jeremy to come home with him, so he could experience the wonder of floating matzo balls for himself, but Jeremy had refused. A visit to Smarty's parents seemed like a grievous waste of precious drinking time. He regrets that now. You will never lie on your deathbed and wish you'd gotten drunk just once more. But you will rue the fact that you didn't linger over a bowl of chicken soup with matzo balls floating in it.

There will be wet T-shirt contests in downtown Dubai before Jeremy drives Rico's car anywhere again. He takes the subway to Queens, following a memorized address, asking directions three or four times before finding himself in front of a two-story brownstone that is indistinguishable, to him, from the hundreds of others of which Queens appears to be made.

Inside, it's a museum consecrated to the memory of Ari P. Garfunkel, KIA April 7, 2007, and curated by his parents, Amichai and Leila, who are short and wizened and remind Jeremy of nothing so much as a couple of well-meaning but dysfunctional elves. Jeremy wishes he'd called ahead. His arrival is greeted like an event out of the Bible. They know his name. They even know his face. It's as if they've been waiting all this time for him to show up.

Smarty once claimed that his parents were already ninety years old when he was born. He was their only child, destined from birth either for accounting—his father's preference—or dentistry—his mother's. Smarty had thwarted them both; he'd become a trained killer. It was either that or do something crazy, he'd said with a straight face. Imitating his mother's voice, he would often read aloud from her emails, which were laundry lists of all the things that might possibly go wrong while he was out of her sight. His father's messages were similarly paranoid, cautioning him about the dangers of venereal disease and trench foot, and urging Smarty to go to USO performances to keep his morale up.

"He thinks I'm fighting World War II," Smarty had explained. "Next thing you know, he'll be sending me a pinup of the Andrews Sisters."

"Who're the Andrews Sisters?" Jeremy had asked. "And what's a pinup?"

"The Andrews Sisters were hot pieces of ass from the forties," Smarty told him. "Pinups were what guys used to whack off to before they invented the Internet."

"I sorta thought people didn't used to whack off in the old days," Jeremy said.

"Yeah, right," Smarty had said. "Whacking off is older than religion. God even mentions it in the Old Testament."

"He does? What does He say?"

"He says, Don't whack off. We need more Jews."

"So it's okay for non-Jews to whack off?"

"Knock yourself out," Smarty told him. "Just use a sock. And not one of mine, either, Shitbird."

Now the three of them sit in the living room, Amichai and Leila on the couch, Jeremy on a wingback chair. Jeremy balances a china cup and saucer on his knee. It is, he believes, the first time he's ever drunk actual tea, and certainly the first time he's ever had occasion to use such a fine receptacle. He's counted no fewer than twenty pictures of their son around the room. In one of them, Jeremy and Smarty have their arms around each other's shoulders. They wear olive drab tank tops. Their heads are shaved except for a stripe of hair down the middle. They're standing before a group of low trees, the Helmand River glimmering behind them.

He remembers the day that picture was taken. They'd only been in country for a week or so. Smarty appears stunned by the heat and the emptiness of the countryside. I'm from New York, he'd said. I've never actually seen dirt before.

That morning, they had called in a drone attack on a house. Afterward, they visited the scene. A whole family had been wiped out: a mother and her three daughters. Only the father survived. He wasn't Taliban. He was just a guy. They'd called in the wrong house. Woot had brought the whole squad along to witness as he offered the man seven thousand dollars cash. This was the going rate for collateral damage on this scale: two grand apiece for the woman and the two older girls and another thousand for the baby. On behalf of the United States of America, said Woot through their translator, I would like to apologize for your loss. We know this money will not bring your wife and daughters back. But we hope it will go some way toward helping you start again.

The man sat limply, the bag of money in his lap. He stared at it like it was a dead fish. After a while he nodded. Woot said he was sorry again. Then they all got up to leave.

The man said something. The other men who were sitting around him, sharing in his grief, nodded in agreement.

What was that? Woot said to the translator.

The translator shrugged.

What did he say? Woot demanded. Tell me.

He said Afghanistan will be your graveyard, said the translator.

Woot and the rest of them looked at the man. He was expressionless, unmoving. The bag of money still sat in his lap. He wasn't looking at them. He was just staring at nothing. It was not a threat. It was just a statement.

Yeah, well, fuck him, said Woot.

And that was that.

Look at it this way, Woot told them all later. Seven grand is a fortune to that guy. Those girls were liabilities to him. That's the way these people think. You gotta put yourself in their head. He would have had to pay that much in dowries just to marry them off someday.

What a bargain, Smarty had muttered to Jeremy.

After that, they'd moved on and stopped to eat, and they'd been drawn to the river, which beckoned them with its coolness and its promise of relaxation. For a moment Jeremy had felt as if they were small boys, as if it would be more natural for them to capture some crayfish and build a miniature battle arena out of some rocks and watch the crayfish fight to the death. Or hunt for tadpoles. Or else maybe strip down to their boxers and go swimming. He'd resented their uniforms then, and their guns, and the whole war, and that was when he realized he had made a horrible mistake in joining an organization that bought the lives of mothers and children out of its petty cash account. In that moment with Smarty by the river, he hadn't wanted to be a soldier anymore; he just wanted to be Jeremy. Things had started to go south for him shortly after that. And Smarty had understood. He didn't want to be a soldier anymore either. It was all a load of bullshit, he'd said. The war, the politics behind it, the lies, the manipulation of the soldiers' minds by their commanders. Patriotism itself. All a bunch of hooey. Seven thousand dollars for a dead wife and three dead little girls.

Most of the pictures in the Garfunkel living room were taken by Smarty himself. He'd always had his camera out. So I can remember my camping trip to hell, he'd explained. He took pictures of everything that moved, everything that burned, everything that flew. And bodies. Lots of bodies. Jeremy wonders whatever happened to those. His trophies, he'd called them. Jeremy had said that was sick, taking pictures of dead people. And Smarty had launched into a lecture on the scalp-taking habits of the Plains Indians, as if that had anything to do with anything.

Someday, he'd said, we'll be old men, and we'll want to remember all this. All of it.

I won't, said Jeremy. Not all of it. Not any of it.

Well, I do, said Smarty. I'm going to write about this when I get home. I'm going to write a book that will blow the whole thing wide open. The *Catch-22* of our generation.

What's a *Catch-22*? Jeremy had asked.

It's a book, Smarty said. A brilliant book. And it's a concept. You and me, Shitbird, we're in a catch-22 right now. We were crazy to join the fucking army and now we're sane enough to want to get out of it. But if you're sane enough to realize how crazy all this shit is, then you're mentally healthy enough to fight. Fit enough to die. Like when they check a prisoner on death row to make sure he's healthy enough to be executed.

They do that? Jeremy had asked.

But Smarty hadn't answered him directly. He just stared glumly into the river, and said, We're fucked.

"You don't like the tea?" Leila suggests. "I'll make you something else." Smarty's imitation of her voice had been dead-on. When she talks, Jeremy hears him doing her. It's discombobulating.

"It's lavender, of course he doesn't like it," says Amichai. "It tastes like soap. A young man should drink beer. I have a six-pack in the fridge, Jeremy."

"No, the tea is fine," says Jeremy. To prove it, he takes another sip. It doesn't taste like soap at all; it tastes like an old lady's neck.

"He likes it, see?" says Leila. "You want some more, honey?"

"No, thanks," says Jeremy.

"Why not? What's the matter with it?"

"Lei," says Amichai in a tone of ultimate weariness, "Jesus Christ."

Amichai is in his mid-sixties, an older, balder version of Smarty. Leila is a handful of years younger. She wears a halter top and shorts, as if defying anyone to point out that at her age she really shouldn't be. The undersides of her arms quiver like turkey wattles as she passes a plate of cookies one more time.

"Ari mentioned you plenty of times to us," she tells Jeremy. "He was always talking about you. So nice that he made such a good friend. Did he ever use that special toothpaste I sent him?"

"Stop with the toothpaste," Amichai says. "It's painful."

"I'm just asking," says Leila. "A mother likes to know these things."

"He didn't come to talk about toothpaste. He came to talk about Ari."

"We're so glad you're here," says Leila. "You're the first person our son knew who's come to see us. Did he have a lot of friends?"

"He was very well liked, ma'am," says Jeremy. "He had a good sense of humor."

"He got that from me," Amichai says. "The Jews are a very humorous people. I'll tell you a joke."

"Oh, no, here we go," says Leila.

"A Jewish boy comes home, tells his mother he's getting married. She says, who is it? Do I know her? He says, I'm gonna bring in three girls and you guess which one she is. So he brings in three girls and lines them up. His mother says, You're gonna marry the one on the right. He says, Ma, how did you know? She says, Because I don't like her."

"This is no time for such jokes," says Leila.

"It's always a time for jokes," says Amichai. "There was never a better time for jokes than this."

"You could at least tell ones I haven't already heard ten thousand times," Leila says.

"I tell jokes so I don't cry," Amichai says to Jeremy. "You can cry, or you can laugh. I do a lot of both. So. You were there on that day."

Jeremy nods. "Yes, sir," he says.

"Tell us about it."

"No, no, don't, I can't," says Leila. "I can't listen."

"To be honest, my memory is pretty hazy," Jeremy says. "I'm not sure I can tell you any more than you already know."

"There was an explosion?" Amichai says. "An IED? This much the army told us."

"Oh my God," says Leila, as if she's hearing this for the first time.

"She wants to hear," Amichai tells Jeremy. "But she's still very upset. We sat shiva for a month. That means mourning. We'd still be doing it, but we would have starved to death by now, and what would be the point of that? We have a duty to our son to stay alive."

"He was our only child. Came to us late in life, when I was already thirty-eight years old. A miracle baby," says Leila. "He wasn't at all healthy when he was born."

"He was fine," says Amichai. "A little on the thin side, maybe."

"He was sick a lot as a boy," Leila says.

"He was never sick a day in his life," Amichai corrects her. "You know anything about Jewish mothers, Jeremy? I'll tell you this one. What's the difference between a Jewish mother and a Rottweiler? Eventually, the Rottweiler lets go."

"You're horrible," says Leila. "Don't listen to him, Jeremy."

"Tell us about that day," says Amichai.

"It happened fast," says Jeremy. "Everything happened fast there. Ari went quickly," he adds, though he has no idea if this is true. "I hope that makes you feel a little better. He didn't feel a thing."

"We didn't know that," Leila says. "We wondered, oh God, we wondered."

"Thank God for that," Amichai says. "Thank you for saying this to us, Jeremy. It brings us some peace." He blows his nose. "This is good for us. Good to have you here. It makes us feel a little closer to Ari again. Tell me something. Was my son a good soldier?"

What was a good soldier? Did they even know? They probably thought a good soldier was someone who stood up straight and kept his uniform neat and clean and charged fearlessly into enemy lines. In reality, it was the Als of the world who were what the army considered good soldiers. He followed orders without asking questions. By that standard, Smarty was the worst soldier in the army. He asked questions about everything. He questioned the very existence of the ground under his feet.

"He was the best soldier I ever met," Jeremy says. "Probably the best in the whole platoon."

Leila nods in satisfaction. "He wanted to do his part to help those people over there," she tells Jeremy. "When the Towers came down, he told us he was joining. He was too young then. But he waited. I was kinda hoping he would forget about it. But he was proud, you know, he loved his country. And he loved being a Jew. My family was wiped out in the Holocaust. He used to get so mad, hearing those stories. He wanted to do something. He almost went to Israel and joined the army there. But Israel doesn't have any good baseball teams."

"We did not think it was advisable for him to join the army," Amichai says. "For obvious reasons."

"But he said he had to do it," Leila says. She grabs a tissue from a box and wipes her eyes. "He wasn't going to sit around and let other people do the fighting."

They're talking about a version of Smarty he never knew, Jeremy realizes. A pre-training Smarty, a Smarty who was still naive enough to think that his good intentions might make a difference.

"A total waste of his brain. He was tops in his class at school," Amichai says. "His uncle is a rabbi. He has three cousins in Israel, all Talmud scholars."

"And another one who's a doctor," Leila says.

"My brother moved there with his family back in the seventies. For me, no thank you. I would miss the Yankees too much. Did Ari ever talk about baseball?"

"All the time."

"We used to go to games, he and I. Every season opener, and as many as we could get to after that. He could pitch, too. What else?"

Jeremy thinks. "I dunno. We just used to talk a lot. It seemed like he knew everything about everything."

"He loved to read," Leila says. "Always with his nose in a book."

"He would have been a great writer," Amichai says, emphasizing this point with a wagging finger. "Of this I'm sure. He used to talk about it all the time. He loved all the great Jewish writers. Roth, Bellow, Singer, Shmollus. He used to write short stories. He would try to imitate them, and he would send them out to those waddaya-call-'em."

"Zines," Leila says. "That's what they call online magazines," she explains to Jeremy, who nods as if he's never heard this term before. "He was a great one for the Internet. He knew all about it. Always on his computer. Tell us more, Jeremy."

"He's telling. Don't push, Lei," says Amichai. "He's a quiet guy. You can see that."

"He talked about you both a lot," Jeremy says. "You were very important to him."

Amichai nods. Tears begin to leak from behind his glasses. Leila folds her hands in front of her face.

"You want a sandwich?" she asks. "A little schmaltz? That's what we call chicken fat."

"When in doubt, offer food," Amichai says dryly. "I was raised on that stuff. Now I can't smell it without wanting to heave."

"I'm fine," says Jeremy.

"You stick around here long enough, you'll be speaking Yiddish. Tell me again. Was Ari a good soldier?" Amichai says.

"He was tough," says Jeremy, wondering how many times he's going to be asked this.

Amichai nods. "I taught him that. You have to be tough to be a Jew." He spreads his arms, shrugs. "And not just because of anti-Semitism. Listen, we have it bad. How bad? I'll tell you. Two old Jewish ladies go out to a restaurant. The waiter comes up to them and says, 'Is *anything* all right?'" He sits back in his chair. "That's how it is," he says, nodding, and then he must wipe his eyes again.

Amichai takes Jeremy upstairs. They go into Smarty's room. It's small, neat, the bed made. More pictures. A bookshelf over-flows. A Stone Age computer sits on the desk, as clean as the day it came out of the box.

"We kept it the same," he says. "We can't bear to change it. Go in, go in. I want to show you something." He fires up the computer. "Pictures," he says, and navigates the Internet clum-sily, an old man in a weird new world, until he comes to a photo-sharing site. "Sit," he says.

Jeremy sits. Peering at the monitor, he sees folders of pho-tos.

Amichai points to one. "Ari took all these. Lots of them from Afghanistan. You want to see?"

"Sure, okay," says Jeremy, though he would rather not. The last thing he wants to see now is one of Smarty's gory battlefield snapshots. His parents think he was a gung ho patriot. Fine. Let them think that. Jeremy knows the truth: every time Smarty took another picture, he got angrier. There were times he grew so disgusted that he would fall silent for hours, just staring.

He opens the folder, wary, and is relieved to see it con-tains nothing but harmless shots of scenery, military vehicles, men standing around in groups smiling. He recognizes many of their faces. Some of their names are tattooed on his shoulder. There are lots of photos of sunsets. The dust in the air created some spectacular colors. Ari had taken hundreds of photos and uploaded them whenever he had a chance. There are perhaps a dozen more folders. He doesn't want to click through them. He hopes Amichai doesn't intend to drag him moment by moment through Smarty's tour. That would be agony.

"This one," Amichai says, tapping the monitor with one stubby finger. "I can't open it. You try."

Jeremy regards the folder in question. It's labeled Personal. He clicks it, and a box pops up, blank, cursor blinking, waiting for a response to its secret prompt. Smarty had protected it.

"It needs a password, see?" says Amichai. "I've tried everything I can think of. No dice."

"I have no idea what it could be," Jeremy says, though he knows very well what it is.

"What's in there, I wonder? Pornography? He liked those big-titted black girls. This much I know. I wouldn't be shocked. A father is curious, that's all."

"Sorry I can't help," says Jeremy.

"Ah, well," Amichai sighs, and turns the computer off again. "Here, I want you to take something of his. To remember him by."

"You don't have to give me anything," says Jeremy. He struggles out of the chair.

"I know, I know. Take a book. Here, look at this one." From the bookcase Amichai picks up a familiar-looking paperback, inches thick. "He used to talk about this book. He had it with him over there." He hands it to Jeremy. "Endless Behest. Shmollus was one of his favorites. Me, I can't read it. My eyes are going. The print is too small. Getting old is a pain in the *tokhes*. That means ass." He presses the book into Jeremy's hands. "It's yours. Something to remember him by."

"Thanks," says Jeremy.

"So, Jeremy, tell me something. In front of his mother, I didn't want to ask this. But I have to know, for my own personal reasons. Did my son kill anyone?"

Jeremy looks down at the book in his hand. He remembers Smarty reading this one. The cover is smeared with dust— Afghanistan dust, he realizes. He opens the book, sees Smarty's cramped handwriting in the margins. He'd been making notes. Analyzing it, the way he analyzed everything else. What does Amichai want to hear? The truth, he realizes.

"Yes," he says.

Amichai nods. "Good. I'm glad he did his part. Don't tell Leila. She doesn't need to know these things. Women don't understand.

And I don't want to know how many. This I don't need to hear. I just want to know he helped his friends."

"You always knew Smarty had your back," says Jeremy.

Amichai nods. "Like Leila said, we raised him on stories of the Holocaust. For years, he was obsessed with it. He got so mad. He used to say, Why didn't we fight back? I had no answer for him. Too complicated to explain to a kid. I don't understand myself. He said when he grew up he was going to fight. I wasn't a fighter. I was too bookish. I don't know where he got this from. Maybe we told him too many stories. But a Jew needs to know these things. And I was proud he wanted to fight. Those people over there, they'd kill all of us if they could. Not just Jews. All of us. Cut our heads off. Animals. If he did his duty, then the world really is a better place." Amichai pats the book, satisfied. "You want anything else of his? Look around."

"No, no," says Jeremy.

"A baseball? One of his hats? You're bigger than him. His mother still washes his clothes once a week. So they don't get musty. It's maybe not healthy. But you know women. A T-shirt?"

"This is enough. Thanks."

"It makes me happy, meeting you," Amichai says. "And what you said—it makes me happy too. Maybe it shouldn't, but it does." He pats the book again. "I picked this book to give you for a reason. It has a lot of stuff in it. Ari's thoughts. He talked about it a lot, how much he admired this writer. Maybe it will help you feel closer to him. You can think of him when you read it. It helped me understand him better, seeing the things he thought about. We're glad you came, Jeremy. You know what your name means in Hebrew?"

"No," says Jeremy.

"It means 'God will raise you up and set you free.' You didn't know you had a Hebrew name?"

"I had no idea."

"See? You learned something new today. All our names have a meaning. My name means 'our people are alive.' My parents named me this because of what happened in Europe. It was a big middle finger to the Nazis. I used to say to my dad, Maybe you should have named me Fuck You Hitler. Now that would be some name." He touches Jeremy on the shoulder, adjusts his glasses. "We picked Ari's name because it means 'lion.' I dreamed he would be a warrior, see, when Leila was pregnant with him. Not a modern soldier. In my dream, he looked like an ancient Israelite. Sword-and-shield-type stuff. Slaying the enemies of God. That was how I thought of him. But I never thought he would become a real soldier. Then he did. And look what happened." He shakes his head. "Look what happened to my beautiful boy," he says, and closes the bedroom door.

On the train back to Manhattan, another headache comes. At first he thinks someone's slapped him on the back of the head. He half turns, ready for a fight, but there's no one behind him except his own reflection, glimpsed sideways out of the corner of his eye, leering emptily like a ghost. Then the knife appears from the deep again, emerging blade first from some part of himself he's never had a name for. He keels forward.

"Stop it," Jeremy whispers. But no one can hear him over the rush of the wheels on the tracks.

15

HE WAKES in some kind of waiting room.

Maybe wakes isn't the right word. He was never asleep. He just gradually falls back into his body. He looks around and sees people sitting in rows of plastic chairs screwed onto long metal beams. Nurses occupy a partitioned desk at the front.

So he's in a hospital. America or Afghanistan?

Neither. New York.

He feels his back pocket. His wallet is still there. The courier bag is still over his shoulder. Jeremy looks inside. The book Amichai gave him is there too. So he hasn't been mugged.

The afternoon comes back to him gradually, trickling down into place like Tetris blocks. But many of the pieces are still missing.

To his right is a young black man with dreadlocks, pressing a bloody gauze pad to his palm. To his left, a young mother sits, a listless child coughing on her lap. The place looks like some kind of third world infirmary.

"Hey," Jeremy says to the guy with dreadlocks. "How did I end up here?"

The guy shrugs his shoulders. "I dunno, man. Just unlucky, I guess."

After a while, his name is called. He follows a nurse into a consultation room and she takes his information. Then she leaves. After another wait, a pretty young Asian woman in a white coat comes in.

"You the doctor?" he asks.

"Physician's assistant," she says. "The doctor will be in shortly. I'm told you don't remember coming in."

"Nope."

"Wanna tell me what happened?"

"I don't really know. I get these headaches," Jeremy says. "They're getting worse all the time."

"How long has that been going on?"

"Last couple of years."

"How did they start?"

"I was in a blast. I guess that's where they come from. But they did an MRI on me in the VA hospital in California. They didn't find anything."

"You're a veteran."

"Yeah." This is the first time he's sat alone with a pretty woman in years, not counting Jeanie. It's almost like a date. He can't help but spin a tale in his mind about how nice it would be to go home with her, play house for a while. She tucks a loose strand of hair behind her ear, and he looks at this ear intently, mapping its terrain as though it were a piece of land he must figure out how to conquer. It's a cross-section of a nautilus shell, a labyrinth in a cornfield, an illustration of the Fibonacci sequence as applied to the perfect geometry of the female body. He wonders what secrets have been whispered into that ear, how many languages it understands, and he marvels at the fact that right now it is bent toward him, absorbing the vibrations made in the air by the twanging of his vocal cords, her own tympanic membrane vibrating in sympathy and transferring these messages to her lovely brain. He has never felt so flattered by an ear before.

"Iraq?"

"Afghanistan."

She nods. "What size was the bomb?"

"Big. Maybe fifty pounds."

"Any fatalities?"

"Why . . . why do you ask?"

She blushes. What an odd thing to do, Jeremy thinks. She's embarrassed.

"Sorry," she says. "We always ask. So we can figure out how close the blast was. How serious it was."

"Oh, it was serious. It was a very serious bomb. The people who made it really meant business."

"So . . ."

"Three," he says. "Ari Garfunkel, Zachary Smith, and Thomas Jefferson. No relation to the president." He smiles, to show this was a joke. But she doesn't get it. How could she? She doesn't know Jefferson was black, though he'd claimed direct lineage to the famous Thomas Jefferson anyway. That was Smarty's doing. He'd told Jefferson how they'd proved through DNA that the famous Jefferson had living black descendants, a result of his affair with one of his slaves. Jefferson had never been able to let that one go. He'd insisted everyone call him Mr. President after that.

The physician's assistant takes a penlight from the breast pocket of her coat and holds it up. "Follow?" she says. He follows the beam with his eyes. "Look straight ahead?" she says, and she peers closely into him. She clicks the light off. "Any pain now?"

"Not in my head."

"Where?"

"My back," he says. "But that's always there."

"Any other head injuries in your history?"

"I've never had a head injury at all."

"None that you know of, you mean. Taking any drugs? Drink a lot?"

"No," says Jeremy. I'd be safe to bring home to your parents.

"Then how do you deal?" she says, and looks at him, waiting.

I'll never lie to you, he thinks. Our marriage will be based on trust. I'll be home every night at five-thirty from the office, and you will meet me at the door of our perfect little house with a drink in your perfect little hand. No, wait, you're a doctor. I'll be the one waiting for you. I'll be a househusband. A glass of wine on the counter with your name on it, a pot of something bubbling on the stove. I'll be the one in the apron. I'll learn to cook for you. I'll change all the diapers. I'll give you a foot rub after a long day in the operating room.

"I smoke a lot of pot," he says. "I mean, I drink a lot of pot. I make tea out of it. I don't like smoking it very much."

"I thought you said you don't take drugs."

"Pot isn't a drug. It's a flower." I'll give you flowers every day, he thinks. I'll grow a flower garden just for you.

"You should quit," she says softly.

"It's the only thing that helps the pain. Pills messed up my stomach. Too many side effects."

She writes on a clipboard. Then she snaps the pen down and faces him, hands prim in her lap. She has a good doctor face. It's a face that lets him know he's going to believe completely in whatever she's about to tell him.

"I can tell you a few things, based on what we know now. Just because they didn't find anything in the imaging doesn't mean there wasn't damage. There could be a kind of invisible damage. Blast waves can have effects on you that we can't pick up yet. We don't know how to see them. We only know from the symptoms."

"Invisible damage?"

"If you were badly concussed, yes. And it sounds like you were. The latest research shows that blast waves can change your brain forever." He loves the way she pronounces "research." English is not her first language. He reimagines her childhood to have taken place in crazed, traffic-packed streets in some sweltering, far-off city. Men whipping around on mopeds; crowds of women coming home from the market with live chickens under their arms, or baskets of flopping fish balanced on their heads.

"Change it how?"

"Well, there can be debilitating neurological conditions. Loss of motor function, balance, consciousness. These inhibit your ability to operate equipment, such as cars. Headaches, such as you're experiencing now. In the worst-case scenario, some men die of their injuries, years after they were inflicted."

"Are you serious? They die?"

"That's the worst case," the woman explains.

"But how?"

"When this does happen, it's usually due to an aneurysm. But I don't want to worry you unnecessarily. This is highly infrequent. If you feel yourself getting stressed or exhausted, you should stop and rest. To be honest, a bigger worry with veterans is suicide. Are you having any thoughts like that? Like you want to . . ."

"Off myself? No," Jeremy says. He decides not to tell her that he feels like blowing his brains out every time a headache comes.

"You having any mood swings?"

"Sometimes I get mad. Like, really mad. Beyond-all-reason mad. And I have these panic attacks, too."

She nods. "You need to go back to the VA as soon as possible. If your headaches are getting worse, there may be a big event on the way. Unfortunately, we can't do anything for you here. This is just an emergency clinic."

"What can they do for me at the VA?"

"To be honest, I don't know. You're going to have to wait for medical technology to catch up with you. There's a lot of guys in your situation."

"You mean other guys having headaches? Other vets?"

"Yeah."

"How many?"

"Thousands. Maybe tens of thousands."

"Oh," says Jeremy. "That many?"

"It's an epidemic," she says as she stands. "If you wait here, the doctor will be in to see you. He can tell you more. I have to go now. I wish you the best of luck."

"Wait," he says, and she sits on the stool again. "What's your name?"

"I'm PA Zhang," she says.

"No, I mean your first name."

"Why do you want to know my first name?"

"So I know how to think of you," Jeremy says.

She doesn't want to tell him, he can see that. But for a moment she drops her guard. She trusts him. Maybe because he's so broken she knows he's not dangerous.

"Evelyn," she says.

"Evelyn. You're about the prettiest doctor I've ever seen."

She looks at him sharply. "I'm a physician's assistant," she says.

"What's the difference?"

"The difference is I'm not a physician."

"You want to grab a cup of coffee sometime?"

"Are you asking me on a date?"

"Yes. No. Wait. Nothing too heavy-duty. Just to talk some more. I like talking to you."

"I am not permitted to date patients."

"Call it a consultation, then," Jeremy says. "You can tell me more about what's going on inside my head. You seem to know more than I do."

"I'm extremely busy," says Evelyn. "I need to go now. Please remember what I said. Get back to the VA as soon as you can." She almost smiles at him, her eyes lingering on his face for a moment. But then she gets up and leaves, breaking his heart like a frozen glass shattering on a tile floor.

When she's gone, Jeremy walks out. Whatever happens to me next in this hospital will be a letdown after that, he thinks. Better quit while I'm ahead.

Outside, he discovers he's on 14th Street. It's a warm day, and after a couple of blocks he's sweating. He has no idea where he's going. Sweat doesn't evaporate here in the East; it just clings to you like a film. He feels the need to squeegee himself.

He hears Smarty's voice suddenly, as if he's standing right beside him, or in his head: the Romans used to strigil themselves in the public baths. That's like a kind of body scraper. They would scrape off all the sweat and dirt and let it drip on the floor. And then they'd gather it up and make medicine out of it. The Romans were pretty smart in some ways, but in other ways they were complete morons.

That was Smarty for you. Only he could get away with calling the Romans morons.

He walks for a while longer. Up ahead he sees a park. It's got a broad, shallow fountain in it, around which people are sitting. On the pavement, other people are walking or Rollerblading or skating, enjoying the sunshine.

He sits on the edge of the fountain, feeling the cool breeze from the spray on his back and watching all the people. He wonders if he could ever get used to this much humanity. Within the space of minutes, he hears at least five different languages being spoken among the passersby, French and German and Spanish and some other Romance language, maybe Italian, plus something Asian he's not able to identify. His heart is broken at least three more times, and they are perfect, all three of them, crisp and tight and sweaty in their shorts and tank tops, and utterly unaware of his existence.

A middle-aged man with wild hair, wearing filthy clothes, is walking along mumbling to himself. When he sees Jeremy, he approaches and says:

"They're coming."

Jeremy looks around. Naturally, no one is paying attention. "Who?" he says.

"The ones who are following you," says the wild-haired man. "They're getting closer."

"Okay," says Jeremy. "Thanks."

"Hundreds of them," says the wild-haired man. "Trying to tell you something."

"Thank you very much. You have a nice day."

"Watch out," says the man. Then he shuffles on, still mumbling.

Moments later, a clean-cut guy in a tracksuit sits down next to him. He says something unintelligible. Jeremy looks at him out of the corner of his eye. Apparently he's a crazy magnet today.

"What did you say?" says Jeremy.

"I said, green buds," the guy says, patting his bag. "Right here."

He's a messenger from the gods. Jeremy looks around. No one is paying attention to this encounter either. You can dance around with a lampshade on your head and no one will notice. He's such a bumpkin. How does one do this? He's never bought pot from anyone except Rico. He doesn't even know how much pot is actually supposed to cost.

"I've got about fifty bucks," he says. "How much will that get me?"

The guy smiles. "For fifty bucks, I can set you up. This is nice stuff, hydroponic." He looks around then opens his bag. Jeremy can smell it from where he's sitting. Suddenly, a memory from television occurs to him. There's something he's supposed to be asking.

"Are you a cop?"

"What? Hell, no, I ain't no cop." The guy closes his bag and prepares to stand up. "Never mind," he says.

"Okay, okay. Wait. I'm sorry. How do we do this?" Jeremy says.

"Just slide me the cash," says the guy. "Be discreet about it."

Jeremy takes his money out of his wallet, crumples it in his fist, slides it along the fountain's edge to the guy's waiting hand. There's already a fat Baggie in it, and Jeremy takes it and stuffs it in the pocket of his jeans.

"Have a nice day," says the guy, and gets up and walks away.

"And a very fine day to you too, sir," says Jeremy.

Now he needs to get back to Jeanie's. He'll make himself a nice pot of tea and kick back on her couch for a couple of hours. They can hang out and talk. Talk about anything but penises. That's fine with him; that's not really one of his favorite topics anyway.

He stands up and makes it about twenty feet before he feels a hand on his shoulder, and something hard presses into his back. Automatically he begins to struggle, and the hand moves from his shoulder to clamp down on his throat.

"That's a nine-millimeter you feel there, so go ahead and fight me," a voice says. "Go ahead, motherfucker. See what happens to you then."

Jeremy freezes. "Let go," he croaks.

"Put your hands behind your back."

Jeremy does as he's told. The hand releases his throat. Two cops appear out of nowhere in front of him. It's as if they've simply levitated out of the pavement. His bag is removed from his shoulder. He feels something encircling his wrists, pulling his back into an unwelcome contortion.

The guy in the tracksuit appears. His demeanor is different now: he's snappy, bouncing on his toes, all business.

"Yeah, that's him," he says.

"Good work, officer," says one of the cops. To the guy in the tracksuit.

"You said you weren't a cop!" Jeremy says through his aching larynx.

"I lied," says the guy in the tracksuit, and then he's gone.

A cop reaches into Jeremy's pocket and pulls out the bag of weed.

"I have a prescription for that," Jeremy says.

"That's nice," says one of the cops. "I have a twelve-inch cock."

The other cop grins broadly at that. "You're under arrest," he says.

"This is insane," Jeremy says. "I'm a decorated veteran."

"Are you resisting?" says one of the cops. "Because if you're resisting, I'm going to pound the shit out of you."

"I'm not—"

"Shut up," the other cop advises him kindly. "Just shut up."

The first cop goes through his other pockets, removing his phone and his wallet. The other goes through his courier bag. For a heart-stopping moment Jeremy wonders if there's a stray ounce or two of Rico's in one of the zippered compartments. They might think he's the dealer. But there's nothing in there except the book Amichai gave him. They put his wallet into a plastic Baggie and seal it.

"You recording any of this?" asks one cop, holding up his smartphone.

"No," says Jeremy.

The cop looks at the phone. He fiddles with the screen, but it's locked. "What's your password?"

"I'm not telling you my password," says Jeremy.

"Fine," says the cop, and tosses the phone onto the pavement and comes down on it with his heel. It shatters into several pieces.

"Hey!" says Jeremy. "What the fuck!"

"That's what you get for recording cops," says the cop.

He knows these types. Arguing is useless. It's like talking to two Als. They frog-march him toward the street. A paddy wagon pulls up and screeches to a halt. Another cop gets out and unlocks the rear doors. Inside, Jeremy sees three other people, blinking in the bright light. All are zip-tied like him. They half escort and half shove him into the rear of the wagon, and he sits down heavily on the bench. His spine shoots up and rebounds off the top of his skull. He nearly faints from the pain. The man on that side scoots over to make room for him. The door slams shut.

When his head clears, Jeremy looks at his new friends. One of them looks like a secretary, a plump woman with a mannish haircut, maybe forty years old. She's weeping quietly, face down. The other two are black men, one in a khaki shirt and chinos, the other in sagging shorts and a sideways baseball hat. They stare straight ahead, a couple of stoics. They look as if they know the drill.

"What the fuck," says Jeremy.

"What the fuck indeed," says the man in chinos.

"I thought cops had to tell you if they were cops."

"That is Hollywood, my friend," says Chino Man. "And this is real life. Welcome to the difference."

The other man says nothing. He radiates a rage that fills the compartment, which is made of riveted sheet metal. It's the kind of vehicle one would use to transport dangerous people. He'd loaded prisoners into similar vehicles himself, after a successful raid. On those rare occasions they took prisoners, that is.

They sit there for a long time. Then the wagon takes off. The driver seems to be making a game of how fast he can take the corners. The four in the back brace themselves against the floor, but they're helpless to keep from smashing into each other. They travel what appears to be only a few blocks, and the wagon screeches to a halt again. Then they just sit.

Time passes, quite a bit of it. It's very hot. There is no air except what comes in through a tiny barred slit in each of the double doors. They sit for so long that Jeremy becomes convinced they've just left them here to die.

"I want a fucking lawyer!" he shouts. "I want a phone call!"

"Hey, man, shut up," says Chino Man. "They'll pound your ass for sure."

"They can't just beat me up," Jeremy says. "That's illegal."

Both of the black men laugh at that.

"Man," says the large angry one, "you really don't know shit, do you."

"No," says Jeremy. "I guess I don't."

The secretary has stopped crying and is now sagging forward in defeat. Either that or she's fainting.

"Hey, lady, you all right?" Jeremy says to her.

"No," she says.

After a long time the door opens, and they get another friend, a young Latino-looking guy whose hands are also zip-tied. He sits across from Jeremy, and they exchange looks.

"Man, what the fuck?" says the Latino guy.

"What the fuck indeed," says Jeremy.

"I wasn't doing nothing! They just fucking grabbed me and went through my shit!"

"You have any weed on you?" says Chino Man.

"I ain't sayin' nothing," Latino Man says.

"Yeah, good," says Chino Man.

"Cleaning up the city," says the larger black man. "Stop and frisk. Make the world a better place." He shakes his head. "Ima kill me every one of these motherfuckers someday."

"Don't say that," says Chino Man, shaking his head. "They hear you, they can charge you."

"Man, what is you, a lawyer?" says the larger man.

"Yes," says Chino Man. "As a matter of fact, I'm a lawyer."

"They arrested a frigging lawyer?" Jeremy says. "Didn't you tell them who you are?"

"No," says Chino Man.

"Why not?"

"Because they didn't arrest a lawyer. They arrested a nigger."

"Straight up," says the larger man. "We all niggers now."

"Stop talking!" a cop screams in the open door.

Then he slams the doors again. More racing through the streets, siren whooping. This ride is longer, and even faster. Then they stop, and the doors open again, and there are cops waiting outside for all of them.

16

A **HANGOVER** when you're twenty years old is one thing. It's a gnat to be swatted away without even thinking about it. A hangover at seventy is quite another. The gnat becomes a dragon, and one must move quietly around it, lest it be roused and unleash a jet of fire from its innards.

Al wakes on the couch without the slightest clue where he is, or even who he is. When he was young and in his prime, he could drink an entire case of beer in a night and wake up at dawn the next morning, maybe even skip sleeping altogether, and work a full day with no apparent ill effects. Now he feels as if he's a can of paint in one of those mixers they have at the hardware store, shaken until all his atoms have been jostled out of place. Maybe, he thinks, this is how Henry used to feel during his seizures. Off his axis. As if he'd been plucked up by the nape of his neck and the world had been shifted six inches to the left. Unsure if it's everything else that's vibrating or just him, he reaches out to touch something, anything, the first thing that comes to hand. This happens to be his own crotch. This is how he discovers he's wet himself.

He slides to the floor. More comfortable there. Must remember to take the couch cushions outside, let them bake in the sun for a few hours. He hopes Rita doesn't come home before then.

Otherwise she'll know he's off the wagon again. Then he remembers: Rita said she wasn't coming home. She's left. As the women in this family do. As everyone does, apparently.

Then he remembers something else. It's the thing he's been remembering for the last three days: Jeremy knows what happened over there. His deepest secret is out, a tiger that's broken free of its cage and is roaming around the house. It was this that had occasioned his first beer in roughly twenty-five years. Maybe more. He stopped counting after a certain point. He was not one of those AA types—couldn't be bothered with the God stuff, or the twelve steps, or the laborious counting of days, or the forgiveness that they were supposed to beg from those they'd wronged during their drinking years. Maybe he'd hurt some people, notably Helen—this he knows and will not deny—but the things he'd done drunk were nothing compared with the things he'd done sober.

It had come as less of a surprise than it should have, that Jeremy'd found out his secret. For many years he'd believed that everyone knew anyway, every person he passed on the street, every colleague and underling at work, every cop who ever eyed him suspiciously. His sins written on his forehead for all the world to see. It had only been a matter of time before these things escaped from his head and became visible. He'd hoped to make it to the end of his life without anyone finding out. And he'd nearly made it.

But the old defensiveness rears its head again. He has nothing to feel guilty about. No more than anyone else who was there, that is. No reason for him to bear the whole thing on his shoulders. He hadn't been an officer, anyway. He was a soldier, and a good one. Which meant that he followed orders.

It takes several minutes for him to have any more coherent thoughts. When he can get up, he goes to the fridge, takes out a beer, and guzzles it greedily. There. Now a man can think.

He peels off his underwear and throws it down the basement stairs, in the general direction of the washing machine. Naked, he sits at the dining room table, his bare ass sticky on the vinyl seat cover. He drinks a second beer at a more leisurely pace and tries to piece together what might have happened the night before. There'd been a conversation with Rita on the phone. That's right. He'd wanted her to come home and make dinner. He doesn't remember what was said, by her or by him. She must have known he was drunk. She could tell. Always could, even when she was little. Judging by the state of the kitchen, and the state of his stomach, no dinner has been made. A package of steaks sits on the counter. He has no idea how long they've been there. In this climate, it doesn't take meat long to turn. They're warm to the touch. He opens the package, smells them, gags. Puts them in the garbage. Has he really been drunk for three days? Amazing how he'd slid right back into it as if he'd never stopped. Just like riding a bicycle.

He must eat something. A frantic search in the pantry yields a can of chicken noodle soup and a package of dried noodles. He puts these together in a pan and heats them up. He manages three bites before he throws up in the sink. Well, good. Let the old poison out to make room for the new. At least he's not hungry anymore. Too sick to eat. But not too sick to drink.

By the third beer, outrage boils up in Al, an anger he hasn't tasted in years.

Nobody understood what had happened there, nobody. The rest of the world had judged them unfairly. The enemy took many forms; he didn't just look like a man in black pajamas with an AK-47 in his arms. That was the way idiots thought. That was the way you got dead. Sometimes the enemy looked like a woman. Sometimes he looked like an old man in one of those pointy straw hats they used to wear, a hat that blocked the sun or shed rain or could be used to carry rice in. Practical little bastards, he had to give them that. Or the enemy might even be a twelve-year-old girl. Anyone could pull a trigger. All you needed was a working finger. By the time they'd rolled into that village, Al had lost count of his friends whose tags had been yanked.

As for the children, well. Children grew up into soldiers. You were not killing them, you were delivering them. Like pulling up a weed before it had a chance to go to seed. You had to stomp evil out before it could take root. That was all it was. A kid was better off dead than growing up Communist. He did not enjoy it. Some of the other guys seemed to. Acted as if the whole thing were some kind of arcade game. That had sickened him at the time, but after a while he made room for the memory of it, and it settled down. Which was not the same as forgetting.

And hadn't he been vindicated? They were no war criminals. Even Jimmy fucking Carter had said so. Of all the people you wouldn't expect to be on your side, he had to be top of the list. But somehow Carter understood better than anyone, that big-toothed frog-gigging peanut farmer, the same clown who'd pardoned the draft dodgers who fucked off up to Canada to play hockey and trap beaver while the brave ones, the real Americans, stayed behind. Al's feelings toward Carter were complicated. He would have preferred to have been understood by a Republican. But he'd take it. Because Carter knew that was the way war went. Either all of them were criminals or none of them were. You didn't train guys to kill and then accuse them of murder. You just let them kill. Nothing else made any sense.

All the same, he knew his reckoning was coming. Because what had happened was wrong. And because Jeremy was right. As soon as you find yourself pointing a gun at women and children, hey presto, you've become a bad guy.

No. No. You couldn't just look at a snapshot and judge it that way. You had to look at the whole thing. You had to play the whole movie from beginning to end.

But he's not going to do that again. He's already done that a thousand times. All he'd learned from that was that looking for the beginning of such an event was as complicated as trying to unravel a world of string. It didn't just start with the rendezvous that morning with Calley, the lieutenant who'd later become famous in the news. Or infamous. It didn't even start with the day he first walked off the transport plane into that country. It was far older than any of that. It started with the war itself; and who knew where that really started?

It would have been better, Al thinks, if he'd never come home from Vietnam. War is like booze: once it has you, it has you forever.

He listens as the swamp cooler kicks into life. Its damp breath blows through the empty house, as hollow-sounding as a child learning to whistle. Everyone's abandoned him. So, this is to be his reward for a lifetime of sacrifice. This is what he fought for— the right to sit naked at his kitchen table and get drunk all by himself. Hardly seems worth it. He must be missing something. There must be some aspect of his freedom that he's overlooked.

Oh, well. Maybe it will occur to him later.

By his sixth beer, which is consumed at ten a.m. according to the clock on the microwave, he knows only one thing: today is the day. The real day. S-hour. No more around-fucking. He's attended to everything, filled out all the papers, had the lawyer double-check everything, got everything notarized. It's iron-clad. He's left nothing undone. Rita will get the house. Jeremy will get what's left of his pension, despite all the things he said. Despite that rain of saliva in his face. Too late to undo it now. There's a clause in the will that he has to take care of Henry. But that, he knew, was unnecessary. Because even though he couldn't be relied on to take out the goddamn garbage, in the end you knew Jeremy was going to do the right thing.

He wishes he could have one more conversation with the boy. Wishes they didn't have to leave things like this between them. But Jeremy will understand. He will never understand the other thing, and that's what makes Jeremy Jeremy.

I'm going to have the last laugh, Al thinks. I'm going to show him what kind of person his grandfather really is.

He thinks of cleaning the house up first, hiding the evidence of his latest fall from the wagon and the piss-soaked couch cushions, but then he realizes this is no longer his problem. Nothing is. He doesn't have any problems anymore.

Oh, wait. Except the hearts.

Dammit. He still hasn't figured out what to do about those.

The box is still sitting in the garage. The garbage hasn't been emptied in two weeks now, and the smell is so bad that for a moment he thinks someone's died in here. Well, this is not his problem either. He doesn't have to worry about any of this crap. Time to pass the torch. He holds his breath, grabs the box of hearts, goes back into the house.

He debates showering, but rejects this as pointless. He also considers dressing up, but that would require showering first. He puts on a pair of shorts and some flip-flops. The less he tries to prepare himself, the better. It has to look unplanned. It has to look as if he got confused and just wandered off. He's old enough for this to be believable, though he's not quite sure how he's gotten to this point. Seems like just yesterday he and Helen were getting married. Rita running around the old Lancaster house in diapers. Jeanie cutting her baby teeth. Just the blink of an eye. You blinked again and the babies were women with babies of their own. How did such things happen?

He walks across the street to the home of Mr. Richard Belton. He rings the doorbell. After an age, he rings it again. Finally one of the Belton kids comes to the door. He's maybe ten years old, a plump maggot of a child, skin as pale as if he's spent his entire life in the sewers. Al doesn't remember having seen him before. For all he knows, Belton has a thousand of them in here. You would never know anyway. Kids don't go outside anymore.

"Hi, kid, who are you?" Al asks.

The kid just looks at him.

"Your dad home? Your mom?"

No answer, just a shake of the head.

"Here," Al says. "This is for you." He takes a heart out of the box, hands it to him.

The kid opens the screen door a crack and takes it. Then he closes the screen door again. Just looking at him.

"Your parents teach you any goddamn manners?" Al asks. "You speak English, kid? *Sprechen sie Deutsch? Parlez-vous français? Có ai đây biết nói tiếng Anh không?*"

"What the heck does that mean?" the kid says.

"See, I knew you were an American. How many brothers and sisters you have?" Al digs around in the box. "Two, three? Eleven? And your parents. Here, take some more. My wife made them. I'm giving them away, free. Okay? Take a whole handful. Tell your folks, those are a present in memory of Helen Merkin. Handmade. One-of-a-kind items. Worth three-fifty apiece. That's a lot of money to a kid like you. I bet you never had three-fifty in your life."

"I get ten dollars a week for my allowance," the kid says.

"Oho. Ten bucks a week. Listen, big shot. You know what minimum wage was when I started working? A dollar an hour. It took me a whole day to earn ten bucks. And that was before the goddamn government took its bite."

"Wow," says the kid dully.

"Yeah, wow," says Al. Jesus, they learned sarcasm young these days. "Lemme ask you something. What do you wanna be when you grow up, kid? A doctor? An insurance salesman? A mime?"

The kid shrugs.

"That's the spirit," says Al. "Listen, in case nobody ever told you this, you know what that flag right there means?"

He turns and points to Old Glory, flapping on a pole in the Beltons' front yard, as it does on nearly every other yard on the street—all panels in a quilt of suburban patriotism, and all no doubt made in China. But the Beltons' pole is cockeyed, and the flag whisks against the withered lawn with the sound of palms rubbing together.

"It means freedom," Al says. "It's a precious gift. So don't fuck—I mean, don't mess it up. It's something you gotta hang on to. Freedom is not a thing, see? It's a way of life. And tell your dad to straighten that pole. It should be straight, right? If the flag touches the ground, it has to be burned. Did you know that?"

"No," says the kid. "I'm not supposed to talk to strangers."

"Stranger? I'm your neighbor," says Al. "I've lived in this house for twenty-three years. That's how much of a stranger I am. Al Merkin's the name. Nice to meet you, kid. Have a good life. And tell your dad he needs to get a new flag. That one's been desecrated. It has to be burned."

He walks down the street. He doesn't bother ringing any more doorbells. He can't handle any more conversations like that. Too depressing. What will America look like when that kid is his age? Who knows. Not his problem anymore. He opens mailboxes, shoves a handful of hearts into each one.

"Compliments of the Merkin family," he says, slamming the little metal doors and putting up the flags. "There. Don't say we never did anything for you."

He keeps this up until the box is empty, except for one. It's a heart that Helen had turned into a brooch, with a kind of clip on the back. As if anyone would ever wear one of these things. He drops the box on the corner and tries several times to pin the heart to his T-shirt. Finally, he succeeds.

"There," he says. "That's the last medal that'll ever get pinned to my chest. Ten-hut!"

He straightens up and salutes. Then he looks around to see if anyone is watching the crazy old man talk to himself, but the street is deserted. People should be out standing in their yards, staring at him, pointing, calling the men in white coats, pulling their children away to safety. He could be walking around with his cock hanging out and nobody would even notice. It feels like noon. It's goddamn hot for September. What day is it? Saturday. Where the hell is everyone?

Oh well, it doesn't matter.

He wishes he'd brought one last beer along with him. But that doesn't matter anymore either.

He turns left at the corner. This takes him into the fake neighborhoods.

"Ouranakis, you genius," he says. "You never had any goddamn intention of building a city. You were a master con man. But I out-conned you, you little Greek fuck. I was actually happy here. I short-sold you. I bet you would lose, and I won. So fuck you, you ouzo-swilling motherfucker."

He comes to the place where the road ends and the desert begins. He takes a few steps on the dirt, but it's too soft, and his flip-flops hamper him. The dirt is painfully hot on his feet when he kicks them off. This doesn't matter either. He's gleeful at the prospect of going to the place where things don't matter, nothing at all—not vanished retirement funds, not pissed-off grandsons, not ungrateful daughters, not even wet couch cushions or overflowing garbage cans.

They won't ever know of his final sacrifice. That he's doing this for them. That it's not an accident. But they can't know. No one can. A real soldier doesn't brag about what he gives up to help the cause. He just gives it.

He walks for a long time. When he turns to look behind him, the town is already a distant memory, barely visible. He looks ahead again, shielding his eyes with his hand. Jesus, it's hot. Too hot. Or is this normal? The way they talk about the weather these days, he doesn't even know anymore. It's gotten to the point where even the temperature is a source of hysteria. The country's full of old women wringing their hands. Let's panic over everything. Why not? We can if we want. That's what it means to be free, too.

The hills are before him now. He stops to contemplate them. Something moves out there. Squinting through the glare, he sees what it is: a dog. It's looking right at him.

"Proton," Al says. "Holy shit. C'mere, dog."

The dog, if it is Proton, seems to have heard him. It takes a few steps in his direction, tail wagging, tongue lolling. Then it runs back the way it came, stops, turns, looks at him.

"All right," Al says. "You wanna play, we'll play. I thought you were dead, dog. I thought you had it for sure." He laughs, then laughs again at the way his laugh sounds, a wheezy old man's cackle. How ridiculous to be this age.

"You are Proton, aren't you? Not a coyote? Or a wolf? Or a monster? Gonna eat me? Huh? Gonna eat me, boy? Just make it fast. That's all I ask. None of this lingering around for days and days. I might have to crack if that's the way it's gonna be. I might be too much of a pussy for that. I never was tortured or anything. I used to wonder how I would handle it, if they ever got their hands on me. They never did, though. I was too quick for them. Too quick for everybody."

The dog comes closer. It cocks its head at him, just the way Proton used to do. It's him for sure.

Then it turns and heads back toward the hills, looking once over its shoulder.

"All right," says Al. "I get your message. I'm coming. I'm gonna follow you, Proton. Just go slow. Have a little mercy on an old man, Proton. Have just a little mercy."

17

AT FIRST, Jeremy's in a cell that's crammed so full there's
no room for anyone to be anything other than extremely
irritable. There's one toilet, which is exposed to the world,
and it stinks of every bodily substance, every excretion, every bit
of despair that has ever been exuded. After a while Jeremy works
his way into a corner, where he grabs the bars above his head,
trying to stretch his back out. At least they'd taken those damn
zip ties off. Judging from the conversations he overhears, everyone was in the middle of doing something else when they ended
up here. It's never a convenient time to be arrested.

Sometimes a couple of guards appear and call someone's
name, and then that person is taken away and there's more space
in the cell. It seems to be a special day. They're arresting lots of
people. Cleaning up the city. Across the corridor is another cage,
full of women in their twenties. They're from some kind of protest. They're chanting about Wall Street. How do you protest a
street? Jeremy wonders. If Smarty were here, he would explain.
Several of the women seem to have been maced, and they beg
for water to rinse their eyes out. But no water is forthcoming.

He has no idea how long he's in there, but it's a very long
time. Eventually most of the people are taken away. Then it's
just him and two other guys. One of them is Chino Lawyer Man.

The other is an old bum who was the source of much of the original odor that had been driving everyone crazy. He gets a whole corner to himself. Jeremy and Chino Lawyer Man huddle as far away from him as possible and breathe with their hands over their mouths. Jeremy would like to converse with him, out of idle curiosity, but the women across the corridor are chanting again and their voices echo so loudly off the walls that his ears are ringing. A cop comes in and tells them to shut up, but they ignore him, so he comes back with a canister of mace and threatens them with it. One of the girls begins to cry. The others fall silent. The cop goes away again, muttering to himself.

Soon Chino Lawyer Man is taken away. He gives Jeremy a fist bump on his way out.

"You got anyone to bail you out?" he asks.

"My aunt, maybe," says Jeremy. "But they haven't even let me call her yet."

"This man hasn't gotten his phone call yet," Chino Lawyer Man says to the guard.

"Boo fuckin' hoo," says the guard. "We're busy, in case you hadn't noticed."

"Good luck, son," Chino Lawyer Man says to Jeremy. "My advice, don't say anything to anybody about anything."

"Thanks," says Jeremy.

Then it's just Jeremy and the bum. The bum is talking to himself, moving his lips almost silently. Jeremy's lost track of how long he's been sitting here. It must be night by now. Jeanie will be wondering where he is, trying to call him on his destroyed phone. Henry will be scared, thinking Jeremy has left him.

Well, maybe that'll be good practice for him too.

Finally, two guards show up.

"Merkin?" says one of them. "Let's go."

He stands.

"Turn around and put your hands through the door," says one of the guards.

Jeremy does as he's told. They put handcuffs on him.

"I didn't get a phone call yet," says Jeremy.

"You'll get one when you get one," says the other guard.

They march him out of the holding area and down a hallway to an elevator.

"Where are you taking me?" he asks.

"Somewhere very special," says a guard. "You must be important."

"I'm not important," says Jeremy. "I'm just very confused."

This elicits no response. They get in the elevator and go up. Then another walk down a long hallway, until they stop at a reinforced door with a small Plexiglas window. By now Jeremy's heart is racing. He feels an attack coming on, but with a power he hadn't known he possessed, he wills it into submission. Something tells him these guys will be less than sympathetic to his special needs.

One of the guards unlocks the door and they bring him into the room. He can tell immediately it's an interrogation cell. There's nothing but a table with a steel loop welded to it and a couple of chairs. They push him down in a chair and handcuff him to the steel loop. Then they leave. There's a barred window in the wall opposite the door, and through it Jeremy can see the weak light of dawn.

They really take marijuana seriously in this city, he thinks. Even more seriously than they take their matzo balls.

After another interminable wait, the door opens. A slight, bespectacled man in a pinstripe shirt and neatly pressed pants walks in, carrying a file folder. He's accompanied by yet another cop, who stands in a corner, holding a billy club. He looks furious. The pin-striped man sits in the chair across from him and lays the folder on the table.

"Oh, my goodness," he says. His voice is mild and reedy. "Officer, would you please take these handcuffs off right now? You should never have been restrained like that."

The cop steps forward and takes off Jeremy's handcuffs. Then he retreats to the corner again.

"Thanks," says Jeremy, rubbing his wrists. "Those are not exactly comfortable."

"I wouldn't know, but I guess they were just being careful," says the man. "So, Jeremy. Jeremy Merkin."

"Yes, sir," says Jeremy. "I'd like some answers here, please."

The pin-striped man opens the folder. Jeremy recognizes documents with U.S. Army headings on them.

"Listen, about that pot," he says. "I have a prescription for it. I have chronic back pain. It's the only thing that helps. I'm really not a criminal."

"I know you're not," says the man. "You were caught up in a random sweep. An NYPD sting operation. But when they ran your name through the database, a few flags popped up, and I was called. We have to ask you some questions, that's all."

"Okay. Who is we?"

"Did I forget to introduce myself?" says the man, sounding surprised at his own absentmindedness. "I work for the Department of Homeland Security. Terrence Moppus is the name."

Time begins doing that funny thing again, slowing down until each instant becomes as elongated as a rubber band.

"Homeland Security?" Jeremy croaks.

"That's right," says the man.

"What does Homeland Security want with me?"

"Maybe you can tell *me* what Homeland Security wants with you."

"No, sir," says Jeremy. "I have no idea, sir. Am I still under arrest, sir? Because if I'm not, I'd like to leave right now. I haven't been given a phone call or anything. I have somewhere to be." All of this comes to him as he remembers Rico's advice on what to do if he was ever arrested. Admit nothing. Insist on your rights. Above all, don't be an asshole. Be polite. "Sir," he adds.

"Well, here's the thing," says Moppus. "Under the provisions of the Patriot Act, I can hold you here indefinitely." He sounds almost apologetic about it. "I would rather not do that, of course."

"I thought the Patriot Act was for terrorists," Jeremy says.

"The Patriot Act is to help keep America safe. From within and without. We can hold anyone we want, for any length of time. That's not a threat, of course. I'm just telling you how it is. So, bearing that in mind, we would really appreciate your help."

"Sure," says Jeremy. "Whatever you say. Sir."

"Excellent. It says here you served with distinction in the Third Brigade Combat Team, Tenth Mountain Division," says the man.

"Yes, sir."

"That's impressive. You were in Afghanistan from October 2006 to April of 2007."

"That's right."

"Wounded on April 7. Very sorry to hear it. I hope you've recovered nicely."

"Sort of," says Jeremy.

"Now, Mr. Merkin, I'll get to the point. There are some questions we'd like to ask you about one of your friends."

"Which friend? I don't have many left."

"His name is Ricardo Estevez," says the man.

Jeremy looks at him in disbelief. "Rico? This is about Rico?"

"So you admit you know him?"

"Yes, I know him. I've known him for, like, fifteen years. He's my best friend."

"I see." Terrence Moppus takes out a pad of paper and a pen and notes this down. "That's very helpful, thanks. Specifically, it's about certain activities your best friend Rico engages in. And even more specifically, it's about your best friend Rico's website."

"I don't . . . I don't understand."

"Let's start with how you met."

"We met in fifth grade," says Jeremy.

"I see," says Moppus. He picks up his pen again. "Do go on."

He's in that room for another very long time. It has the feeling of an awkward first date. Sometimes long minutes go by when no one speaks. Sometimes Jeremy slumps over the table and words come out of him, though he's only half aware of what they are. Sometimes he weeps, though he doesn't know why. Moppus seems unsurprised by this. He must be used to people crying in front of him. Or maybe it already says something about this in his military file: Cries a lot. A total pussy.

Some food is brought in, but he can't touch it. A pack of cig-arettes is offered, though he didn't ask for it. He smokes half of one and has a violent coughing fit. The second one goes down a lot easier. Soon the pack is half gone.

There are lots of questions. Some of them he knows the answers to, though he can't tell of what possible significance they might be. They're almost like trivia questions, with Rico as the subject. What does he eat? How does he dress? Where does he go? How does he support himself? But Jeremy has the feel-ing that the answers to these questions are already known.

Eventually, Moppus gets to the point.

"Here's what I need your help with, Mr. Merkin. All you have to do is agree, and you'll be free to go."

"Okay," says Jeremy.

"Here's what I'd like to ask you to do. When you go back to Elysium, you're going to keep on spending lots of time with your friend Rico. You're going to find out who writes to him. I'm especially interested in who is sending him these photos he keeps posting. You know the ones I mean?"

"I think so," says Jeremy. "But I try not to look at them. They're pretty gory, some of them. I get these panic attacks, see. My therapist told me not to look at things like that, or they might set me off."

"I would like to suggest that you start looking at them," says the pin-striped man. "You're going to get names and email addresses. And you're going to send this information to me. Do you understand?"

"Yes. You want me to spy on Rico."

"Don't think of it as spying," says Moppus. "Think of it as helping your country. You helped us once, by fighting the Taliban. You can help us again, this time by helping to keep us safe from what we like to call domestic terrorism."

"Rico's not a terrorist," says Jeremy.

"No, he's not," agrees Moppus. "But the people who are sending him these pictures are the kind of people we need to know about. They're breaking quite a large number of laws. Some of these photos are classified, which means someone has been breaking their secrecy oaths. And we don't like this very much. When people can't keep secrets, it's bad for everyone. Do you agree?"

For about a nanosecond, Jeremy considers arguing this point. In fact, he strongly believes that keeping too many secrets is one of the things that's deeply wrong with the world. Or at least with his family. But he finds, to his dismay, that he's utterly willing to discard his sense of moral outrage in favor of saying whatever will get him out of this room the fastest. His fear doesn't just have a scent; the reek of it fills the room, and it's as strong as if a skunk had been run over and deposited under the table.

"Sure, I agree," says Jeremy. "Wholeheartedly."

"Well then," says Moppus, "I think we're done here." He takes a business card from his pocket and slides it across the table. "Keep in touch, Jeremy. I'll be waiting to hear from you."

He folds up his paperwork and leaves. Jeremy picks up the business card and looks at it. It strikes him as ridiculous that this whole encounter should terminate in the giving of a business card. As if they were just two guys networking. He slides it into his pocket.

The cop in the corner leads Jeremy down the hall, a hand clamped firmly on his arm.

"Don't give me a reason to put the cuffs back on you," says the cop.

"No, sir," says Jeremy.

"Or I'll beat your fucking head in," adds the cop.

"Yes, sir," says Jeremy.

He's walked back through the booking area to a desk. Here his courier bag and wallet are returned to him. Then the cop walks him out into the parking lot where he'd disembarked. Judging by the position of the sun, nearly a whole day has gone by since he was arrested. Yet another cop puts him in the back of a waiting cruiser. He's driven back to the park where they'd gotten him. The cop lets him out.

"So this is where I give you a speech about how this never happened," says the cop.

"Somehow I knew you were going to say that," says Jeremy.

18

EXCUSE ME, young lady. Would you like to be part of a conceptual art piece?"

The man who is speaking is middle-aged, clad in a velour bathrobe with bulging pockets. In one hand he holds a digital camera; in the other, a notebook. His expression is kind and solicitous, with a touch of serenity to it. His skin is so pale it's nearly translucent. It seems he hasn't been outside in a very long time.

Jenn looks up at him in bewilderment. She's been in the hospital only a few hours, and she isn't at all sure what is what. Since her arrival, she's been sitting dumbly in a chair near the reception desk, waiting for someone to tell her what to do. There was supposed to be a room ready for her. This is where she's going to spend the next thirty days. But the room isn't ready yet, and while they clean it, they seem to have forgotten all about her. No matter. The way she feels, she could sit here for the next month without moving a muscle.

"Are you a doctor?" she asks. He has that air about him. He's either a doctor or some kind of priest, she supposes, except he isn't dressed like either one.

The man smiles. "Quite the opposite. I'm a permanent guest here. Will you be joining us?"

Jenn doesn't answer. She doesn't mean to be rude; she simply has no energy.

"May I?" Without waiting for her reply, the man sits next to her. To her relief, he puts his camera back in one of his pockets. "Everything all right?"

"No," says Jenn. "Nothing is all right."

The man nods and sighs. She can feel him looking at the fresh bandages on her wrists. She went further this time than she'd ever dared to go before. Her latest cut was beyond decorative. Apparently this time she'd meant business. She doesn't remember doing it, nor does she even remember deciding to do it. That's the scariest part. She'd woken up in a regular hospital, where they kept her overnight, and now she's here. Probably better off, she thinks. Major damage has been done this time, not just to herself but to lots of other people as well. She can't remember much of that either. The last week or so can only be viewed as if through a blood-streaked windshield. She knows she said some things that weren't right. Stirring up trouble again, the way she always does during her low periods. She hopes they will decide to keep her here forever. She doesn't think she can face anyone ever again.

"I know it probably seems that way now," the man says. "But eventually you'll realize that things can be all right again. You're very young. You've got time on your side."

"Nothing is on my side," says Jenn. "Nothing and no one."

"When I first arrived here, I felt just the same way," says the man. "I feel better now, though. You'll feel better too someday."

"No, I won't."

The man nods. He's utterly nonthreatening, and appears uninterested in trying to convince her of anything. Jenn finds this reassuring.

"I understand," he says.

"I was born this way," Jenn tells him. "I've always been like this."

He smiles. "Of course. We're all born the way we are. Our personalities are already there when we're babies, like the seeds of an apple tree. You can do anything you want to an apple tree, you know. You can prune it or deform it. You can keep it short or let it grow nice and tall. No matter what the world does to it, it's still the apple tree it was born to be."

"I was born to die," Jenn says.

"We were all born to die," says the man.

"Then what's the point?"

The man shifts in his chair so he can look at her directly. She looks back at him, and sees that his face is like a father's, or perhaps a grandfather's. There's something familiar about it, too, but she can't put her finger on it.

"What's the point of what?" he asks.

"Of being born. If we're only going to die."

"There is no point," he says. "The point of being born is to be born. The point of being alive is to live. The point of dying is to die."

"They said I was gonna die when I was born," Jenn says. "I was premature. I've never been right. Never in my whole life. I do these horrible things, and then I don't remember them. That's why my mother left."

"Maybe she had her own reasons," says the man.

"Sure," Jenn says. "Sure, she did. Gulf War syndrome. Do you know what that is?"

"I've heard of it."

"It's why my father went crazy. And it's why I was born the way I was. The government won't admit it, but it's true."

"I see," says the man.

"Mom couldn't take it anymore. My brother got lucky. He was born before the war. I was born after my dad came back. So I got the messed-up genes. From plutonium, he says. Spent plutonium shells, lying around everywhere. Or the experimental vaccines they made them take. Or nerve agents. Or all of them put together. So I end up spending the first three months of my life in an incubator and having all kinds of problems. I'm bipolar. I'm a pathological liar. I'm suicidal. I never thought that was fair, that I got handed all that stuff, while my brother got away with nothing. Maybe that's why I said those things about him. Because I'm mad at him." She feels that perhaps she ought to cry here to make her point, but she has no emotions left. She's not even sure if she feels like crying, or if she simply thinks that she should. Something tells her this man doesn't care, though. Not in a cold way. She could cry or not cry, and it would be all the same to him. "I did some really bad things," she adds. "I wish I could undo them, but I can't."

"You're another casualty of war, that's all," says the man. "It's not your fault."

"How could I be a casualty of war? I wasn't in the army."

"No, but your father was. And he brought it home. It's not his fault either. That's what war does, you know. It spreads damage. Long after the fighting is over, the damage is still being done."

"Great," says Jenn. "So whose fault is it?"

The man shrugs. "Everyone's. All of us."

"But how could that be?"

"A good question to ponder," he says. "What role do people like us play in all these wars? This is what I ask myself all the time. Maybe I'll never find the answer. But I still keep asking the question. It's the children I really feel bad for. Nothing is their fault, and they get handed all the mistakes their parents made. But," he says, "we were all children once."

They sit for a while. A sunbeam makes its way in through a window and shines on the linoleum. Jenn stares at it.

The man pats the camera in his pocket. "Conceptual art can take a break for today," he says, and gets to his feet. "You've got more important things to think about. It was nice talking to you, young lady. I'll see you around, I expect. If I can do anything to help you, let me know. I know all the ins and outs of this place. One of the perks of being a long-timer." He holds out his hand. "My name is Wilkins, by the way."

After a long moment, she reaches out and takes his hand. "Jenn," she says.

"Jenn," says Wilkins, "the fact that you shook my hand just now tells me you're still in there. So don't be afraid. Everything is still possible. Look at me. I destroyed everything in my life that was good and beautiful. I don't expect forgiveness, except maybe someday from myself. I'm still working on that. But I'm still here. And so are you. And for us, that's all that matters." He smiles, does a funny little sort of bow. "Good luck with everything," he says, and turns and leaves.

Jenn watches him shuffle off down the hall. After a while she returns her gaze to the sunbeam.

19

JEREMY has one goal: to get back to Jeanie's. But first, he's very very thirsty, and he needs to sit down for a while. So he walks until he comes to a café, a tiny place about the size of a shipping container.

Every place in this city is either large beyond belief or small enough to induce claustrophobia. This place looks like an Internet café. There's a row of computers along the wall. He orders a glass of water, but when the girl behind the counter looks at him like are-you-fuckin'-serious, he adds a sandwich he doesn't want. He has to learn to look at people that way, he thinks. It's a great look. Very expressive. Not a word needed.

I just got arrested, he thinks. Arrested and interrogated and given a mission and then cut loose.

The whole situation is so weird it defies further contemplation. He looks around. Everyone else in here is tapping away on one of the computers, or is deep in some hipster conversation, hands carving profound shapes in the air.

He sits at a table, and then, because he hasn't the slightest idea what to do with himself, and because he feels dangerously close to tears again, he takes out Smarty's book. He runs his finger over the cover, feeling the grit that had once snuck into everything, every part of his body and every piece of equipment for which he was responsible, including the crevices of his ball sack. He'd once hoped never to touch Afghani soil again. Well, here he is doing it, in a New York café. He rubs it between his fingers, touches his finger to his tongue. Yup. Just like old times.

He tries to read the first page, but for some reason the words are blurred. He lays the book on the table and bends over it, trying to decipher the notes Smarty made in the margins. Then he notices there is more writing on the flyleaf. Smarty's name, his real name that is, and various other cryptic notes in some kind of code. Computer stuff. And a URL. After a moment, Jeremy recognizes it as belonging to the photo site Amichai showed him.

He goes over to one of the computers and types it in. Once again he sees the rows of folders, each one jammed with dozens upon dozens of photographs. They're labeled with single words: ARUBA. CONEY. BASIC. PLATOON. He clicks that one and finds perhaps a dozen pictures of familiar faces, standing in casual poses. Jeremy himself is in a few of them. Automatically he categorizes the other faces according to status: Dead. Wounded. Dead. Okay. Okay. Okay. Legless. Dead.

He clicks out of that folder. He clicks the one marked CONEY. These photos are old, scanned-in snapshots from the days of film. Smarty with his parents at Coney Island. He was a funny-looking kid, with a big nose and a prominent set of ears. Leila is wearing a halter top in these too. Amichai has more hair.

Then he spots the folder Amichai asked him about, toward the bottom of the screen:

PERSONAL.

Oh, yeah. That.

The reason he didn't tell Amichai how to get in is that he knows what's in here. A day ago he didn't want to see any of these pictures. But now he wants to see them very much, because he knows just what he's going to do with them. He will send them to Rico. A big middle finger to Terrence Moppus.

The password, he knows, will be *shibboleth*. Because this was the password they had always used to relieve each other on watch. They were supposed to change it every night, but they never did. *Shibboleth* itself means a kind of password. An old Israelite thing. Smarty had told him a story about it, but Jeremy can't remember what it was. It doesn't matter now. He only needs to remember how to spell it.

It works.

Inside are sub-folders. These are labeled only by date. He opens the first one, DECEMBER_06, and sees a single photo. A burned-out car with a charred corpse inside. The photo is dated too, a digital imprint adorning the lower-right corner. December 25. Merry Christmas, crispy. That was what they used to call the burned ones: crispies. He closes that quickly.

He looks at the rest of the sub-folders. All of them are dated. All of them contain pictures of bodies. Smarty's efforts at documenting the cost of war, so he could come home and look at them and remember the way they looked and the way they smelled and write his great antiwar book.

Then he spots one labeled APRIL.

This folder has lots of pictures in it.

He clicks the first one. He recognizes himself and Smarty. And Woot. And Jefferson. Seated on the ground in front of them is a black man in a turban and shalwar kameez. His hands are bound in front of him. One eye is swollen shut.

There's a date imprinted in the lower right-hand corner of the photo: April 6, 2007. The day before he was wounded, the day before the bomb went off.

The missing day.

In the next picture, the man has been caught in the act of falling to the ground, holding up his bound hands defensively. Smarty is laughing. His foot is still in midair from having kicked him onto his back.

The third file, Jeremy realizes, is not a picture. It's a movie.

The images are bad, low quality. But there's sound. The man is upright again, kneeling. Talking.

"... traitor," says whoever is holding the camera. "Tell us your name, traitor."

"Faisal ben Mohammed al-Haj," the man says, in an American accent.

"No, your real name, not your raghead name." Jeremy recognizes his own voice. He is the one holding the camera now. "Tell us and we'll go easy on you."

"Yeah, real easy," says Woot, winking at the camera.

Charlie Cooper, Jeremy says to himself.

"Charlie Cooper," the kneeling man says.

"Where you from, Charlie?" asks Smarty.

Detroit, Jeremy whispers.

"Detroit," says Charlie Cooper.

"How'd you end up in the 'Stan, man?" Jefferson asks.

"I came to fight for Islam," says Charlie Cooper.

"How's that working out for ya?" Woot says.

"Not too good," says Charlie Cooper. He looks around, desperate, practically panting with fear. He knows what's about to happen to him.

"What we got here," says Woot to the camera, "is an American Taliban."

The movie jitters to an end. There are more pictures. He clicks them all open.

Charlie Cooper getting the water method treatment. Jeremy gleefully assisting.

Charlie Cooper kneeling, with Jeremy behind him, holding his gun to the back of his head.

Charlie Cooper, dead on the ground. Smoke issuing from the muzzle of Jeremy's gun. Gore issuing from the hole in Charlie Cooper's forehead.

Jeremy hoisting Charlie Cooper up by his turban, as if he were a prize deer. Giving a thumbs-up. The other guys standing behind him, laughing at their trophy. All their thumbs up. A-OK. A good kill.

Charlie Cooper had done something horrible. What was it? He'd shot someone, Jeremy remembers. He'd been hiding in some kind of hole. Waiting, with other Taliban. Ambushed their patrol. He'd shot Lance Corporal Dinkins. That was it. Who was, irony of ironies, from Detroit. Jeremy was the one who flushed him out. His prisoner. His life to do with as he wished, by the ancient law of combat. Woot had said so. Which practically made it an order.

Does he remember this? No. Yes.

It doesn't matter. It happened. Pictures don't lie.

The day after this episode, they'd been in their Hummer going through the village, and that was when the bomb went off. He remembers now. Or at least he thinks he does.

How could he have done such a thing?

Oh, yeah. Because by then he'd given up any thought of ever going home again. And he had believed in only one thing: that nothing mattered anymore.

Lola Linker had told him over and over: if you can remember whatever it is you've forgotten, you'll have the key to solving your panic attacks. But maybe she wouldn't have said that if she'd understood what he'd forgotten. It was a crime. He'd tortured and executed an unarmed prisoner.

In Al's time, this had not been a crime. It was par for the course. In every single war in history, in fact, that was how it was done. But these days, they send you to prison for it. Things have changed. Why?

He knows what Al would say about that. He can hear his voice as clearly as if he were standing right beside him. He would say it's because the world is becoming pussified and nancy-boyed.

It's because the feminists and the liberals and the PC thugs have fucked everything up so badly that men cannot even be men anymore. You see it at every level of society. A kid gets ragged on for being gay or fat or Chinese, and the next thing you know the counselors have to be called in, and the lawyers, and the media. Two guys have a fight in a bar, and if one of them loses a tooth, he starts a lawsuit instead of just admitting he got his ass kicked. A soldier does what he's trained to do, and suddenly he's a war criminal.

Al is full of theories as to why things are this way. His favorite theory is that life in America is simply too easy. Nobody knows what it is to struggle anymore. Nobody knows how to survive. In his father's time, every man had known how to catch a fish, gut a deer, grow crops, make things with his hands. Women could birth a baby, churn butter, kill a chicken, set a broken bone. People who knew how to survive didn't stop to ask themselves whether it was right; they just did it. Now all anyone knows how to do is press buttons and sit and stare at various screens all day. And nobody knows anything worth knowing.

Now he sees the whole conflict that's been raging inside him as if from high above. He's in a helicopter, flying over the terrain of his own psyche. He's never felt this clear before. He can see his whole life in an instant—the role he has played, the things he has done, his part in the whole machine.

He needs to think. Think think think.

These pictures need to be erased. That much is beyond question. Eventually, someone will find them, somehow. The technological tentacles of Terrence Moppus are long and powerful. Jeremy knew when he walked out of that interrogation room that Moppus wasn't done with him. He will be watching him forever. At some point, he'll find out about Smarty's pictures. And a simple password will prove no obstacle to him.

What will Moppus do with them?

There are two possibilities. Either he will find a way to use them against Jeremy, or he will simply delete them. In the first case, Jeremy will find himself even more beholden to Moppus. In the second, it will be as if the whole incident never happened.

The latter is the far more beneficial scenario to Jeremy. He's been living as if it never happened anyway. Up until now, he had a good reason. But now that he remembers, what's he going to do? Spend the rest of his life trying to forget about it? Get some stupid job somewhere, maybe get married and have kids, drink a cocktail every night at six o'clock, mow the lawn on Saturdays, work until he retires or drops dead? Hold his babies and grand-kids in the same hands that pulled the trigger that killed Charlie Cooper?

In other words, become Al?

It's just as Wilkins told him. Every once in a while a person comes along who sees things clearly, who has a vision of a bet-ter way. That person will be shouted down and persecuted, but eventually, other people will see that he is onto something. They will admit, however grudgingly, that he is right. And the human race will have made an inch of progress.

Suppose these images did get out. Suppose they became public somehow. What would happen? There would be con-sequences. He would be easily identifiable. People would see them and be outraged. They would demand justice. He would be charged. There would be a trial. He would be found guilty. He would go to prison.

That's what he would want, if he saw someone else doing the things he's done. He spit in his own grandfather's face when he learned he was a murderer. If he wanted justice for those poor people in My Lai, then shouldn't he want it for Charlie Cooper of Detroit, no matter whose side he was on?

The Jeremy who pulled the trigger that day would have dif-ferent thoughts on the matter. But that Jeremy doesn't exist anymore. He died five years ago, the day after this video was taken. And the world is better off without him.

And then, from the vantage point of his mental helicopter, he spies the solution—not just to this situation, but to the problem of what to do with the rest of his life. He can go somewhere else. Like Mexico. Get a fake name, learn a new language, become part of a new culture. That sounds far better than going to jail. He has just enough money to get there. He can rent an apartment or a little house. He can teach children who have nothing, who want to learn, who will be grateful instead of resentful. He might meet a woman, settle down. Live in a real place instead of an imaginary one. Live a real life, instead of a fake one.

The more he thinks about this plan, the more appealing it becomes. For the first time in a very long time, he's excited about the future. This is the only thing that makes sense. "Love it or leave it," is Al's mantra about America. But the America he loved does not exist anymore. It never did.

So he will leave it. And he'll never come back.

But first there is something else he needs to do.

Jeremy logs into his email account. He wants to do this fast, before he can think about it any further. He finds Rico's address in his address book. He clicks it and it appears in the *To:* box. He attaches the picture files, just the ones that show only him and the dead Charlie Cooper. No need to make the families of the other guys suffer. Woot he doesn't care about, but the Garfunkel and Jefferson families don't need this.

Rico, he writes. U were always asking me what it was like over there. I think u shld know the truth. Put these up on yr site. I didnt remember this until today b/c of the blast. But I remember now. Dont try to protect me. Dont blur my face. And you should know DHS was asking me about u. Long story. Ill tell u about it some other time. I had to tell them I would spy on u. Maybe time for u and yr mom to move. Gracias para todo. J

Well, he thinks, that ought to send Rico's paranoia into high gear. Then he remembers Rico's car. Oops. He hastily includes the address of the parking garage, along with some sort of promise to make right all the automotive-related elements of this chapter in his life, eventually, somehow. Then he hits Send. He waits until the progress bar finishes creeping across the screen.

Your email has been sent.

There, he thinks. At least I won't live my life like Al has lived his. Hiding from the ghosts that follow me around, demanding to have their stories heard. Wading in the shallowness of whatever fucked-up version of the American Dream he needs to believe in to get through his days. Pretending like nothing he did over there mattered, because he was just following orders.

It mattered. All of it mattered.

I'm going to Mexico, he thinks. I'll teach in a little schoolhouse and marry a woman who makes her own tortillas and have babies with her.

Next he deletes the file marked PERSONAL from Smarty's archives. Are you sure? the program asks him. Yes, he clicks. Amichai will notice it's gone. And he will wonder. But he's better off wondering than knowing.

My children will grow up speaking both Spanish and English, and they'll ask me about my life in America. And I'll tell them they've got it better in Mexico. No matter how poor we are, our life will be a good one. Because it will be real.

His hands are shaking, his breath is coming fast. He needs to get out of this place now. He can feel the walls moving closer. He gets up and throws a twenty on the table, next to his untouched sandwich.

Outside, he hails a cab. Suddenly he doesn't want to go back to Jeanie's apartment. He can't have her and Henry seeing him like this. He needs to relax for a while. Find somewhere cool and open to chill out. Central Park, maybe. He wants to feel grass underneath him. He'll call Jeanie in a little while. Right now he really needs to get high.

"Hey," he says to the driver. "You wouldn't have a joint you could sell me, would you?"

The driver is an old Chinese man. He looks at him in the rearview mirror. He doesn't answer. He thinks Jeremy is making fun of him. His own words aren't making sense, Jeremy realizes, even to himself. They sound like gibberish in his ears. Something is happening to his ability to talk.

The cabbie drops him at the entrance to the park. It takes him forever to pull the money out of his wallet. His fingers are thick and ungainly. His hands feel as if they've been cut off and sewn on backwards. Finally he just pushes a handful of bills through the slot in the Plexiglas. He doesn't know how much. It's only stupid money.

He gets out of the cab.

It's another beautiful day. The kind of day you want to take pictures of, so you can remember it forever. There are people everywhere, lying on the grass, playing Frisbee, walking their dogs. His legs seem to be giving him trouble. He must lift and drag, one after the other. He's walking like Frankenstein. No one gives him a second glance. This city must be full of weird-looking guys who walk funny. Just like it must be full of guys who have invisible head injuries. Guys who get strange headaches that come out of nowhere.

This one he can feel sneaking up behind him, can practically hear its footsteps, almost as if it's an animal. A horse. But he can't move fast enough to get out of the way, and this time it doesn't feel like a knife or a slap on the head. It feels as if the horse is kicking his skull in. But he knows there's nothing there.

He makes it to the base of a tree. He just wants to rest and ride this one out. It's bad. Like something in his head just popped.

He just needs to rest here awhile. He wants to sit, but instead he falls.

He can't get up.

He can't even roll over.

He doesn't work anymore.

The horse comes down hard on him again. Something shatters in the back of his head. It's a mighty sound, but it doesn't hurt. First he feels warm everywhere. Then he feels nothing.

He listens to his heartbeat as it fades softly against the cool grass.

EPILOGUE:
THE VILLAGE

AMONG THE MANY LIES they told me was that your life passes before you at the end. But I've already forgotten my life. I could remember it if I wanted to, but I don't. Because I'm not there anymore and none of it matters. All that matters is now. Even though I don't know when now is.

I'm back in the village. I still can't remember the name of it. That doesn't matter either. I know where I am. I'm standing outside the house where it all happened, only it's as if it never happened. There's no crater in the road. No bullets whistling or mortars thumping. The fear is gone from the eyes of the people. It's like the war never came here. This is some other time, then. Maybe far in the future. Maybe all the Americans have gone home. Except for me.

The village is full of people. Kids are playing in the road, but they don't ask me for candy. Maybe they can't see me. Of course they can't see me. I'm a ghost.

I see her as she comes out of her house: the little girl in the yellow shalwar kameez who sat watching me with her fingers in her mouth. I'd know her anywhere, even though I only saw her that one time. She's stuck with me ever since, and now I know that the sight of me was important for her too, the day I played with her brothers in the road. Because she remembers me. She's older now, a young woman instead of a tiny child. Years have gone by. Not sure how that happened. Doesn't matter. She's outgrown the yellow shalwar kameez. Now she wears a different one of green and white that glistens as if it's woven from strands of water. The edges are embroidered. But she still has the same big, dark eyes.

She's looking at me. She smiles. She can see me.

So she must be dead too.

I wave.

She points down the road. That's where I'm supposed to go.

So I start walking. There's a crowd in the street. It's some kind of market day. My senses are working. I can smell spiced lamb sizzling over a fire. I can even feel the people, each one a rush of warmth and flow and energy as I pass through them and through the market and out the other side.

Ahead in the shimmer of heat, I can see men standing. They're waiting for me to catch up. I know these guys. I'd know them anywhere. I know them the way I'd know my brother, if I had one. Jorgensen, Cowbell, Squiddy, Ape, Rocks, the Bean. They are my brothers. They were waiting for me so I wouldn't have to make this walk alone. They knew all along I was coming.

I walk next to Smarty. Our shoulders touch. We don't talk. There's no need. The road winds gently over a slight hill. On the other side, the Helmand River flows through the land that claimed all of us. We'll take our time getting there. We're in no hurry. When we get to the river, we'll take our clothes off and dive in. We'll splash each other with water and float on our backs and hunt for tadpoles and laze around until the sun goes down. And what comes after that, I have no idea.

Acknowledgments

Thanks to my parents, Kathleen Siepel and William Kowal-ski, Jr.; my mother-in-law, Geraldine Nedergaard; my brilliant editor, Janice Zawerbny; my dedicated agent, Shaun Bradley; and to my friends Aaron Garza, Keir Lowther, Don Sedgwick, Philip Slayton, and Cynthia Wine for their assistance and encouragement. For all that these people and many more have done for me, I feel boundless gratitude.

The quote from *The Odyssey* is adapted from the Samuel Butler translation (1900).

I also wish to thank the Nova Scotia Department of Communities, Culture and Heritage Grants to Individuals Program for their support.